THE PALACE OF HONEYMOONS

THE PALACE OF HONEYMOONS

Delver Maddingley

First published in 1993 by
Nexus
332 Ladbroke Grove
London W10 5AH

Typeset by TW Typesetting, Plymouth, Devon
Printed and bound by
Cox & Wyman Ltd, Reading, Berks

ISBN 0 352 33855 X

A catalogue record for this book is available from the
British Library.

To Agnetha, Andrea, Antoine, Aran,
Cyrian, Esme and Maria

– try beating that lot for fun and excitement!

This book is a work of fiction.
In real life, make sure you practise safe sex.

ONE

A LESSON IN LOVE

'It's all right,' calls Sally. 'You can come and fuck me now.'

At seventeen Sally is still a virgin. During the months of courtship and engagement Rod has been allowed to enjoy all her soft smoothness above the waist, but everything below has been out of bounds. She has saved herself for their wedding night. Her mother told her it would be better that way, but right now it feels quite a bit worse. Although she has more or less got control of her shivering and keeps telling herself that she really does want Rod to make love to her properly at last, Sally is still a bit apprehensive.

She has not done too badly so far, she reminds herself. Not only did she manage to preserve her girlhood until her wedding night, she still has it now, four nights later. This place was not available on Saturday, only from Tuesday, so they had to spend the first few days together at her mum's. And in that crowded semi in East Acton, together didn't really mean *together*. Not together like they are now, as man and wife.

At least she feels confident about her appearance. Before getting into bed she took as long as seemed decently possible in the bathroom, where she had insisted on undressing, out of Rod's sight. When she was as ready for the moment of truth as she would ever be, she stood looking at herself in the full-length mirror.

She knows that what she saw will please him, though that is not much comfort in her present situation as she cringes under the single sheet. The night before, while her golden hair was

1

still damp from being washed, she plaited it in dozens of tight ropes hanging to well below her shoulders. The resultant effect after sleeping with it like that is one of ripples rather than waves, ripples she saw flowing down over her bare shoulders as she admired herself in the bathroom mirror. Now they flow all over the pillow. For her wedding night attire she has chosen a simple negligé of transparent white. It has no sleeves, leaving her arms and shoulders bare. At the front it is secured with a pink bow at the throat and another just below her bosom – a pretty picture as she gazed at her reflection. The show of demureness was a sham, of course. Sally's small pink nipples were perfectly visible peeping through the thin material, as were the contours of her decent-sized round breasts. Below the second bow the garment had fallen open, exposing the dimpled belly-button, the soft creamy thighs and the tiny white G-string with wisps of blonde hair escaping around the edges and through the intricate open-work of the lace.

Admittedly, Sally is no hourglass goddess of classical proportions. Some men would find her too short. And before slipping on the negligé she had to acknowledge to herself that her sides curved only slightly in at the waist and out at the hips as her eyes ran down from armpits to thighs. But Rod likes her that way. He says he likes the broad, flat expanse of belly above those belts and waistbands that have until tonight been the limit of his explorations.

Beneath the sheet she places her palms on her breasts. She can just feel the tips of the nipples through their covering but the little buds remain dormant. She slips a hand down and wriggles her fingers under the lace of the G-string; her sex feels dry and unresponsive even though right inside she can feel her womb heaving with excitement. At least the bed is comfortable, as it ought to be, considering what they have paid for their month – yes, a full month – at the Honeymoon Palace Motel.

In the subdued light shed by the bedside lamp, which Rod has insisted she should leave on, the room looks softly romantic. This is meant to be the happiest day of Sally's life. So far it has indeed been pretty good but this part could spoil everything. Rod does tend to get carried away. He doesn't always show the kind of respect for her as a *person* that she expects from someone who wants her to share her life with him. Sometimes she has to throw a tantrum to stop him overstepping the limit. Oh dear! It will be difficult to insist on any limits tonight.

The bathroom door opens and Rod steps naked round the corner into the outer reaches of the pool of light cast by the lamp beside the bed. He stands with his back to the wide mirror on the wall, his features obscurely menacing. Sally has often wished she could forget what one of her girlfriends once told her: that his pale narrow face makes him look like a rat. Ratrod. Rodrat. Silly Sally Buxton. That wasn't how she had seen him when they first met and that wasn't how she saw him as he smiled at her after the wedding. Mr and Mrs Roderick Larby Nugent.

The rat's rod stands up like a red-tipped cosh. He crosses the room and stands right above her at the bedside. And now, lit from below, his appearance is definitely not romantically knee-trembling; it is positively diabolical. Just for a moment she wonders how she ever thought she could be alone with this man, let alone marry him. His wagging *erection* – she has read enough in the women's magazines to know this is what it must be, quite apart from what the girls in the office have told her – his erection casts a stripe of shadow up his hairy belly and smooth chest and right up the centre of his face. He can, of course, be quite charming. She likes going to smart restaurants with him. And when after those occasions she lets him stroke her breasts the sensation is almost one of spiritual uplift after the first rude shock of contact; but he always wants to go too far. Rude Rod. Tonight nothing will be too far. Everything is much too near.

Rod comes even closer, stooping to kiss her. He leans there for a moment with his arm on the pillow. Sally turns her head away as the kiss becomes a little fierce for her taste and she squeals as a strand of hair trapped beneath his forearm tugs at her scalp. It nips like a rat-bite. But she wants him to love her, she really does. Only not too quickly.

All the same, there is not much she can do about it when he takes the edge of the sheet and folds it right down to her knees. His eyes glitter and his features grow sharper. Instead of

3

touching her, though, he climbs in beside her and draws the sheet up again over both of them. Mr and Mrs Nugent. Mrs Roderick Nugent and her twenty-three-year-old husband, her licensed lover. The length of his naked body presses against her side. Against the flimsy negligé. *The delights and intimacies of married love.*

It's her own fault. She remembers how in the office she always used to lead him on, driving him crazy whenever he walked past her desk by letting him glimpse a flash of cleavage or thigh flesh. The other girls were convinced that he was having it off with her, even before he started taking her out. In fact, one of the most annoying things about the collapse of the property market was when Rod had fired the other three girls. Sally had basked in their prurient curiosity, and their presence had discouraged Rod from getting too fresh with her during working hours.

Sally's job, too, had soon had to go. There just wasn't the demand for estate agents when there didn't even seem to be a need for flats and houses. She thought this would be the end of all the hassle she was getting from Rod. But on her last morning he had asked her to make coffee for both of them and proposed to her. They had only been engaged a couple of months when head office closed the Goldhawk Road branch down and Rod had joined her on the dole. At least he had his severance pay; they can just about afford this honeymoon, he says.

She hopes she's going to enjoy the four weeks here on the south coast, once the nasty bit's over – well, you know, the necessary bit. If she'd had her way they'd have flown to Tenerife or somewhere a bit lively with lots of discos. Rod can be a scream when he's got a few lagers down him. He supports Chelsea. Sally doesn't much care for the culture of the terraces herself. She'll put on the blue and white scarf sometimes when he gets her to prance about topless after a match, but only for him. She's never let him persuade her to do it in front of his mates. Mind you, she might have let herself go a bit on a noisy night in Tenerife if they'd gone there for their honeymoon, but Rod had other ideas. He'd heard about this place from one of the lads that time he went over to Fulham to shoot pool – this seaside motel had just opened and special rates were being offered up to the end of the month, so he'd gone ahead and made the booking. And here they are.

This is going to hurt.

Rod pulls back from her a little, does something to himself down there with his hand and pushes himself against her again. He has forced down his big thing, which had been squashed up between his stomach and Sally's side, so that it presses angrily against her thigh. If he's leaking, like they say can happen during foreplay, he'll mess up her negligé. He lifts his head and starts kissing her lips.

Rod's mouth excites her. Instead of those rather antiseptic mints he usually sucks before kissing, it's got a more interesting smell now that really turns her on. Lager or catpiss or something. That's it, she thinks: catmint. Some people might not find the smell too appealing but Sally doesn't give a five-X about that. She loves it. It's what's going to happen down below that bothers her. If only she'd listened to her mum and gone to college.

First he turns the sheet down again as far as her waist, unfastens the two pink bows and opens the garment to expose her firm boobs with their little pink teats. Rod drools hungrily before licking up between them. Then he starts teasing the breast nearest to him by poking it with little stabbing flicks from the tip of his tongue. The breast shakes like a kid's birthday jelly. He pulls her on to her side so that she lies facing him and nearly all of the other boob falls into his open mouth. The mouth floods with saliva; his tongue laves the slipperiness of Sally's captive tit.

At the same time Rod's upper hand has slid down under the sheet to find its way through the opening of her negligé and round over her hip to her bottom. He pinches the soft flesh and hooks a finger under the narrow thong of the G-string that has become lost between her bum cheeks. He tugs at it playfully and Sally winces as the pretty lace at the front is pulled into the reluctant folds of her thingie.

She feels she is uncomfortably close to the end of her days as a virgin. Can she find some way to put him off his stroke, this bloke she has just married but who now seems even more disconcerting – even menacing in a romantic kind of way –

than when she first met him? Maybe if she gets him talking he'll go off the boil a bit. He has a finger pressed in along the length of the crease between her arse cheeks and has sucked out her nipple into a long, hard tube. What you could call harassment, these days. Only this isn't the office and there's nobody to complain to, no more than there was when Rod was her boss.

'Tell me about the first time you did it,' she gasps, in a bid to defer the fatal moment.

He lets the breast slide out of his mouth. It feels deliciously cool as the coating of spittle begins to evaporate. Rod's chin is all wet. 'Did what?' he asks.

'The first time you – you know – had sex.'

'Hard to say. Wasn't really a first time. Came on sort of gradual. You go through this sort of phase when you keep getting hard-ons wherever you go. And then it all spills out in wet dreams. My mum used to whack me when she thought I'd been blowing my nose in the bedclothes. When my pyjamas went in the washing basket the bathroom had that lovely fresh smell of the seaside. Had to spray loads of stuff from an aerosol so she wouldn't notice.'

He rolls Sally over on her front, turns the sheet all the way down to her ankles and the hem of her negligé up to her shoulders. Now he can admire her legs and explore her bottom properly. She can feel the slippery tip of his ramrod nudging against her thigh, down near the back of her knee. He goes on talking.

'Used to go to school by bus. Must've been about twelve, I suppose. That's it – the headlines people on the bus were looking at were all stuff like "UP YOURS GALTIERI". Well, I always sat upstairs on the left because there was this bus-stop, see, right next to an electrical shop, one of those little places stuffed full of dodgy videos and car radios. It was winter. The bus windows used to get all steamed up, so I had to wipe a place with my sleeve when we got to this particular stop.'

'Bet your mum whacked you for that as well.'

Rod has pulled Sally's buttocks apart and hooked the G-string to one side to give access to her arsehole, which he sniffs as he continues his reminiscences.

6

'The point is that in the shop window they had a sort of cardboard cut-out to advertise light bulbs. It was a blonde in a white one-piece swimsuit kneeling and holding up a bulb like it was some sort of sex toy, like one of those gadgets we found in the drawer over there. Course, I knew fuck all about sex toys in those days. But this girl – she wasn't even in a bikini, mind, but a one-piece thing – looked so sexy I just sort of fell in love with her, know what I mean? Every morning when the bus stopped outside this shop I got hard as a fucking rock. We had to get off at the next stop, me and my mates, so I was always terrified I'd have to stand up and walk to the stairs with this big thing poking up in my trousers. Knew I could cure it by thinking about the homework I hadn't done – they used to give you homework in those days – but all I wanted to think about was this smashing blonde – what it would feel like to touch her.'

Sally feels a fleeting twinge of jealousy. The memory of this cardboard cut-out, this paper doll that he could call his own, seems to be getting him even more worked up than the sight of her bare bum. But once more she remembers what they say about handling hostage-takers and other people who want to do dreadful things to you: keep them talking. 'That doesn't count,' she says. 'I want you to tell me about doing it with somebody else.'

Rod lifts himself up and plonks a knee down between her ankles. He slides the knee up the bed, forcing her legs apart as he tries to work it between her thighs. The higher he gets the less leverage he has; Sally's resistance is quite effective even though her pussy is burning and she is dying to let the air get at it.

Her husband, too, is impatient. 'Come on, Sal,' he pleads. 'Thought you said it was OK to fuck you now.'

'When I'm ready. I don't mind you playing with my bottom while you tell me about your first time.'

But Rod is impatient. In a rambling incoherent way he starts muttering about his schooldays, when he had a sentimental attachment to this chum of his, Craddock, and they locked themselves in a stock cupboard while this teacher, old Shaggers, was droning on in the background about sheep farming in New South Wales and that.

Rod never gets round to telling Sally what it was they got up to in this cupboard. He's stroking her all over and she too is finding it quite hard to concentrate. She presses him rather half-heartedly for details.

'That's all that happened,' he lies. 'One day we had a row about sharing a bar of chocolate and Craddock started spreading rumours about me. "Nugent's a girl," he kept saying, till I got so sick of it I punched him in the mouth and that shut him up.'

Rod is using his knee to apply pressure to the soft, fur-fringed flesh between the tops of Sally's thighs. She quite likes the feeling. The petals of her sex seem to have come open, trying to wrap themselves round the knee. She can tell she's not dry down there any more. Is it her imagination, or can she feel the short bristles on his kneecap scouring her tender wetness? His hands are scrabbling at her hips and worming their way underneath her until they are playing with the lace of her G-string. Maybe she'd be ready for him now. Maybe she could relax enough to let her Rod and his rod skewer her without shrieking out.

Rod seems to be in no hurry now as he teases her with his fingers and knee. But Sally knows it's not her imagination when the head of her husband's penis, a gorgeous piece of flesh that feels as big as a sheep's kidney, presses up hard against her dripping vulva. She wriggles out from under him, tearing the elastic of the pretty G-string in the process, and sits with her back to the headboard of the bed, hugging her knees. She sees Rod staring at the swollen purse with its silky hairs that must be showing down there between her thighs. The alluring obscenity between his own legs looks like it's ready to take off for Mars. She peeps shyly at him from under fluttering eyelashes, and speaks.

'Look, Rod, I'm still not quite ready.' She knows, and she knows he knows, that she is in fact perfectly ready in the physical sense. Her oozing cunt is a literally open invitation to her partner. Any partner. She's just dying for some relief to the sensations building up down there but cannot bear the thought of Rod ripping through her unruptured hymen. She's got to keep the chat flowing. 'You still haven't told me about the first time you slept with a girl,' she purrs. 'You can touch me just here while you tell me.' She lowers her knees while keeping them pressed together and places his index finger at the top of her slit, the place she has often found herself rubbing on waking up from dreams about getting married.

'I'll tell you all about that another time,' he promises. 'Just lie back and try to enjoy this, for fuck's sake.'

Sally feels the tip of Rod's finger tentatively teasing the outside of her sex. The finger resumes its rather inept frotting of her clitoris. After a time he moves his finger from the fleshy bud which is slowly getting worked up. Sally can feel him scratching in her curls and tugging at the plump outer lips. All the time she holds her legs together as tight as she can. There it is – the bony length of a finger curving down from the furry mound along the line of her central rift. The first joint of the finger wriggles and tries to press into the entrance of her vagina. Sally takes his wrist, pulls the hand away and places it firmly back over her mound and clitty.

'Listen,' she complains, 'you were supposed to be telling me about your life history and you never actually got to the first time you stuck your thing into a girl. When did you start, well, having intercourse? And did you screw around much before you met me?'

Rod is vague and non-committal. 'Had the odd girlfriend. Nothing steady, usually just a bit of a fling when I went on holiday. But what about you, Sal? Tell us about when you first started doing it.'

Sally is caught in a bit of a dilemma. She's never actually told Rod she's a virgin, and she's never given him the chance to find out. What she has said is that she thinks what they've got going between them is something special she doesn't want to spoil. She used to tell him she wanted to stop putting herself about and keep herself for him, for their wedding night. He is afraid of upsetting her and has never questioned the logic of keeping something she has already given away or had taken from her. Not that she's indicated in so many words that she's been screwing or anything like that. She would not want to lie to him. But she has never contradicted him when he's dropped remarks implying that she's had a bit of experience. It makes her feel more grown up.

Expectations of the confession he hopes to extract from Sally have aroused Rod. He gets on top of her and attempts to prise her thighs apart with the inflamed knob of his member. She winces, grabs it and encourages him to rub the tip against her clitoris. Another ten minutes or so of this sort of treatment and she'll be ready for anything, she reckons. 'Go on,' he breathes. 'Let's hear about the first boy who had you.'

'Wasn't a boy,' she replies. 'He was a man, thirtyish.' She's blowed if she's going to tell Rod the whole story. It was less than a year ago, when she had just turned seventeen and was looking for work after leaving school. She remembers how she used to serve in this corner shop that's been taken over now by the friendly Indian family. At the time the bloke who ran it looked really weedy. Seedy. He had thinning hair, a narrow, unconvincing moustache and a stye on his eyelid. She can see all that now but at the time she thought he was like a rock star, just because of the fascinating bulge in his jeans. She used to flirt with him every morning, brushing up against him all the time and flaunting herself in a little top that left her tummy bare and denim shorts that cut into her crotch. Well, one day this Reg had left his pregnant wife in charge of the shop and took Sally out to the garage on some pretext.

'He got me in his garage,' she confides. 'Made me stand right in front of his car and bend over the bonnet.' She remembers how dusty the car had been. Rather than dirty her white top she had yanked it up and rested her bare chest and tummy on the cold metal. Afterwards her tits had looked disgusting. 'Then he started playing with my thighs and feeling my bottom. He reached round to the front and unfastened my shorts so he could pull them down and the panties with them and lifted one of my feet clear – he wanted me with my legs wide.'

Rod, too, wants Sally with her legs wide, but she makes sure he just goes on frigging her clit with his cock. She seems to be getting worked up, so he keeps at it optimistically as she approaches the climax of her story.

'All of a sudden I felt him sticking it in.' This is the bit she really must censor. No way is she going to tell Rod about the shameful way Reg had abused her bottom, even though it was so exciting. She couldn't believe it when she'd felt him licking her bum and using his fingers to work the spittle into the groove. He licked her again with his wet tongue and paddled the soothing liquid right into the opening of her bottom. And then came the awesome penetration. That wasn't his finger. Not even his thumb. She had felt herself going deep red as his throbbing monster split her open to the quick. 'It wasn't much fun, Rod,' she fibs. 'I gave up the paper round after that.'

At the time the discomfort had given way to quite an agreeable sensation as Reg grew inside her till he came. But all she can remember clearly now is the initial shock of that anal deflowering and her sense of shame and embarrassment afterwards. Well, the way she has told the story has spared her the ignominy of sharing the dirty details with Rod. Without actually lying outright she's given her husband the impression that this old guy had slipped her a proper fuck. Clever.

Or not so clever! How's she going to explain her virginity to Rod when it comes to the crunch, as it surely must in the next few minutes? Either she'll have to tell him her guilty secret after all or he'll think she really was lying to him even when, technically, she wasn't.

By now the insistent friction of glans on clitoris has worked her up into such a lather that all her scruples evaporate. This is her wedding night, her honeymoon, and if a girl can't enjoy giving herself to her husband . . .

Sally is quite unable to pursue this line of speculation; she loses the thread of her thoughts along with control of her body. She is all cunt. The rest of her flesh is here for the sole purpose of enticing the male into her vagina. The only function of her eyes is to seduce. Her limbs and muscles are efficient tools designed to be thrown open to lure him to her body and then to grip him, to force his hot hardness up inside her so that his seed can sate the craving of her womb. She is blessed with a sudden intimation of the delights of being a married woman.

And now she spreads her thighs and draws them back as far as they will go, this gaping cunt called Sally. Rod gasps above her, overcome with fierce desire. She has chosen him to service the wanting which is now so urgent. Or, strictly speaking, he has chosen her from the other girls in the office as a receptacle to slake his lust, but it comes to the same thing. The head of

11

his cock thrusts painfully into the tender membranes between cunt-hole and clit; surely it will slide down the oily trench between the lovelips and be sucked into its destination by the mighty force of nature. Sally the Cunt – Cunty Sal – shoves her hips up to assist this process. But instead of plunging into the now convulsing sleeve of flesh, the huge knob slides upwards. She feels it move against her sticky wetness. At this very moment, which is also the moment of her juddering climax, a mass of something moist and warm bursts into the slight gap between her loins and Rod's. Rod has shot his load and still doesn't know his pretty young bride is a virgin.

When he rolls off her it is noticeable that the pubic hair of both partners has become darker, slicked down by the salty paste that gives off its heavy fragrance to revive their flagging spirits. Round the edges the gloss on their bellies is already starting to dry into a flaky white crust.

Sally thinks quickly. She hits on a plan and acts. Her first move is to send her deflated husband to the bathroom, telling him to wipe that stuff off himself. As soon as she hears the water running she jumps up herself and nips over to the mock-rococo cabinet in the corner. When they first arrived and looked the place over they found the top drawer full of really weird articles, some of them with a vaguely sporting appearance while others arouse more medical associations. Surgical supports? A weight-lifter's harness? Equestrian accessories? Rod had a knowing grin on his face as they rummaged but it was a little time before Sally cottoned on.

It was the unmistakable shape of a jumbo-sized pink rubber penis that put her on the right track. Near where her mum lives there used to be a nondescript shop with its windows blanked out. The signboard advertised it discreetly as an outlet for martial aids. Or so she had always thought – if not dyslexic, Sally is certainly a little short-sighted. One day, at a time when she was obsessed with the fear of being attacked or felt up by blokes on her way home from work, her curiosity got the better of her. She opened the door and pushed past the blanket-like curtain hanging behind it. For a few minutes she had persisted in the misconception that the masks, chains and truncheons displayed around her were all adjuncts of specialised arts of self-defence rather than being designed for the softer combat of the boudoir. Then, as now, it was the shock of being confronted with an outsize phallus that exposed her mistake. The man in charge of the shop asked if he could help her. She mumbled some words of explanation. He was an old soldier himself, he told her with a wink and a lopsided leer, quoting his favourite adage: *the penis mightier than the sword.* 'Mind you,' he added, 'if it's a well-fleshed pork sword you're looking for, dear, I dare say I could help you out.' Sally was clean out of her depth and had not needed helping out of that dreadful shop. It was enough to put you right off marital life, she told herself, as she hurried out into the embarrassing glare of the sunlight in the busy street.

Well, Rod and Sally have decided to leave the drawer of toys until they get a bit tired of just playing with each other, if that ever happens during this honeymoon. But now young Mrs Nugent has an idea. She's got to hurry or Rod will be back to catch her at it. There's so much in the drawer, all jumbled up, that it's hard to know which implement would be most suitable. That rubber thing's far too big. Maybe after a couple of weeks here . . . No, this one's better. She slips the shiny plastic object into her handbag and shuts the drawer.

When Rod is ready, Sally, still wearing the pretty negligé which now hangs open at the front, takes her turn in the bathroom. She cleans herself up a bit and sprays some Seduction on her tummy and newly fluffed-up fur. Then she turns on the tap in case the operation proves noisy, smears cream on the cigar-shaped vibrator and the lips of her pussy, and places one foot on the edge of the bidet. It will go in like a tampon, she thinks, or maybe not quite so easily. The rounded end presents no problem and the first half inch slides up quite smoothly. But now it's really painful when she pushes against the resistance.

Without moving the heavy object she holds at the entrance to her quim, Sally spreads a thick towel on the floor and lies back on it with her thighs wide open. She shuts her eyes and fiddles about down there. Suddenly her thumb finds a plastic button which slides under the pressure. It is the switch operating this battery-powered vibrator, which now bores into her with a sound like a dentist's drill. Wow! At first she thought it was going to hurt as much as what old Reg used to do to her in his garage, but after the first shove it's as easy as falling off a log. It feels great now. She lies back, luxuriating under the influence of this vigorous internal massage.

Careful, Sally! Her cunt freezes as she recalls a paperback she read in which an American girl electrocuted herself with a thing like this. As far as she remembers, though, that device was plugged into the mains and wrongly wired up. This bugger's much tamer. She must have another go with it some time, but right now she'd better get back to Reg – no, to Rod.

Hell, the vibrator comes out of her all bloody and there's blood on the towel. It would be a bit too obvious to make out she's had a nosebleed, so she rinses out the towel and hangs it up. Rod must be getting impatient again.

But when she returns to the bedroom she finds him lying on his back, snoring. She joins him on the bed and switches off the lamp. Unlike him, in her freshly deflowered state she is far too aroused to sleep. After what seems like an hour or so she realises that a chink of light somewhere up to her left is keeping her awake. It's really annoying. Anyway, what's a light doing up on the wall beside the bed? When she gets up to investigate she sees the light is leaking from behind the frame of a picture hanging at eye level and measuring about two feet by three. Right now the picture is lost in darkness but she remembers it shows a rather rude scene involving Cupid and – who was it on the label? Physicky? Sukie? Psychic? Piskie? How she wishes she had gone on to college. Anyway, she lifts the picture off its hook and lays it on the bed.

What's this? The picture has been concealing a sliding panel that covers a little window, or would cover it if it had not been left partly open. Sally peers through into the room beyond, which is a mirror image of the room she stands in. Mirror? Yes, this must be one of those two-way mirrors she's looking through. For a moment she is alarmed at the possibility that she and Rod have themselves been under scrutiny from unseen eyes, but the thought is banished by the sight before her.

The couple on the bed, which in this room is just below the secret window, must be about thirty. They are both completely nude, dark in colouring, lean and handsome. But what on earth are they doing?

To begin with they kneel belly to belly, kissing. Then the man piles up the pillows against the headboard, too close to the wall below her for Sally to see. The woman lies back, propping herself up against the pillows so that Sally is looking almost directly down on her; the woman's head is outside her field of vision but the view of her cleavage, belly, bush and thighs is almost the view Sally would have of herself if she were sitting up in bed, different though her own young body is. The man kneels on the bed beside his companion. His whole person is a shaggy pelt of tight black curls interrupted by the relatively smooth patches of face, shoulders and upper arms, upper back, sides and buttocks. A gold medallion winks from the mat of his chest. But Sally's attention is mainly drawn to the upward and sideways curving length of hairless cock that sprouts from the dense undergrowth at the base of his belly. It is tipped with a shining purple plum and a drop of transparent fluid is plainly visible gathering at the slot. Without ceremony this bloke grabs the woman by the ears, pulls her forward so that her head just comes into view, and shoves that cockhead into her open mouth.

Shocked and tearful, Sally turns away, shakes the snoring Rod and drags him over to the little window. Rod quickly perks up when he gets an eyeful of what is going on next door. Standing beside Sally at the window he slips a hand under the hem of her negligé and runs it up between her thighs until it presses edgewise into her crotch.

The guy on the bed takes his cock out of the woman's mouth. It is still enormous – he hasn't come yet. He seizes her thighs and drags her down the bed so that she lies flat on her back, her face fully visible now to the couple spying on them. The woman lifts her arms as he places a knee on each side of her; then she lowers her hands so they rest on the backs of his bulging calves. She reaches up and strokes his flanks. The man stoops forward. His hairy hands have gently opened her thighs. He stares hard at her pussy as he smooths aside the black fleece and teases open the flaps of flesh. Sally notices that his nose is twitching.

He sticks out his tongue and plunges his face down into the waiting cunt. Poor Sally feels terribly embarrassed. Somehow she feels implicated in the dirty act and her sense of defilement is aggravated when she realises that her own Rod is poking a finger into her.

Meanwhile, the woman on the bed is responding to the man's intimate attentions by grasping the prick which had stuck up stiffly along his belly. She draws it down and opens her mouth wide to take it in, or as much of it as she can. With one hand she tickles his testicles as they dangle on her nose and with the other she fondles one of her breasts. The couple heave and rock. They roll over on one side, still maintaining their two-ended connection, and explode in orgasm. When the man removes his prick from the woman's mouth a trail of residual semen dribbles from the corner of her lips. The rest of it has gone down her throat.

Sally cannot bear to watch any more of this display. She slides the panel shut and makes for the bed. 'Let's do it,' she says. 'Let's do it like them. After all, we're married now.'

She lies back and opens her thighs to Rod's rather tentative tongue. He kneels over her, licks all round the outer lips, avoiding the exposed pinkness, and chokes as he chews on the pubic hair. Sally, too, finds it hard to do what the woman in the next room was doing. Taking the hard prick between thumb and forefinger she bends it downwards and opens her mouth, but can only bring herself to run the tip of her tongue along the shaft. The salty-sweet taste of the knob is just too much for her. Sally wants it in her cunt.

'Come on,' she says. 'I want it in my cunt.'

The unemployed estate agent turns round and slides his well-oiled rod towards its snug bijou accommodation. Just as the soft curtains of flesh fall apart to admit it, this unskilled bridegroom disgraces himself once more by letting his seed gush all over the outer approaches. Sally's belly, thighs, buttocks, thatch, clit and sexlips are awash. And so is her cunt, but only with her own bitter-sweet juices.

The Captain grinned at Gloria and wriggled his thumb in her arse. They had really enjoyed the performance of the unwitting

16

Nugents. It will be no surprise to the reader that the long wall-mirror above the dressing table opposite the bed on which Rod and Sally were disporting themselves was not the innocent reflecting surface it seemed. Sally's momentary suspicions had been quite right.

Although narrow and windowless, the compartment in which the Captain and his assistant lurked was quite comfortably appointed. It was certainly warm enough on an evening like this in the middle of July. A specially elevated upholstered bench allowed them to lie and fondle each other while they contemplated the action and commented on it in whispers. First-time honeymooners were always putting on a good show and when they didn't the Captain had ways of livening things up. He always made sure, for example, that the couple in the bedroom adjoining theirs were mature and experienced.

Gloria was so excited she wanted to go round and join the Nugents. Her companion had to restrain her by slipping a couple of fingers up her vagina and squeezing them against the thumb in her anal passage. She winced and gasped. 'You can forget Mr and Mrs Roderick Larby Nugent,' he chuckled. 'At least, you can forget them till the morning.'

TWO

COTTAGE AND PALACE

When Melanie Winspur lifted the corner of the sheet the deliciously suggestive aroma of spent female lust was overpowering. She was tempted to stay and engage her companion in yet another bout, but Miss MacDonald was already sleeping, oblivious to the early morning sunlight and the clamour of birdsong out in the cottage garden.

Melanie swung her slim legs down to the floor and wriggled her feet into her slippers. She stood up, yawned and stretched. The bed was large and the bedroom small under its sloping ceiling, so she was only a couple of feet away from the full-length mirror on the door of the wardrobe. She avoided eye contact with her own reflection, knowing that the blonde hair hanging to her shoulders was tangled and her features crushed and creased from being forced down into the pillow by Mac's last furious assault on her behind. Everything between neck and knees, however, was reassuringly perfect in its twenty-year-old beauty. The pink nipples that tipped the little rounded cones of her breasts winked up and slightly outwards; the navel dimpled an otherwise smooth, almost flat belly that just began to curve down and inwards where the triangle of gingery curls shaded the mound of her sex.

She slipped her arms into the sleeves of a flimsy white housecoat which hung on a hook behind the door. Not bothering to fasten it at the front, she stepped across the landing and entered her own little room with its dormer window that looked out on the secluded garden and the orchard beyond.

Melanie no longer slept in this room, except when she wished Miss MacDonald to understand she was not best pleased with her, or when Derrick, to whom she had entrusted a key without Mac's knowledge, was paying her one of his early morning calls on his way to work. She used the room mainly as a den, a place where she could be private, get her head together and write her diary. It was the diary that she now took out of a drawer as she sat at the small desk under the window.

Wed, July 15

This letter came yesterday from the Captain, addressed to both of us. We'd already had card at Xmas, so guessed he was back from USA, but he's been too busy to contact us. I felt miffed about this but now he's making up for it and I can't wait to see him again. Letter gave full account of what he's been up to, if you can believe a word he says.

Well, he made tons of money from the Californian end of that scam last year and says he's going to give us cash for our part in it – lots and lots of lovely cash! But he had to get out of Banesville and start new life back here. Fly in ointment: that PA of his, that Gloria. She insisted on coming with him. He regrets having had her in with him from the start. She knows too much and doesn't want the same things as him. Mainly she wants him to marry her and settle down and have kids. As if that was the Captain's scene!

OK, so when they got to UK he started looking round for suitable location for this next scheme of his. Wanted somewhere on coast. Now I'd thought whole of south coast from Margate or wherever to John-o'-Groats (Do I mean Land's End? Are they the same? – must ask Mac) was either all concrete and buildings or National Trust land closed to public so army can practise on it. I was wrong, wasn't I? Even in this county there are some secluded coves with lovely sandy beaches and not a road or house in sight. It's just that they're private property so you never get to see them. Anyway, he found just the place, not thirty miles from here, he says. Owner's business was threatened with going under in recession and Captain had heard things about dodgy

19

dealings he'd had on stock market – that wheeler dealer or insider dealer stuff – so he got a real bargain.

Captain seems to know lots of cases like that. He got this bent architect just out of jail to draw up the plans for him, and a tax-ducking builder to do the work in double-quick time: three months start to finish, he says. He reckons it's a bit flimsy, just plywood and cardboard (hardboard?) mostly. They cut corners where they could, but that's the way it goes these days. Doesn't really matter because there's no upstairs to collapse on people and in any case the cliffs are eroding so fast there's no point in building for posterity – another reason why he got the land cheapish.

He calls it the Honeymoon Palace Motel and it's got this sort of American look about it with its clapboard (?) and fancy wedding-cakey woodwork and boardwalks (?) and hitching posts for tying up your nag if you've got one or your new wife if she nags you. Or so he says. He had motel designed as a special facility for voyeurs and eventually plans to build up discreet network of clients: droolers and amateur photographers as well as couples who get off on watching others at it. All the rooms have see-through mirrors and are bugged with hidden mikes and video cameras. And between the pairs of rooms and round behind them he's got passageways with padded benches you can lie on while you spy on what's happening on other side of wall.

Of course, it's not a motel at all, strictly speaking. Nowhere near a main road, though Captain says he's having a small signboard put up at nearest crossroads. He doesn't cater to casual trade, he says, unless he likes the look of them. A couple of times he's caught couples trespassing on the private beach and persuaded them to spend night as his guests – always keeps a couple of rooms free for that kind of thing. Otherwise it's all arranged by word of mouth or by punters enquiring about small ads he puts in *Time Out* and *Private Eye* and whatever. Usually insists on four-week bookings, because 'honeymoon' was originally 'honeymonth', according to him, but doesn't charge for days when brides have their periods, so it's like a discount if you have the full whack. Also pretends to be very strict about only taking newly-weds, though they don't have to be first-timers. Asks to see copy of marriage certificate. But all these rules can be got round if you've got the money and he takes a fancy to you. Oh, and you have to send him pictures so he only gets to take on good-looking couples.

Sent us his glossy illustrated brochure, printed by that Benny (or was it Kenny?) in Amsterdam. It makes place look and sound really inviting and sexy but, knowing him, I'm sure it only gives half the picture.

> *Every suite equipped with a wide range of ergonomically designed and medically approved appliances to guarantee the gratification of all tastes from middle-of-the-road to exotically bizarre. Watch one of our 'in-flight movies' while waiting for that magic moment with your newly legal lover! Hire of specialised costumes on request: ask for catalogue at reception. Enrol for our courses in marital harmony; group sessions or private tuition at beginners', intermediate and advanced levels. Get to know your fellow-honeymooners at weekly barbecues and dances. Also computer-matching for foursomes and moresomes. Enjoy yourself! Enjoy your partner! Enjoy our facilities! Enjoy these unique opportunities for enjoyment!*

And much more like that, with all these pictures of happy couples in wedding clothes and nighties and bikinis and starkers (as far as you could see) in bubble baths. He's invited Mac and me to go and stay there when we can get away – I can hardly wait. Wonder if we'd have to bring a couple of men with us so we'd sort of blend into the background . . .

'Say, Captain, don't I get to fuck you on a daily basis no more? You think I left California just to do a boring job like this? Guess I'd rather go back to my folks in New Hampshire if you're gonna spend all your time in back with them monitors and switches and tapes.'

It was the day after the Captain had amused himself watching the Nugents at play and the speaker was his pretty assistant, Gloria Sweetbutts. She was now installed as motel receptionist, and he was becoming sensitive to her increasingly whinging disposition. Ought he to feel guilty about this? It was true that she had abandoned her doctoral studies at the University of Banesville in order to accompany him to England. But in this country, he reflected rather illogically, she would never have made it to university in the first place. Her supple body with its soft cream-coloured flesh still appealed to him. So did that dainty head with its thick braid of chestnut hair enshrining a mind that was lively but hardly, as he had often remarked, of Nobel quality. That combination of the puritanical and the richly sensual had a real piquancy. All the same, he didn't altogether like the direction things were beginning to take. At bottom, Gloria was as domestic as apple pie, whereas the Captain was your proverbial rolling stone. Why couldn't she give him space when he wanted to enjoy his fantasies in private, and just be available once or twice a day and most nights for a bit of the old one-on-one?

'Take it easy,' he said, breathing into the side of her neck and allowing her nipple to rise and press against the fingertip he had rested lightly on the front of her high-necked blouse. 'You know the commitment we have to our guests. Mr Pelham in Number Three is already threatening legal action if we can't meet his extravagant requirements on the Intercoupling facility – says our brochure's a legally binding document and he intends to have his pound of flesh.'

'You mean he'll get the lawyers after us?'

'I mean he *is* a lawyer. And very particular about the kind of flesh he enjoys and how it's presented, the randy bugger.'

Gloria pouted and tilted her head back to look up at the Captain from her chair. 'But do you really have to spend so much time getting off on all those electronic gizmos you have in there? You used to have time for me, honey.'

'I've still got plenty of time for you,' he growled, economising slightly with the truth. 'All I ask is that you look after the front-of-house business by yourself from six to eight. You know why, don't you – that's the time I've undertaken to operate the Intercoupling and monitor all the other facilities offered in the brochure. Can't afford to give Pelham any more grounds for complaint.' He tweaked the hardened nipple and passed into the adjoining office. They could still see each other through the glazed upper half of the partition separating his inner sanctum from the reception counter, but the Captain now had more interesting material to contemplate than his assistant's head and shoulders. This material, on the other hand, was concealed from Gloria, as the bank of video monitors on which it was generally displayed above his control console presented only its reverse side, sprouting a tangle of boring cables, in her direction.

A buzzer was sounding as he eased his lean though no longer youthful frame into the swivel chair, and he observed that the flashing red light belonged to suite Number Eight. By pressing the appropriate switch he activated one of the smaller screens in the array before him. After a few moments a sharply focused image snapped into life. Side by side on a small two-seater sofa sat Rod and Sally Nugent, demurely clad in white shirts and blue jeans. They were gazing rather sheepishly into the lens of their apartment's intercamera, just below the screen which could also bring them piped adult movies at the touch of a button.

The Captain jammed his lightweight headset on, directed a somewhat predatory smile at his own intercamera and spoke into the little microphone. 'Happy honeymoon, Mr and Mrs Nugent. This is your manager. How can I help you?'

The eyes of the young couple lifted slightly as their attention was caught by the image of the Captain that now appeared on their screen. It was the pale-faced Rod with his narrow features who undertook to reply. 'Well, your brochure says something about, er, about "Intercoupling",' he began. 'We wondered whether . . .'

'That's quite right, sir. No problem. Now, I have in front of me a list of guests who have also registered their interest in this facility. In fact, most of the guests who have been here more than a week are on the register. Quite unusual for someone who's only been with us three days to apply. They're usually too – oh, I didn't mean to embarrass your charming wife.'

Sally was blushing becomingly and staring at her hands, which were clasped modestly in her lap.

'You can either take pot luck,' the Captain continued, 'or give me the name of anyone you're interested in, or their room number if you don't know the name, and I'll put you in touch with them right away if they're in their rooms.'

Rod opened his rodent-like mouth and was about to speak but Sally threw an arm round his shoulders and whispered something in his ear before letting him proceed. 'Well,' he said, 'we do have a particular couple in mind but Mrs Nugent says she feels a bit nervous about going right into it. Could we possibly . . .?'

'No problem, sir. We can look up two or three of the others for you first and you can get yourselves in the mood by just chatting to them. Who knows, you might fancy them more than the ones you've already got your eyes on. Now, if I might make a suggestion, sir, most of our clients find it a good idea to present themselves in, well, in a fairly *provocative* way when they make their first contacts. As informal as possible. To be blunt with you, as a rule they take their clothes off before I put them through.'

Sally was looking distinctly uncomfortable. Since he could just see at the bottom of the screen that her husband was gripping her wrist to prevent her from getting up and dodging out of the picture, the Captain revised his regular patter to reassure her.

'I think in your case a slightly different presentation might be in order. If I may say so, madam has a certain *je ne sais quoi* about her which calls for – how to put it? – a slightly reserved approach. Just a touch of coyness. You too, sir, could exploit your position as a first-time bridegroom to some advantage. As a couple, you might almost do just as you are now. On the other hand, whatever virtues and other attributes our guests can boast, they're not always blessed with a discerning taste. You are, of course, quite free to disregard my advice, but I think I would recommend underwear or beach attire as a starting position. Just let me know when you're ready, sir, and I'll access one of our willing couples for you.'

Rod and Sally stood up and moved out of the picture. Simply by flicking a switch the Captain could have brought into play two or three other cameras concealed around the edges of the room, but he preferred the mild excitement of waiting to see how they would look when they returned to the little sofa, ready to confront their potential partners.

Rod was the first to resume his place. It could not be said

that his appearance had become more seductive as a result of his undressing. His ribs were visible beneath the pale and almost hairless skin of his narrow chest. His navel formed the apex of a gradually broadening trail of dark scrub leading down under the waistband of his white Y-fronts, a stray tuft of it emerging negligently through the opening.

Sally rejoined him on the sofa. A rush of blood to the Captain's privates confirmed his judgement that she, unlike her husband, had succeeded in improving the suitability of her appearance for the operation about to be undertaken. Her scant, snug panties were of pale blue with diagonal stripes of slightly darker blue and pink emphasising the contours of her bulging mound. Around her breasts she had tied a flimsy black scarf interwoven with lines of silver thread. The Captain was quite surprised when she clasped her hands behind her head to display the wisps of golden hair she allowed to flourish in her armpits. She let her bottom slide forward just a little on the seat and stretched her legs out languorously so that, although the thighs were pressed together, her plump pubis was pushed into prominence.

'That's quite charming, my dear,' he commented. 'Perhaps you could just hold that position while I put you in touch with – let's see – with the couple in Twenty-four.'

He activated the appropriate switches so that the dot-dot-dot-dash signal of their buzzer would prepare the recipients for the nature of the incoming call. Contrary to the account of this service given in the motel brochure, which described it as confidential, the Captain was able to watch and hear both couples throughout their conversation. No wonder, he thought, that British Telecom had brought in digital exchanges and other cost-cutting technology to displace the old village operators at their switchboards before the expected advent of video phones.

Although his office contained an impressively large array of screens, the system was so arranged that for most purposes including the present one the Captain did not need to look beyond the 'active' monitors immediately before him. The one next to that on which Rod and Sally were displaying themselves now lit up. A rather stout, balding man with a moustache blinked at the camera. A small white towel was wrapped

25

precariously round his loins. His chest and belly put the Captain in mind of a gorilla and made him wonder how he could have cleared such a monster for admission. Everything from his shoulders down was covered with a dense mat of greying hair. The man's breasts were sizeable flaps of fatty flesh resting on the outswelling curve of the stomach. A pair of small but outrageously prominent nipples stuck out from the hair, looking as if they had just been snatched from the apish lips and gums of prehensile-tailed offspring. How come this guy had not been vetted and weeded out on application? He appeared to be annoyed and was directing impatient gestures at his unseen partner.

Suddenly this partner joined him on the two-seater. She was a delightful young creature from Hong Kong and it was for the sake of her attractions, the Captain recalled, that he had admitted her and her husband, who had identified himself as a police officer recently 'retired' from the colonial force. The young lady wore a black silk robe adorned with gold dragons. As she sat down she casually untied the cord around her waist and parted the front to reveal the neat, round breasts with their dark teats. The Captain was interested to note that although her general colouring was a deep honey-brown, the breasts were more lightly tanned. He inferred that her lower parts would sport the complementary negative image of a bikini bottom, but she had crossed her thighs before allowing the robe to fall open and he was unable to confirm the conjecture.

For a moment both couples contemplated each other. Then Rod spoke. 'A very desirable wife you've got yourself there, Mr, er . . .'

'Call me Des. Yeah, I think so too. She's got a funny Chinese name but I call her Doris. And you and your good lady?'

'Oh, Rod. Rod and Sally.'

'Well, Rodney . . .'

'Roderick.'

'Let me tell you something, Roddy old chap. This Doris here may not smile overmuch but, boy, is she a goer. How about yours? Knows how to enjoy herself, does she?'

Rod gulped. 'We've only been married three days . . .'

'Don't you worry about that, squire. I'll give you a hint. Try

26

your chances with my Doris and you won't need to bother with all that foreplay and stuff to get her opened up. Just has to see a man and as long as he looks reasonably European the fuck-juice starts pouring down her legs. Stand up, Doris, and show them.'

Doris rose to her feet and Des pushed her towards the camera so that her pubic region filled the entire screen. As the focus adjusted itself the Captain now saw that she did indeed have that small, lighter-coloured bikini mark. But what struck him most forcefully was the fact that she was completely hairless. The mound bulged out, a pale, curving wedge between the deeply tanned thightops. The vertical slit could be seen in all its succulent detail: the outer lips gaping wide, the inner ones inflating puffily between them, their moist inner surfaces peeling away from each other to release the flow of sexual honey which had already, while she was sitting, lubricated the underhanging curves of her buttocks. Now that she was standing upright the flood had begun to slide down the inside of her right thigh. The Captain was enchanted.

Rod, on the other hand, cringed back in the seat as if he had just discovered a reptile in his bed. When he had sufficiently recovered his composure he addressed Des in tones devoid of bravado.

'Look, I think we probably won't make a date right now if you don't mind. To be frank with you, Des, I don't really go for those bald ones.'

Des raised a chubby hand to his head and glared for a moment before realising what was meant. 'Please yourself, old son,' he replied. 'Not everybody's cup of PG tips, of course. It's a kind of hygienic measure, see. She used to get all caked up from that stuff leaking out of her. I do have this bit of fur I stick on her now and then for a lark but it's not the same thing. A pity, though. Wouldn't mind having the use of your Sal some time if that suits you. Yeah, I could really fancy a fresh young blonde.'

Rod switched Des and Doris off and re-established contact with the Captain. Sally lounged back and parted her thighs, looking relieved. The Captain glanced at the register in front of him and said he would put them through to the couple in

Fifteen. The same procedure was gone through as with the appalling Des and his Doris. This time it was Sally who called a halt to the negotiations. Although she could not bring herself to say so in so many words, the huge boobs of the woman were so upsetting that the thought of Rod touching them quenched the small fire that had been kindled when she first caught sight of the burly hunk this wife was attached to.

The Captain tactfully refrained from demanding an explanation. Everyone involved in Intercoupling appreciated the arbitrariness of taste and understood how much harder it had to be to match two couples than two individuals. Fortunately the stock of registered participants was large enough for everyone to have a fair chance of getting lucky before their honeymoon was over.

Now that the ice was broken, Sally smiled at the Captain (or at a point just above his head) and asked if the pair they had had in mind all along had put their names down.

'Who are they?' he asked.

'We don't know their names. The ones next door to us, in Seven.'

The Yglesiases were indeed on the register, but instead of slowing down proceedings by passing on this information, the Captain flicked the switch at once, hoping the girl would be carried away by the immediate realisation of her dreams. As soon as the screen lit up, the darkly handsome couple were already in position on their sofa as if they had been waiting for the call. Or, the Captain reflected cynically, as if they had been on the point of accessing someone else. They wore nothing but little pouches of imitation leopard skin, and the man had thrown a thigh over his wife's leg.

Rod seemed to have lost his voice. Maintaining her seductive pose but wriggling slightly to draw attention to her appetising young body, Sally spoke up. 'Hi there,' she began. 'I'm Sally and this is Rod. I don't know if you've noticed, but we're next door to you. We're very much in love, but we want to have lots of fun while we're here. I wouldn't mind sharing my Rod once in a while and he says he'd like to see me really let myself go. You see, we're not really very good at . . .'

Rod interrupted brusquely. 'What I say is, they give us this facility and we'd be stupid not to use it. Young Sally here fancies you two.'

The lean, handsome faces of the older couple lit up eagerly. The man put an arm round the woman's shoulders, kissed her cheek and spoke. 'We take that as a compliment, believe me, Rod and Sally. Yes, we have noticed you, indeed we have. It's lovely to see newly-weds enjoying themselves so much.'

'You're just married yourselves, presumably?' asked Sally.

'Yes, but it's not our first time,' the man replied. 'We were divorced for a few years and we've just remarried.'

'And you're getting on better than with your first partners?'

The dark woman smiled. 'We were married to each other,' she explained in velvet tones. 'It'll be nice to meet you, Sally. I'm Yvonne, by the way, and this is Talbot. Talbot's a big boy and curves up a bit at the end if you know what I mean. He can fuck like a corkscrew. What's your Rod like in that department when he's not all tied up in the Bigbuys underwear?'

Sally was embarrassed. She knew it was not her fault. Now she was with Rod on a full-time basis she would get rid of all the old junk from his bachelor days and kit him out in new things from Next or somewhere. But in the meantime she would have to put up with well-meant advice and sneers from the other wives they were bound to run into. This Yvonne wasn't really sneering, of course, but there was something just a bit superior about the way she had made the remark. Sally couldn't help glancing down at Rod's Y-fronts and saw that his tool had stiffened and worked its way out at the front. 'You can see for yourself,' she said with an air of rather petulant bragging.

'Looks like he's got what it takes,' Yvonne observed. 'I like them slim for a change, as long as they've got the length on them. We're all going to get on fine. Just fine. Don't you think so, Talbot?'

Talbot frotted one of his wife's dark nipples with a languid circular motion. 'I get on fine with anyone,' he said. 'One's adaptable, my love.' His glittering eyes locked on to the screen and his nostrils twitched as he addressed the younger couple. 'Yvonne here will tell you just how adaptable I am. But you'll be finding out for yourselves soon enough, won't you, if we decide to go ahead with this Intercoupling. Speaking for

29

Yvonne and myself, I'd say we're on to a winner with you folks. What sort of knockers has she got under that scarf, Rod?'

Rod gave a tug at the black material and it fell away. He poked and prodded at the medium-sized round breasts to demonstrate their firmness; the pink tips puckered into rigid pegs.

'Perfectly satisfactory,' Talbot commented. 'And I like the look of that bulge in her knickers. Not mistaken, am I – that is a damp patch just where she's got her legs pressed together, isn't it?'

Sally, who had been biting her lip and looking around shyly rather than focus on the camera, raised her bottom slightly as Rod eased the garment down over her thighs and pulled it right off. He parted her knees and laid his palm over the little blonde bush. She blushed as his middle finger sank into the sexual aperture.

'Yes,' said Rod. 'She's quite wet – not used to all this excitement.'

Yvonne seemed to be getting impatient. 'Oh, come on, for heaven's sake,' she cried. 'Let's show them what we're offering and see if we can arrange a meet.'

Standing up, she peeled off her mottled pouch, which had concealed a triangle of dense black curls. She sat down again, placed her heels on the edge of the sofa and let her knees hang apart while she used both hands to open her sex to the camera. Talbot sat as far forward as he could and pulled his own pouch aside to let his bollocks swing free. Then he tugged it outwards until the massive purple-headed corkscrew sprang out. Sally quailed at the sight and Rod felt his own organ drooping. But the games Yvonne was playing with her fingers gave him fresh heart, and he took a deep breath before clinching the deal.

'OK,' he said hoarsely. 'Why don't we get together – what about tonight?'

'My, we *are* eager,' laughed Yvonne.

Talbot grinned. 'We'll take you out to dinner,' he offered. 'Where do you fancy?'

Sally pondered a moment before speaking. 'Well, last night we found quite a decent little Italian restaurant a couple of miles up the main road, just before all those bungalows.'

30

Talbot appeared to be unenthusiastic. 'What about something a little more exotic?' he suggested. 'There's a classy joint that specialises in Singapore cuisine quite near the town centre. The mouth waters. You'll love it, Sally.'

'So what sort of stuff do they do?' she asked.

'You know, all the usual things. Gulai Ayam, Rendang, Baba Alia – you name it. Always go for the Udang Nanas myself. Tiger prawns work wonders for the old love-life.'

Rod would have been quite happy to settle for a jumbo burger with chips but as the gastronomically more adventurous Sally seemed to have been seduced by the promise of these outlandish dishes he grunted his assent.

Both screens in the office went blank as the couples completed their transaction. Immediately, the Captain's attention was caught by a flashing red light. It was the third in the row – Mr Pelham was keeping up the pressure. What an irony: he had only taken the Pelhams on because he thought the old jerk would be a useful contact. The Captain accessed the grey-haired, buttoned-down solicitor and asked politely how he could help him this time.

'Now look here, Haggler,' the caller began. For commercial and legal reasons, the Captain had retained the name he had assumed in America, but discouraged its use in conversation. 'This is the last time I shall approach you on an informal, friendly basis with my demand. Got me fitted up yet?'

'I'm still doing my best, sir.'

'There's no doubt the courts would support me in the way I read your brochure. It's no good you stocking your so-called honeymoon apartments with manacles and whips if you won't take the trouble to provide bums to wallop. Your small print gives an unequivocal commitment to providing for every taste.'

'I can't just . . .'

'With all the couples you've got here there must be someone who'd be glad of a few sharp lashes.'

The Captain was horrified. 'But you saw for yourself on the Intercoupling network how little demand there was for that kind of thing. Believe me, sir, anyone who knows anything about the leisure and recreation industry these days will tell you it's hard enough to get bums on seats, let alone to have them on offer for flogging.'

'Come on, Haggler. Everyone fancies a bit of that from time to time, don't they? It's a natural urge. I've explained to you about Mrs Pelham, of course. She's not robust – gets these migraines. Got one now, in fact. Twenty-four hours I'm giving you, Haggler, and then I'm holding you to the letter of your contract.'

A low, off-camera moan could be heard as he was speaking, becoming quaveringly articulate when he fell silent. 'What are you doing, Danvers? I can't stand the light from that television.'

Pelham craned round, presenting his hawk-like profile to the camera. 'Just claiming our dues, Nance. I'm glad to say Captain Haggler's beginning to see things the way we see them.'

The monitor in front of the Captain went dark as the sadistic lawyer logged off. He leaned back in his chair and became aware of Gloria gazing down at him from behind. She laid her hands on his shoulders and kissed his brow sympathetically. 'You got problems, Doc,' she commiserated. 'You gonna let me help you forget them?'

'Captain,' he said. 'You agreed to call me Captain. This isn't the campus, it's a motel, remember? And I don't just want these problems forgotten. I want them solved.'

THREE

INTERCOUPLING

It was warm in the restaurant, and almost impossible in the dim rosy light to read the names of the dishes, which were printed in red on pink paper. Talbot, the medallion winking in the open front of his shirt, closed his menu ostentatiously, summoned the waiter and took it on himself without consulting the others to order for all of them.

Sally was still feeling breathless after the drive. Talbot had insisted on having her in the front of his swanky Alfa Romeo with Rod and Yvonne in the back. She did not know what had been going on behind her, but she was amazed at how much this dark charmer had been able to achieve with one hand up her skirt while driving at speed. And now he was at it again under the tablecloth while the other two were engaged in whispered conversation.

'What does your husband *do*, dear?' Talbot inquired.

She did not want to say Rod was on the dole. 'Property,' she said. 'That's it – he's into estate agency. And what about you?'

'Oh, I make movies. Got my own production company.'

'How fascinating. Would I have seen any of your films?'

'I very much doubt that, Sally. One works at the specialist end of the market. Low budget but high turnover. And what do you do – devote yourself to household duties?'

Sally shivered deliciously as his hand clamped the softness of her upper thigh. 'Actively seeking employment, as they say.'

'And you'd like a part in one of my highly specialised productions, is that it? I'll set up a screen test for you if your husband agrees,' he leered. 'By the way, ours is going to be an open marriage this time round. How about you two?'

'Well, we haven't really – you know . . .'

She did not remember too much about the meal as they raced back afterwards through the gathering twilight of a balmy mid-July evening dominated by a huge moon, except that she had not been able to eat more than a few mouthfuls of the food. On the other hand, she had undoubtedly drunk more than she intended of a rough, potent liquor served in little china cups. Back at the motel they tumbled out of the car and headed for Number Seven. Talbot unlocked the door and they all piled in, the younger couple nervous and unsteady after the meal and drive, and the older ones loud and eager.

Yvonne Yglesias closed the door. Her husband grinned. 'In these situations one usually has a bath or a shower,' he said, peeling off his shirt. 'I'm afraid our facilities here are rather cramped but no doubt the management will mop up any mess we leave.'

'Later,' laughed Yvonne. 'First it's the beach, for skinny-dipping and fucky-ducking. There are no clouds and you saw how big the moon is tonight.'

The four of them removed their clothes. Sally couldn't help noticing the way the corners of Rod's mouth drew back as he ran a lascivious eye down Yvonne's body. She felt too shy herself to look at their new friends below the level of their necks and was thankful when Yvonne came out of the bathroom with a pile of soft white towels. They wrapped these round themselves, the women choosing bathtowels which they secured under their armpits while the men contented themselves with smaller coverings for their loins. Talbot's tanned skin with its pelt of wiry black hair made a rather striking contrast with the white towelling, especially when he allowed a muscular leg to emerge negligently from the opening down the side. Sally feared that the sophisticated Yvonne might be less attracted to Rod than she herself had been to Talbot ever since she first spied on him through the mirror two nights before. She liked to think of the colour of Rod's body as a kind of ivory. Really, though, she was afraid it might strike other people as being not unlike putty.

34

The little party hurried across the brightly illuminated area in front of the motel and over the small sloping meadow where the grass had been allowed to grow long for the benefit of amorous couples. Yvonne's towel came unwound as she ran, so she trailed it behind her. They came to the hedge that marked the top of the cliff and crossed the stile. Some care was needed to negotiate the crude steps cut into the crumbling sandstone but soon they all reached the beach safely. Talbot snatched off Sally's towel, loosened his own and stood with it hanging rudely from the rigid peg that curved up between his thighs. She was quite glad when Rod took her by the hand and dragged her purposefully towards the gently breaking waves.

After the first shock of entry the water felt agreeably warm. Rod, a floundering non-swimmer, lingered on the edge but Sally preferred to wade out rather more briskly than was usual with her in order to dip down and conceal her pussy, bottom and breasts. Not that these charms would have been visible from more than a few yards away (would they, she wondered), except as indistinct, pale shapes like those of the others splashing about in the shallow water. She lay back and floated, rising and falling on the gentle swell as if drawn into and released from the embrace of the moon.

Before Sally knew what was happening, busy hands were sliding over her limbs, attacking her from underneath. Body slipped voluptuously against body in a submarine dance that forced her to hold her breath, not just out of astonishment at the sheer beauty of the encounter but in order to survive each time she was drawn under. In this free interplay it was as if every part of her person was touched and caressed underwater by every part of Talbot's. The tide carried them towards the beach and the sound of the breaking waves grew more distinct each time they broke the surface.

And now they were back in Sally's depth, the black sea around them flecked with sparkles of silver. They stood facing each other, up to their shoulders in water that made Sally rise on each incoming wave while her partner's feet remained planted in the shifting sand. Her arms went round his neck and she felt his upstanding hardness first stab against her stomach and then corkscrew its way up into her sex. 'Tiger prawns are all very well,' he shouted. 'But to finish off the meal you can't beat a succulent mollusc. No "R" in the month, of course, so how about adding a solid whelk to a fat, juicy mussel?'

Her legs floated up round his hips. She revelled in her lightness, her buoyancy. Sex might feel like this, she thought, if we had the benefit of an extra dimension. Well, actually it was gravity that usually stopped you doing what you wanted to, wasn't it? Space flight would be fun . . .

Talbot Yglesias was wading towards the shore, boring up into her with each moonwalking stride. She had quickly discovered that she didn't like this Talbot as a person. But he certainly knew how to make you feel like a grown-up woman. By now the water was rising and falling around his waist. He bent forward, his lips sucking wetly on hers, until she was floating on her back. Then he straightened up and the water streamed from the glistening black shag plastered down his front. The gold medallion shone wet in the moonlight. His hands cupped her buttocks and his proud figurehead was securely rammed into a sheath tightened by the tang of the ocean. Their pubic hair swirled round the point of connection like fine seaweed.

Tight she might be, and Sally was conscious of her tightness, but she also felt unusually oily and elastic inside. She was beginning to enjoy sex, if only Rod could soon get the hang of doing it properly. Maybe Yvonne would put him on the right track. Sally squeezed and relaxed, squeezed and relaxed. The age-old action of the ocean, lifting her and letting her fall, lifting and falling, procured a fucking motion between the two of them which the outer muscles of her cunt resisted, while deep within her the intrusive flesh swelled and stirred with the heave of each wave. And Talbot's hands were all over her floating body, stroking her face, plucking her nipples, teasing her clitoris. She took a huge breath and plunged backwards until her head touched the bottom. Her thighs gripped Talbot's slippery hips as her hands thrashed about wildly in the water. Her cunt clenched, loosened and clenched again and yet again as the waves of orgasm swept over her, displacing the marine waves as movers of their lust and causing Talbot's seacock to open in a surge of salty foam. Sally felt her bilges flooding and overflowing into the life-giving, devouring ocean.

At some point in this process Talbot's temporarily diminished tiger prawn was expelled. Sally rose giddily to her feet and stumbled shorewards in happy oblivion. As she waded, a seemingly endless store of spawn slid down the insides of her wet thighs, twisting away into the water in viscous ropes and hanks.

On the firm wet sand repeatedly washed by the tame, crisping curves of the exhausted waves she found Rod and Yvonne. The latter lay on her back, knees spread, heels dug into the sand and toes pointing out to sea. The silvery, moonlit slimness of Rod was stretched above her, his bum bouncing as he rammed in and out of her. It must have been the cool salt slap of the sea that had enabled him to hold back long enough to effect penetration.

Sally dropped to her knees, which sank down into the yielding sand on each side of Rod's legs and between Yvonne's feet. She fondled her husband's white buttocks and handled his tight, cold scrotum as he fucked. He responded with more violent thrusts. As he withdrew on each stroke, the sticky stiffness of his ratrod slipped through her fingers; as he plunged in again the fingers were trapped between his sodden hairs and Yvonne's speared flesh.

It was impossible to know if Rod realised it was his own wife who was tickling his balls. But Yvonne opened her eyes and saw at once what was going on. She reached up under Rod's arm to grasp Sally's breasts.

At the same instant Sally felt strong hands on her bottom. She squealed with joy as the burning tip of Talbot's unseen penis began to batter her brine-shrunken outer sex. A finger prised her open and her newly gushing juices flushed out still more of the semen left from their first encounter. And then the whole crazily crooked length bored into her and began pounding with a fury that communicated itself through the jiggling of her breasts to Yvonne's fingertips and womb, and through the frenzied movements of her own hands to Rod's testicles.

As if to show that the tide would not be cheated, a rogue breaker crashed down just behind the intercoupling foursome. Thousands of gallons exploded exultantly, lifting them bodily and hurling them a dozen yards up the beach. Its fury spent, the water sucked back, leaving them stranded. So tightly had they clung to each other under the buffeting welter of foam that their fourfold embrace was still intact. Sally, still twitching as her own climactic waves subsided, could tell that Talbot had burst inside her, and the couple pinned beneath them were clearly in a state of post-coital deflation, flattened into the cool sand and gasping like freshly landed fish.

After a pause for recovery and a couple of minor wettings they all got up, stepped a short way out into the sea again and splashed each other playfully to wash off the sand. Yvonne's bottom in particular required a good deal of attention; her husband insisted on using his hands to grope between her legs and scoop out anything still silting up her intimate inlets. The Yglesiases seemed to be as randy as rutting walruses after their dalliance with the Nugents and soon abandoned drying each other to get down on the towel and fuck.

Rod gave Sally a look she could not interpret with any certainty in the light of the moon. He took her hand and led her up the beach to the steps. Both of them were still dripping, their towels hanging loose from their free hands.

Sally toiled up the stairs behind her lean husband. Her eyes were fixed on his glistening buttocks and the darkly glimpsed bunch of fruit hanging and dripping beneath them as he raised his foot to each high step. On the final bend of the climb, however, she looked up at the stile which was now suddenly revealed some ten feet above them. Silhouetted black against the pale sky towered the figure of a man. The figure drew back and she clasped her towel in front of her.

As she followed Rod over the stile the man emerged from the shadows of the hedge and was seen to be none other than the manager, Captain Haggler. 'Lovely night, sir, madam,' he said in a low and possibly insinuating voice. 'Just checking security. Don't want trespassers barging in on our little games, do we?'

When the Captain returned to Reception ten minutes later after watching Talbot and Yvonne obtain mutual satisfaction, he found a sulky-looking Gloria standing bent forward, her elbows resting on the counter. He raised the flap and passed through, slapping her lightly on the behind as he made for the door of the back office. To his surprise, for he had not bothered to look at her properly and had administered the friendly pat as a semi-automatic gesture, the behind turned out to be bare. He was even more surprised when he saw that it was flushed bright pink and was cross-crossed with red lines.

He turned her to face him and raised his eyebrows interrogatively. The tears welled in her eyes and trickled down her freckled cheeks. 'Oh, Doc,' she sobbed. 'Captain, I mean. Your problems with Mr Pelham? I guess I was trying to come up with a solution.'

Melanie flicked through her diary. Although still early, this was going to be a hot day, so she had stripped off her flimsy nightdress and sprawled lazily on the little couch in her room. She stretched and yawned contentedly. After nearly two years she had still not tired of life in this cramped cottage on the outskirts of Upchester. It had to be better than going out to earn a living, didn't it? During term time the MacDonald was off to the college in her old Morris Minor most of the day. Then Melanie had the place to herself. Herself and anyone else she cared to have round to swan about nude with or, in the warmer months, to sunbathe in the sheltered garden. It was true that Mac's absences were also the cause of some grief, as Melanie's suspicions that the older woman was indulging in flirtations with her young students received frequent corroboration. And *flirtation*, of course, was something of an understatement. Last year Mac had engaged in a full-blown affair with little Anne Amory and her chum Carla Merryweather. At least the situation had become bearable after she brought the pair home with her for that rave of a tea-party – from then on Melanie had been enlisted to make up regular quartets and had even been encouraged to bring Derrick's talents into the circle occasionally. But since Anne and Carla took their A-levels and left Cunlip College last summer, those happy sessions had come to an end. Melanie now thought she had reason to suspect her mistress was carrying on with a younger girl, that greasy-haired slut Helen. Well, Helen Lascelles' hair had always looked greasy two years ago, before Melanie had been obliged to leave

Cunlip under a cloud. Now the girl was eighteen she had probably glammed herself up a bit. All the same, Helen had always had a very distinctive scent. Not at all off-putting, but, well, distinctive. And these days that scent often seemed to cling to Mac's mouth, tits and fanny.

Still, apart from such minor irritants, mostly connected with Mac and Derrick, and a certain boring sameness about her daily routine, life was not too bad. Now that the Captain was back in the country there was a chance things would start to liven up. She had not seen him since that fantastic business last summer.

After licking the finger with which she had been unconsciously probing the outer intricacies of her sex, Melanie opened the diary, replaced the finger – consciously this time – and more or less randomly selected the penultimate entry, the one before her account of the Captain's current activities. She began to read.

Mon, July 13

Really pissed off with Derrick when he called round Saturday morning and couldn't get it up. I had to spend more than an hour tickling his balls and licking and sucking him. In the end he just rested his thing, all swollen but quite soft, on my tummy, half lying on me and half propping himself up on his hands so he could look down at my face and boobs. I winked at him and stuck a finger up his arse. He came, but it was like two-dimensional. Instead of squirting up in the air the stuff shot out across my skin and spread all over my tum. Rather like when you chuck a carton of yogurt on the floor and suddenly it's everywhere. Made him lick me clean but he seemed less enthusiastic than usual. Just wanted me to leave him alone and let him kip for half an hour. Anyway, his defences were down – easy to get truth out of him, or part of it at least.

ME: You went with someone before you came here, you scumbag.

DERRICK: I never. I come straight here, didn't I?

ME: You came with drained bollocks.

DERRICK: I was just tired. Plenty of juice in the old nuts – saw it yourself. Old Rover here was just a bit too tired to sit up and beg for it. Give us a break, Mel.

ME: Tired, were you? What were you up to last night, then?

DERRICK: Nothing. Went down the drinker and threw some arrows. It give me a fucking stiff wrist.

ME: And a non-fucking limp prick? What do you take me for, you pathetic cunt? Don't you find me attractive any more?

DERRICK: Course I do. I mean, you're a real woman compared with that Susie O'Flammery, the little whore.

ME: Susie? Been pestering her again, have you? Look, Susie and Darcy are good friends of mine. They wouldn't be married if I hadn't fixed it for them – no way. Ever since that business last year with the Captain and his American friends she's been right off men. Except Darce, of course. You're not her type, she told me. Unless they're at least forty she can't stand them all hairy like you. And she prefers them tall, like most of us do.

DERRICK: Cool it, won't you? She give me the eye the other day in Upchester, outside Bigbuys. She let me go in with her to push her trolley round and then I took her home on the old Yamaha with all the stuff she'd bought – they still can't afford a fucking car. Oh yes, I'm her type all right. She made a mistake with that poncy Darcy.

ME: Let me tell you, Derrick, I've never known Darce unable to get a hard-on when it was needed. Maybe he still looks the innocent choirboy, but since he's been married he fucks like a space shuttle. They make a lovely couple. You just lay off sweet little Susie. Believe me, she's not ready for a hairy bugger like you.

That afternoon I went round to D's digs to pick him up because we were going into town to see a movie. Well, he was out but his landlady let me into his room to wait. Mess everywhere as per usual. Door of walk-in cupboard he uses as darkroom open. Strips of negative hanging from sort of clothes-line in there. Held them up to light – they were all females, and a lot of them nude, but no way of recognising who they were. Could have been me except that I haven't let him take any of me lately.

Got on D's bed to wait for him, fuming. When I shifted

pillow found pile of finished photos under it. Oh no! I might have known – he'd been taking pix of little Susie. There she was posing for him in her 'wedding' outfit: head-dress and veil, open sleeveless top and little hankies front and back to cover bum and pussy. He'd taken a sequence of these, starting with the veil wrapped round her quite modestly and ending with the suntop pulled to sides to show tits and with Susie holding up front handkerchief. Wondered what young Darcy would think if he saw them. Turned over photo and next one *was* Darce, dressed just in the hankies like at the wedding. He was grinning and waving his stiff prick at camera. In next picture both of them kneeling – Darce and his bride still in wedding togs with him fucking her from behind.

At least they were only doing what they're entitled to do as a married couple. It was Derrick I was mad with, not them, the poor lambs. But there were still more photos. Imagine how I felt when I saw half a dozen of Susie wearing *my* clothes! Nighties, bikinis, hats, leotards, G-strings, T-shirts without bottoms – you name it. Now I understood why I thought I'd been getting absent-minded lately and mislaying my things. Sometimes they'd turned up in dirty washing and I was sure I hadn't even had them on.

More to come. Susie nude with another girl I didn't recognise at first. Then it came to me. Those tiny breasts she used to have had swelled out into proper knockers and her hair wasn't straight and brown any more but blonde and frizzy, but I was sure it was that Nikki, the one who'd been Susie's bridesmaid at her 'wedding'. What put me on right track was the fact that her twat was still hairless and shiny like we had it for the big day. Anyway, in these pix D had taken the girls kissing and playing with each other. Then he must have given camera to Susie. Last couple of shots sort of crooked and a bit blurry. But no doubt about it. My Derrick was screwing that hot-tailed bitch Nikki Culpepper.

Heard D coming up the stairs so shoved photos back under pillow and pretended to be all smiles and sweetness. But came straight out with it when he kissed me and tried to put hand on cunt.

ME: OK, you hairy bastard – when did you last have her?

DERRICK: Have who?

ME: Nikki, of course. Who else?

DERRICK: Nikki? What Nikki's that, then? With a CK or two Cs?

ME: Cut the crap, lover. I mean the Nikki you slipped a length to on your way to the cottage this morning. The one who took the wind out of your sails so you couldn't do the business with me – remember?

DERRICK: OK, so I had this quickie with Nikki. So what? She was standing there on the canal bridge watching the water. I stopped the bike right by her and revved up the engine to show I was serious. Well, she was asking for it, wasn't she? Only wanted to do her a favour. Said she hadn't had a bloke since last weekend, so we went down under the bridge and I unzipped my leathers and went in up the leg of her hotpants. Knickerless Nikki, that's what the lads call her. Just a slag. No reflection on you, Mel. After all, I come on straight up to your place after, didn't I?

ME: 'Straight up' maybe isn't the best way of putting it. You were a flop.

Anyway, for all his bluster he was so deflated I thought there wasn't much point in going on at him about Susie – that would keep. I stripped off for him and this time he reinflated and performed without a hitch. I made him spunk up me three times without taking it out, then sucked last dribblings out of him.

Melanie sighed and wiggled her finger. For some reason, reading this entry was not having much effect on her yet. She was lubricating, but nowhere near orgasm. Perhaps it would be a better idea to go back to bed for a cuddle with the MacDonald and everything a cuddle was likely to lead to. But by this time Mac would already be thinking about getting up, preoccupied with the day's programme and trying to work out what to do with the girls in her English and Physical Development classes. She was never at a loss, of course – it wasn't that. But she was as keen on variety as her young charges were and didn't like them to feel let down because what they did one day didn't measure up to the lesson they'd had the day before. Melanie sighed again, licked her sticky finger, turned a couple of pages of the yellow notebook and found the end of yesterday's entry summarising the letter she and Mac had received from the Captain. Moving across to her desk she took her ballpoint and began to write a continuation.

Thu, July 16

Which reminds me. There I was, rattling on about Palace of Honeymoons, as I keep wanting to call it, and completely forgetting to write up what happened Monday afternoon. It was getting on for four o'clock. I'd just finished with diary after writing that bit about sucking last dribblings out of Derrick's dick when I heard car outside, then front door opening and Mac calling out to see if I was home. *Very* unusual for her to get back so early.

I had on just my yellow T-shirt. Ran downstairs without thinking, really pleased to see her so soon. Oh dear! She wasn't alone but had that awful Helen in tow. When I made a point of not giving Mac my usual hug she just gave me a cool look and asked me to make tea for the three of us. All so matter of fact – only jarring note my bare bum and fanny. Mac quite homely-looking in purple tracksuit. Helen, in spite of sluttish reputation, just your typical sixth-former in Cunlip uniform: crisp white shirt, striped tie, shortish grey pleated skirt and long white socks with black sandals. Didn't have that dark greasy hair any more. Now that it's properly washed it's quite a light brown, almost yellow. Very straight, cut in a fringe at front and just down to nape of neck at back. Made her look quite pretty, even with those dark shadows under her eyes, that mouth which keeps turning down at corners and the crooked front teeth. In a way this new prettiness (well, maybe she was always pretty in a nail-biting, shagged-out sort of way) only emphasises that look of sleaziness I can't help associating her with. One way to describe difference between how she is now and how she was two years ago is this: when she was sixteen she looked as if she had bad breath (though when I asked Emily she said there was no trace of it that time she got to fuck her in our famous dorm feast with the Captain), but now the idea wouldn't enter your head. Oh, and she's still rather skinny but at least she's grown a pair of little boobs. They made two separate (spelling?) bumps under her shirt.

Imagine how sour I felt when Mac patted my bare bottom and told me to take some tea out to garden for them. I deliberately let it stew a bit, let tea slop into saucers and put some rather stale biscuits on tray with tea things. Out in garden I found them chatting and laughing – dreadful to think they might be laughing about me but if so I'd have expected guilty hush when I came out. Mac had taken top of tracksuit off and her nipples had puckered into hard orange jewels in the fresh air and sunshine. Helen was sitting on two-seater under the apple tree, facing her across table. She was putting on orange lipstick, making funny mouths and squinting at herself in a little mirror. In fact, lipstick was all she had on apart from socks and sandals. For a moment I was reminded of her mum when she came to the Cunlip open day – not that Mrs Lascelles was nude, of course, but I caught her putting make-up on and that intense sort of expression was just the same. Mrs Lascelles is a single parent who makes ends meet by writing smutty books and I think it shows somehow in her daughter's demeanour (spelling?).

They had their tea and I sat there with them making them feel embarrassed (I can spell that one by now). Pretended not to be looking at Helen but was rather fascinated by her skinny body. Very white skin with lots of moles and a pair of little brown nipples that look rather like moles themselves. Had her legs crossed but every now and then I got glimpse of surprisingly light-coloured silvery-yellow fluff between thighs.

Mac was talking about *Songs of Innocence* – probably her pretext for having the little madam round here – and making Blake sound like a sex maniac and child-abuser. That seemed to work with Helen, who'd thought he wrote wishy-washy kiddies' stuff. All those little lambs and angels and children with white hair. She hadn't heard of things like 'Let the Brothels of Paris Be Opened'. I just sat there picking garbage out of my belly button. The sun was hot. After a time Mac got up, put her tracksuit top on and said she had to pop back to the college to fetch something. She told me to 'look after our visitor'. Well, I just went on sitting and gave that unwelcome visitor a long, cold stare. But Helen seemed to want to be friendly and flashed back that crooked smile of hers. Sometimes you can't win.

HELEN: Remember the time you and your room-mates had that dorm feast and you got four of us sixteen-year-olds to be your partners?

ME (*coldly*): Of course I remember.

HELEN: Old Emily chose me and I think you picked little Anne Amory. I used to be jealous of Anne when she was the MacDonald's pet.

ME (*coolly*): Then you know what it feels like.

HELEN: Look, there's more than enough for everyone, Melanie. Anyway, that was a fantastic night, wasn't it? The eight of us all frigging and licking away like the clappers. And who was that old geezer we had with us? You know, that odd-job man – didn't he call himself the Colonel or something?

ME (*warming up a bit*): The Captain.

HELEN: That's right, the Captain. Well he was with us and after he bit he started fucking us all, remember. You told him to see how many of us he could get into before he came. He got through all eight of us and shot his first load into that Nikki Culpepper.

ME (*flushed with excitement*): Then he went straight on to a second round, with us taking it in turns to squat on top of him, and in no time at all he'd flooded your sweet little cunt. Think he was a bit on the big side for you, wasn't he? It all came sloshing out round the edges while he was still pumping it in.

HELEN: It's just that I've got these incredibly strong muscles down there. If I come with a guy inside me I sometimes squeeze him right out like a champagne cork. Well, I was sitting on this Captain so there was no way I could spit him out. And his thing was so long it felt like I had this huge pole stuck right up into my stomach, or I might have shot up in the air and released him. He had me skewered and when I contracted like that the only place his spunk could go was over my thighs and bum.

Helen could see she'd got me interested in this tightness

and I just knew she wanted me to have a feel for myself. She'd uncrossed her legs to reveal the delicate vertical slit and was pushing her bottom forward on the seat.

Went over and sat next to her. My left leg rubbed against her cool right one, which she lifted and put over my thigh. I looked at the pointy little bumps on her chest, then down her white belly to the narrow hips and fluffy sex-mound. It looked soft and awfully inviting – obvious what she wanted. I laid left hand on it gently and gave little squeeze. Helen did same to me with her right one and we curled middle fingers back to slide up inside each other. Sat there with hands crossed and fingers paddling about in sticky twats. Funny feeling as if I was frigging myself but with twice as much sensation as usual.

Sure enough, Helen's cunt tightened up and seemed to be sucking on my finger, drawing blood into the tip. But not a dry tightness – it got more slippery as well, so I could go on pushing in and out though it was pretty hard work. She must have been enjoying looseness of mine. I felt her cramming three of her fingers into me and churning them about in the juice. Then her thumb found my clit and of course mine homed in on hers. I leaned to the left and bent my head to bring my lips down on her right tit.

We were getting so carried away we didn't hear motorbike pull up or see Derrick striding into garden till he was towering over us. Well, *towering* can't be right word for that shortarsed two-timing cunt. But it will do for the purple-headed monster he'd pulled out of his leathers as soon as he got sight of us doing each other like that and caught a whiff of our intermingled pheromones (spelling?). Why, they were so rank and overpowering that even that tabby tomcat of Mac's had dropped down out of the apple tree and was smarming itself stiff-tailed round both my legs and Helen's left one as if we'd been dabbling our fingers in saucers of milk.

Helen was fascinated by D's tool. He stood there on his squat legs grinning down at us, then slowly opened his other zips and peeled the motorcycling gear off, followed by his string vest and Hawaiian boxer shorts. Not a pretty sight with those spikes sticking up on his head and looking as if his papery skin had had tangles scrawled all over it by intellectually challenged kids with black biros. Helen, though, was eyeing him greedily.

After the way he'd been treating me I wasn't letting him gorge himself on the first bit of cunt-flesh that offered itself, just like that. No. Taking my cue from the dorm feast Helen had reminded me of, I told him he could stick it in us but must do it in turns, once in and out each time with no pumping. He didn't get it, so I made Helen lie beside me to my left on the grass, both of us with legs open, and explained exact sequence to him: H's cunt, my mouth, my cunt, H's mouth, then her cunt and so on over and over again till he came. A kind of musical orifices but with only the sweet music our bodies made with each other.

Derrick stretched out over Helen and entered her in one strong shove, but how he winced as she gripped him! At first I thought she'd drawn him off. He unplugged with sigh of relief, still swollen hard but maybe a bit bruised, and moved up to poke it in my mouth. The lovely thing about playing this game was the way you got the taste of another girl's cunt-juice mingling with the seepings from the prick.

We were halfway through round two, with D fucking my cunt, when Mac got back, carrying a plastic bag from Bigbuys. While she pulled off her tracksuit she was watching us and working out what we were up to. She stepped out of her red knickers and got down beside me on my right – I thought that was a nice gesture because she knows how jealous I get. So now Derrick had three quims and three mouths to service. He went from Helen's cunt straight across me to Mac's mouth, then her cunt, my mouth, my cunt, Helen's mouth and cunt and back to Mac. It was while transporting his equipment from her pussy up to her lips that he spilt his load all over her belly and tits. Helen and I leaned across and licked it up so it wouldn't go to waste, and Mac insisted on kissing both of us to get benefit of coating left on insides of mouths after we'd swallowed it down.

Next job: to wind Derrick up again. Mac made him kneel over Helen with wet willie dangling in her mouth. I came up behind him to lick bollocks while the MacDonald stuck

a lewd finger up his bum. Didn't take long. We had to drag
H out from under him or she would have choked. And there
was that lovely truncheon of his again, all hard and gleaming.

I told Mac it was a pity we had just this one prick to satisfy
three hungry cunts. She smiled and reached for her Bigbuys
bag and guess what – she'd fetched that huge demonstration
dildo from her physical development lab in the college, the
one with that kind of harness attached to it. My first
acquaintance with it goes back to the time I used it on Susie
at her 'wedding', to open her up for Darcy. Derrick had seen
it in action last year when Mac brought Anne and Carla home
for that wild tea party. But from the way Helen's eyes went
as wide as saucers I got the impression it was the first time
she'd encountered it outside of Mac's classes. And as Helen
had always been used in those classes to illustrate smallness
of undeveloped genitals I couldn't suppose Mac would have
compromised her suitability by stuffing a thing like that up
her. Tight twats have a high price on them in these parts.

Well, two pricks better than one even though we still had
a ratio of two to three. But Mac had the answer to that
problem. She strapped the thing on fairly loosely and stood
there looking like a female athlete who'd had too much
testosterone pumped into her to harden her muscles. All
Mac's muscles are in good shape of course but one in
particular – the rubber one – was impressively hard. Made
her look like one of her Highland forefathers ready to toss
the caber.

Next she bent down slightly with feet apart, knees bent
and thighs splayed. She twisted dildo round in harness till
balls were uppermost, then tightened straps a bit. Used both
hands to pull cuntlips open before forcing bulging rubber
scrotum up between them. Brilliant! Final stroke of genius
was to adjust angle of inverted prick till it pointed upwards
with root nestled up against clit. Holding it in that position
she made final adjustment to straps and waved magic wand
in front of us. Now there were only two holes to be filled.

Question was, who was to get live penis and who would
make do with artificial one? Dildo much bigger but Derrick
warmer, more mobile and – we all hoped – primed with hot

spunk. I assumed Mac and D would sort it out between them. But no – surprise. Everything settled when Helen insisted on gettting her fill of dildo. Mac said that was fine as long as we didn't end up as two separate couples. She supervised our linking up to avoid this.

Helen had to lie on her right side with knees pulled up so her pussy stuck out between bum cheeks and upper thighs. How pretty she looked in her sandals and long white socks! Mac got down behind her, curled up against her and nudged knob of dildo into entrance of sex. I helped by applying lots of saliva and forcing the lips really wide open. Once head was jammed into the stretched flesh Mac gave a mighty heave, clutching her firmly round the waist. In it went in one stroke, with poor Helen whimpering and sobbing. Only for a moment, though. As soon as she got used to it she smiled bravely and said the feeling was lovely. Said her own wetness and elastic stretching made it feel as if the hard rubber was melting inside her.

Holding her firmly with both hands on her titties, Mac told me to lie down on my right side too, my pussy level with Helen's mouth and my mouth with her pussy, as per sixty-nine. We each had to lift our left leg so right thigh made pillow for partner's cheek. Then Derrick lay behind me and slid up into quim. The knot was sealed.

Well, not quite – Helen and I still had to go for it with some nimble tongue work. I felt her face and hair moving against skin of my thigh as she adjusted position and started licking. Seemed to be sweeping up and down slit, lingering at top to bore tip into my clitoris and then licking down to lap up liquor welling out of my vagina as D's dick slid in and out of it. He must have felt her tongue too, and probably her fingers on his balls and bum. Every time she slipped down from my clit to operate on the place where we were joined, fingers of his left hand got extra busy with my breasts, pinching and tweaking nipples till my stomach was churning with lust and my own tongue writhing frantically along the slippery gash that ran from Helen's little lovebud to where her flesh was stretched in an oily seal round the thick rubber piston. My right hand was on Mac's behind, working its way down the groove between her buttocks and tickling her arsehole. Funny thing was, her body felt like part of Helen, and what Derrick was doing to me felt like it was being done by her. Maybe I was getting obsessed with the depraved little darling. The one sensation that was nothing like her caresses was fur of tomcat rubbing against my skin – and theirs too, I should think – as it circled round looking for nesting place.

The four of us could have gone on like this for rest of afternoon, or at least the three females. Felt so happy I wished all four of us could go to this Palace of Honeymoons and take advantage of the Captain's facilities. But all good things have to end and obviously it was the defusing of Derrick that did for us. He groaned and squeezed my nipple so hard it felt like it was going to burst. He rammed his cock so hard into me that my splayed-out sexlips were forced tightly against Helen's face and nearly suffocated her. Her reaction was to shove her pussy forward even harder into my face as she juddered into orgasm, dragging her rubber phallus with her so its balls tormented Mac's cunt to climax point. Of course, I was coming myself. I'd been coming continuously for the last few minutes and was now in the final throes of ecstasy. The last thing I remember was feeling the heat of that stream of pressurised sperm Derrick squirted into my womb. He may be screwing around a bit, but he can't be all that drained . . .

Been having second thoughts. If we do make that trip to the Captain's fun palace, best to keep D out of it. He cramps my style.

FOUR

TYING THE KNOT

A couple of days later, heavy rain ensured that most of the motel guests stayed indoors. This meant that the Captain and Gloria were even busier than on most Fridays, which were devoted to providing demonstrations and assistance for those who desired to improve their performance in readiness for the weekend. Calls for room service had been coming through since early morning. The Captain had only survived to the afternoon by holding back from orgasm three times out of four; even Gloria, he had noticed, was beginning to handle like a lettuce that had lost its crispness. And now, to make things worse, she was starting to hassle him again with talk of marriage. He knew she was fond of him in some ways, as she ought to be after all he had done for her. He had taken her on in California as an obscure postgraduate student of erotic photography and ripped apart the veil of prudishness that had still clung to her despite the direction of her studies. He had elevated her to be his personal assistant, given her a generous share of the proceeds of his irregular dealings with the university library and brought her back to England with him when things got dodgy. So maybe when she bared her bum to that brute Pelham she had only been repaying part of what she owed for these favours. At least he had been spared further pestering from the importunate solicitor since her sacrifice.

Yet although he felt sure she had grown fond of him, the Captain was also aware that Gloria had set her heart on acquiring British nationality and staying in this country. Well, that was understandable seeing that she might have to face criminal proceedings if she returned to the States. But he didn't like the idea that he was being used, and he certainly didn't like the idea of being restricted by the shackles of matrimony, however lightly those shackles might chafe. In short, he was preoccupied as he went about the day's business and was beginning to feel a little self-conscious about the angle he could achieve with his prick in front of all these guests clamouring for instruction.

It did not surprise him in the least that even couples who appeared to have long been familiar with the facts of life should be requesting lessons in sexual technique. Probably most of them just wanted an excuse to watch his performance with Gloria. Right now, for example, it was porky Des and his bride from Hong Kong who were looking for some action. As usual on these occasions the Captain used his master key to open the door in order to avoid interrupting any activities already in hand. Clinically attired in white coats with nothing underneath, he and his assistant slipped into the room.

The lithe and well-tanned Doris was lying face down on the bed, her legs stretched at a wide angle and her middle raised on a pile of pillows. Between her legs there puffed and panted a mound of flesh that might have been mistaken for a stranded sea-beast but was in fact fat Des, his face buried in the woman's juicy crotch. Feeling Gloria's cool hand on buttocks that struck the Captain as being disproportionately small, Des withdrew his tongue and nose, and rolled over on his back, using Doris's bum as a pillow. His penis, more of a match in size for his buttocks than for his belly, stuck up like a small red-tipped bone.

'Now then, Des,' began the Captain, who had perched himself on the edge of the bed, 'what would the trouble seem to be?'

The man's beady eyes blazed with a kind of desperation. 'You can see from where you're sitting, mate. This beer gut on me – it sort of gets in the way. I just haven't got the length to reach her any more. The old tongue goes in easy enough. That's another reason why I shave her, see. And boy, can she suck! I've tried to take her by storm, like – rushing across the room and throwing my whole weight at her. I just bounce back.

You're a military man yourself, I take it, Captain Haggler. How would you go about storming her defences?'

'You've tried other positions?'

'Not really. Looked through one of those rude books you supply in these rooms, *The Comfort of Sex* or something. But I'm not much good at following the pictures in it. It's like trying to do up a dicky-bow tie in a mirror.'

This guy was a fool, the Captain decided. Instead of using Gloria for the demonstration, why not have a crack at the lovely Doris? He slipped out of his white coat and got Gloria to kneel and lick him. Thank goodness: it worked. He was standing to attention. A military man indeed! The only uniform the Captain had ever worn had been of a less honourable cut.

'Tried having her from behind? Bend over, Gloria, and show him how your pussy sticks out between your bum cheeks.'

Gloria removed her own coat and complied. She reached a hand back between her thighs to reinforce the point. First she squeezed the outer lips to make them swell and project even further and then she stuck two fingers into the vulva and produced squelching noises by churning them around in the juices.

Des's face flushed dark red. A trickle of saliva appeared on his chin and a drop of clear fluid on the tip of his tool. 'Yeah, I tried it like that, squire,' he said. 'But her bum gets in the way of this low-slung belly of mine. OK, I can go up higher so it sort of fits against her where her back curves in. But then I can only get into her arsehole. That's what we do most of the time when I'm not licking her. Not bad, not bad at all, but it's that cunt of hers I'm really crazy about. That's what I bought – what I brought her here for.'

Des was certainly a fool; no doubt about it. The Captain took the belt of a dressing gown hanging behind the door and used it to tie a plump cushion to his own stomach as an artificial paunch for demonstration purposes. He made Doris get off the bed so that he and Des could lie side by side on their backs. Then Gloria had to kneel astride Des's thighs, looking down into his fat face, while Doris adopted the same position above the Captain.

Des's face lit up as if 50p had dropped into his meter. Where had this guy been, the Captain asked himself, if he had never thought of getting the woman to fuck him instead of the other way round?

Both women hovered expectantly above the men. The Captain grasped Doris by her slender hips and guided her into position. Her inner cuntlips were hanging down, pink and engorged, and she used her fingers to part them for him and mould them round the swollen head of his penis. The exposed flesh felt moist and surprisingly cool against the tip. 'Look at this,' he ordered Des. 'When she slides down on my shaft there's no way this cushion can stop her going all the way. Just watch how we do it, then you do the same with Miss Sweetbutts here.'

He patted Doris's bottom as a signal and quite slowly she let herself down the seven inches or so that separated her buttocks from her thighs. As she descended, the Captain's burning stem forced its way up the entire length of her tight vagina. He felt the initial coolness of the outer sex replaced by a lustful heat equal to his own.

Before the sheathing was complete, Gloria descended on Des. She dropped down in one swift movement, her pupil's prick being both slimmer and shorter than the Captain's. The latter now demonstrated on Doris how handy this position was for playing with the woman's breasts; Gloria bent forward over Des to show how easy it was to let her tits dangle into his mouth. He declared himself well pleased with the lesson and was obviously eager to try out this position with his own woman.

Doris's eagerness was less obvious. She was hardly to be reckoned a beginner in the ways of the world, or at least the ways of the Orient. If she had really been set on consummating her marriage, or whatever kind of relationship it was in reality, she would never have needed this demonstration but would have adopted the superior position as a matter of course.

Gloria lifted herself off Des, unsheathing a weapon in a rather more virile condition than it had been in for some time, its modest but not unserviceable length slick and shining with her foaming juices. With some reluctance Doris followed her example; the Captain was not all that keen on their disjuncture either and pressed his hands down lightly on her honey-coloured thighs as if to resist her rising. The tension generated on both sides between the need to part and the wish to stay proved critical. As more and more of his thick and thickly coated cock emerged into view, the Captain felt the product of his balls gather in an urgent mass at the base. Just as the enlarged knob encountered a ring of muscular resistance near her sexual aperture, this mass gushed upwards with uncontrollable force. He pulled her violently down, ramming against the mouth of her womb as burst after burst of creaming spunk jetted from him. Doris collapsed forwards, climaxing unexpectedly as her bare pussy was thrust into the wiry tangle of his hair and her clitoris was crushed against the pubic bone. It was only when the last slow globs had been eased out from his crushed glans that he patted her bottom and she lifted herself off him.

The emergent prick was still sufficiently erect to avert a jealous husband's suspicion. But when the plum slipped out it was followed by most of his white salty spendings, which continued to join cunt and cock in a slithering viscous sheet. Hoping that Des would not notice this, the Captain seized the cushion he had attached to his waist and released it with a sharp tug. Stuffed between Doris and himself it served as a thick, absorbent pad to soak up most of the effluent. He took it with him as he and Gloria hurried off, and with some reluctance popped it into the dirty linen bag on a trolley left by one of the young 'maids' who spent most of their time hanging about waiting for a chance to get into the rooms.

The next few clients simply wanted demonstrations of classical positions with one or two fancy variants. As the Captain worked through these routines he became increasingly aware of a strange, clinging hostility in Gloria. It was as if she resented wanting him. He knew it was all to do with her thing about marrying him. Maybe it was not just to get a British passport, he flattered himself. But in view of her involvement with him in the Banesville University Library scam it was highly likely that her main motivation, at least, was to avoid harassment by the forces of law and order over there in the States.

Anyway, these bad feelings and niggling doubts were getting the better of his virility again. As he made love to her for the enlightenment of the motel guests, from the front, from behind, from the side and upside down, he had to thrust himself against her the moment he had unbuttoned his coat. In this way, he hoped, the onlookers would not realise that the scenes of passionate intercourse enacted before their eyes were only simulated.

Things got a bit more interesting when he and Gloria were summoned to deal with an emergency by a couple who had checked in as Mr and Mrs Brown of Clapham. It was the beautiful but distraught Mrs Brown who admitted them, looking particularly beautiful and black in particularly white panties and bra. Mr Brown was equally black and even more naked but not at all distraught. In fact, he was slumped back in an armchair, snoring. These details, however, were not what first caught the eyes of the Captain and his assistant.

Spread-eagled on the bed lay one of the hand-picked 'maids', a Swedish blonde called Astrid whose ostensible reason for working here was to acquire a bit of English, though the Captain knew she was by no means averse to a bit of the other as well. Astrid was chained by her wrists and ankles to the four corners of the bed. She sobbed and whimpered in her captivity. Her saucy maid's uniform had been savagely ripped to expose one of her breasts. If she had been wearing knickers when she entered the room, there was no sign of them now.

Mrs Brown explained the difficulty: they had lost the key needed to release poor Astrid from her chains. The Captain found this surprising, as these were not like little luggage keys that could slip between a crack in the floorboards but were attached to coloured plastic tags a good three inches long. 'What exactly happened?' he asked. 'What were your next moves after locking her up?'

Mrs Brown pondered. 'Well, now,' she said. 'Mr Brown here, he threw himself on her in a kind of *fury*. With me he's always really gentle, even when he's angry. But oh my! You should have seen the fur flying. He was on top of her and finished his business before I got my things off. And then he flopped down on that chair and don't want to wake up. You got another key?'

The Captain was too embarrassed to reply. These manacles, chains and padlocks had been picked up cheap from a provincial establishment that had gone under like so many others in the recession. They came without duplicate keys and he had never bothered about having copies made, thinking that the conspicuous tags would be sufficient safeguard against loss. He approached the bed and bent forward over the snivelling Astrid. A sudden flash of insight brought a smile to his face.

Astrid (or 'Astride', as the Captain tended to think of her) was an attractive little piece, though of slighter build, he had to admit, than the stereotypical Scandinavian blonde. He stroked her brow in an attempt to soothe her and then let his hand wander down to her thigh, brushing the exposed nipple on the way.

The palm of his other hand cupped her silvery pubic mound and squeezed very lightly. In response the pink lips pouted and parted, and a sluggish emission of sperm eased itself down to the sheet, coating her arsehole and the curves of her buttocks. The Captain shifted his hand a little and introduced two fingers into the overflowing cunt.

When he withdrew these fingers and held them up, the three women saw that they held the missing key with its yellow tag. Suddenly Mr Brown leapt to his feet with a great guffaw. 'Just keep them chains on her, mister,' he cried. 'Mrs Brown and me, we got a few more fancy tricks to pull before we're done.'

After dealing with the Browns, the Captain and Gloria skirted the open-air pool, in which a few couples were energetically chasing each other, and the crowded and ever-popular hot tub, in which there was no place for coyness and no room for escape. They passed through sliding glass doors and entered the small gym to check that the equipment was functioning properly and the naked guests were deriving full benefit from it.

Some of this equipment was of the conventional lever-pulling kind with weights and pulleys. Apart from promoting peaks of unwonted fitness or troughs of excessive tiredness (both states encouraging the users to think about returning to bed to conclude their work-out), the main contribution of this machinery to the business of honeymooning was to display male and female bodies to advantage from unusual angles, exercising unusual muscles. Care had been taken to situate the machines in pairs, and some of them were equipped with rear-view mirrors so that couples could work out in full view of each other.

A rather plump young wife was giving herself a hard time

and her weedy husband a hard-on by struggling with what looked like an ordinary exercise bicycle. It was in fact an adapted model featuring a thick rubber phallus incorporated in the saddle. As the pedals turned, this self-lubricating phallus was driven up and down in the rider's vagina while a small and supple extension tickled the clitoris and surrounding area. Because the present cyclist was somewhat out of form, the effect was even more striking than usual. She appeared to be almost at the end of her tether in more senses than one. Her large thighs quivered, gleaming with sweat, as she strove to force the pedals round – it must have felt like trying to ride a bike up the side of a house. With each thrust her legs gave notice that they could take no more, while her genitals, overriding her conscious will, urged her on to scale the final summit. Suddenly she slumped forward over the handlebars, spent and dripping.

Her husband dragged her off the bike and pushed her into a kind of upright coffin known as the Rubber Maiden. When he closed it her face stared out through a little window while her entire body was massaged and caressed by thousands of rubber spikes, the points of which moulded themselves to the contours of her form and vibrated in a wavelike rhythm. The shrimp of a husband shut himself into a second Maiden facing the first one, so that they could stare into each other's eyes as he was raised and his wife was restored to a condition of heightened sexual readiness. When they emerged from the coffins, the man's cock looked more like a lobster than a shrimp and his rosy wife seemed to have lost any flesh surplus to the requirements of voluptuousness.

Congratulating the couple on their enterprising approach to these mechanical aids, the Captain recommended that they should complete their workout on a special couch of Japanese design and manufacture which had attracted his interest at a recent exhibition in the Victoria and Albert Museum. Attached to the couch was a notice carrying complicated instructions in Japanese and garbled English, the English version headed 'THE AGONY AND THE ECSTASIS: Chaise Lounge with Earth Moving Plant for Amiable Couplings'. To save time and trouble the Captain undertook to operate the controls himself. The amiable couplers lay down on it in a missionary embrace and the woman announced when her husband had penetrated her. This was the Captain's cue to switch on the machine, varying its speed in response to the surprised expressions that raced in rapid variation over their faces as they were shaken and pummelled by wave after wave of what felt like iron fists punching up through the couch. The pummelling forced them to cling to each other more and more tightly, while the shaking propelled the husband's member in and out of his wife's cunt with such vigour that in no time at all his spunk sluiced into her climaxing loins.

Just as this happened, Gloria's bleeper summoned the management team to the Nugents' suite. In spite of the encouragement they had received from their new friends Talbot and Yvonne, it seemed that Rod and Sally, who lay side by side on their bed with the sheet folded down to their waists, had still not successfully consummated their marriage.

'Tell Dr Haggler what the problem is,' urged Gloria, who had become adept at exploiting the guests' propensity for mistaking the Captain's bogus PhD for a medical degree.

Rod frowned and mumbled. 'Well,' he began, 'it's just that . . .'

'He comes too quickly,' Sally interrupted. 'Every time, as soon as he touches me down there with the tip of his thing, his stuff squirts all over me. He's never going to get it in. We might as well not be married.'

'When did this last happen?' the Captain inquired.

'Just before we called you. Look.'

To Rod's evident embarrassment, Sally sat up and drew the sheet right down to their knees. Although it was on its way back again to the fully extended condition in which it had been maintained by proximity to his bride for most of these early honeymoon days, the size and rigidity of Rod's still weeping tool was nothing compared with the Captain's massive erection. This monster hard-on had been summoned up by the sight of Sally's pretty snatch, the velvety texture of its blonde fur ruined by the masculine spillage that darkened it and slicked it down against her skin. Around the edges this salty puddle had already started to dry into lacy white flakes on her.

Well schooled by now in how to cope with this particular affliction, Gloria unbuttoned her clinical coat, climbed up on the bed and knelt astraddle Rod's thighs. As she peeled apart the sticky leaves of her sex and let the enticing aroma drift out to saturate the air around the little group, Rod stiffened up impressively. Gloria kept her eyes fixed on the empurpled glans, afraid that if her glance fell on his rodent-like features she would freeze and clam up. 'Take the rim of the head between thumb and forefinger like this,' she explained to Sally, 'and give it a bit of a squeeze. That ought to take the pressure out of it just a little bit – enough so he can hold back till you've gotten him inside of you? Watch.' She edged forward and slid down over the upright prick, which was swallowed completely and without ejaculating.

'Don't worry, dear,' said the Captain, gently patting Sally's mound. 'She's not going to have him properly. We're going to see if we can get that stiff dick up you without an accident. Let's just check that you're ready.'

His finger stabbed into Sally and stirred about in such a welter of lovejuice that he could hardly pretend there was a need for lengthy stimulation. Gloria lifted herself up off the panting husband and joined the Captain at the bedside. Sally then took the American girl's place, looking lithe and very nude with her long hair piled up on her head instead of cascading down as usual over her back, shoulders and breasts. The prick towered up angrily right in front of her honeyed slit. The onlookers saw it twitch with Rod's eager pulse as the blood raced through it. A droplet grew and glistened on the very tip.

'Squeeze him,' whispered the Captain. 'Squeeze him and stick the bugger in.'

Sally extended a slender white finger and thumb and pinched the cockhead gingerly between the tips. She gave a little squeeze, at the same time lifting her pretty bottom to elevate the entrance of her vagina until it hovered immediately above Rod's straining knob. She squeezed again.

A thin stream of semen fountained up to irrigate the dry deposit already coating her sexual parts. 'Keep on trying,' said the Captain. 'We'll see if we can get back to you tomorrow.'

* * *

That evening the Captain sat in his office sipping coffee from a polystyrene cup. The monitors were switched off to give him a chance to think; his only distraction was the view through the glass partition of Gloria behind the reception counter. There was no doubt that she was becoming something of a thorn in his flesh and yet, in a kind of detached way, he still found her highly desirable. Yes, he was sort of hooked on that thick chestnut plait, the soft cream-coloured flesh and the fluffy bush of brown curls that decorated her sexual parts. And the parts themselves had a certain silky allure, he had to admit. Was marriage really outside the bounds of possibility?

Well, he thought, the chances of being done for bigamy were slight – he had always taken care. And there would be no chance at all if he could put Gloria through a ceremony and supply a certificate which she mistakenly supposed to be legally valid. Then at last she might relax and stop hassling him. He refilled his cup from the machine and considered.

The part of the United States she originally came from was pretty strict and conventional, of course. Women who had illicit sex there, he had read, had a scarlet letter A tattooed on their breast, or something of the sort. Probably it was because of this puritanical background, apart from anything else, that Gloria was so keen to marry him. But more recently she had lived in California and assimilated the golden lifestyle of the Coast, hadn't she? You could get married out there any old how, easy as kiss your arse and not much longer lasting. The Captain seemed to remember accounts of bizarre nuptials which Gloria had probably become conditioned to seeing as the norm. Those underwater ceremonies with a choir of electronically amplified dolphins and a top-hatted penguin as officiating rabbi, for example. Skin-divers and sperm whales cavorting around and doing their respective things as the connubial rites were solemnised, not to mention those friendly, fun-loving turtles . . .

Maybe he was letting his imagination run away with him. Still, they had the motel beach out there. Total immersion was not strictly necessary. He would probably be able to root out the genuine-looking marriage certificates his friend Benny de Bok had printed for him in Amsterdam that time when they were needed in some quantity. He even knew just the man to conduct the ceremony, if only he could contact him. Hadn't he heard on the news that the police were trying to break up one of those music festivals not so far away, just the other side of Overy Clister? That was where he would find this guy. Jimbo DeVayne was a New Age traveller, heavily into religion, who styled himself the Titular Archimandrite of Durdle Door.

The Captain called Gloria into the office and broke the good news to her. It was now Friday, July the seventeenth, and he saw no obstacle to naming the happy day as Saturday the twenty-fifth. Neither, of course, did Gloria, who was delighted that he had at last fallen into what she probably saw as her trap. She took him to her bed to give him a physical pledge of her appreciation and he found he now had no difficulty whatever in performing with vigour and gusto.

Mary Muttock tried to relax in the minicab rushing her from the station to the Honeymoon Palace Motel. But the pot-holes disfiguring the unadopted road that formed the last half-mile, as well as her own excitement at the prospect ahead of her, made relaxation difficult, even though she had nearly emptied her silver hip flask. It was always a relief to get away from the grim decay of the Hall, which only came to life when she was visited by the former students or by her old friend Harris Hardbuckle, who had risen higher than he merited in the police force. Wasn't it in this very county, incidentally, that Harris now held the post of deputy chief constable? Of course it was – the Captain's new establishment was not really very far from Upchester and the college.

Far enough, though, to make it unlikely that she would be recognised by the local plods, from whom she could hardly expect the same indulgent treatment she enjoyed at the hands of old Hardbuckle. Ever since her disgrace and enforced resignation as principal of the college two years before, she had kept a low profile, avoiding the law enforcement agencies like the plague. Not too difficult to lie low in her ramshackle inheritance, Cunlip Hall, though even there she sometimes thought of changing the name as a precaution. Anyone aware of the old-time connection between Cunlip Hall and Cunlip

College might start to draw conclusions. But here, she reflected as the vehicle tossed her up with an alarming lurch, she was well off the beaten track and ought to be able to unwind.

It would be lovely to see the Captain again and thank him properly (if the circumstances of his wedding made it possible) for that generous pay-off he said she had earned for her part in the matter of the Victorian erotica. She would be able to renew her acquaintance with the bride, that enchanting American girl – Gloria Softbuds or whatever she was called. And he had said he was inviting some of the others from the old days. With luck these would include Melanie Winspur who, with some more luck, would still find her attractive.

And why not? The passing years had been kind to Mary Muttock, even if a few more had passed than the twenty-nine or so that she acknowledged. Men found her irresistible, and so did women, once the ice had been broken. Even she herself, who had been thrown more and more on her own company recently, flitting about the Hall like a tanked-up Mariana in the Moated Grange, found her own body definitely appealing. To look at her, especially when she removed her glasses and let her hair down, you would never guess she had stalked the corridors of power as the headmistress of a college for young ladies. And when she put the glasses on and tied her hair up again you would be even less likely to guess she had done time turning tricks in a transatlantic cat-house.

It was good to know that her talents were still in demand, though. According to the cryptic note scribbled on her invitation card, the Captain had summoned her and the others not just for old times' sake but to help him out in the face of various oppressive forces threatening his peace of mind. She would be happy (provided that these ominous and undignified hiccups subsided before her arrival) to oblige and to make the most of what promised to be a pampered and sexually rewarding break from routine. The thought of all those young people around her made her nipples itch. As long as she didn't get molested by . . .

You know, she reminded herself: by these – what were they really? – *animals*. Goats and things, yes, goats and well-hung leopards and muttocks – or did she mean mammoths? Big ones, anyway, with fangs and tusks. Big and horny. Animals and men equipped like animals or who turned into animals or who dropped out of trees and crawled into her bed to tusk her. Sometimes it seemed more as if they were animals who turned into men with great horns on them, but there was sure to be a proper scientific explanation. Surely? Miss Muttock was a strict rationalist and always insisted on scientific explanations. That was all you had that you could hold on to, wasn't it? If she abandoned her conviction that she lived in an ordered, logical universe she would begin to doubt her own sanity.

When the cab dropped her off she filled her lungs with sea air and headed for reception. To gain the door she had to squeeze past a derelict caravan hitched to an old Ford Transit. The Captain and Gloria gave her an enthusiastic welcome, kissing her, taking her to her apartment and apologising for being too busy with the last-minute preparations for their wedding to remain with her. They advised her to slip into something cool and find her way to the pool, where she could expect to meet some old friends who had come down on an earlier train.

Attired in a stylish black one-piece swimsuit cut very high at the sides and very low at the back, and with a black straw sunhat adding a touch of extra sophistication to complete the effect already achieved by the use of dark glasses, Miss Muttock stepped out into the sun. Around the pool, trestle tables had been set up and a small army of 'maids' and youthful pages were busying themselves laying out an extensive cold buffet. One of these pages, cute in his pillbox hat, bum-freezer jacket and red ballet tights, offered her a dry sherry.

Apart from servants, the only people at the poolside were three half-familiar female figures standing chatting at the far end. Everybody else was probably getting ready for the imminent ceremony. As she drew closer to the little group, Mary Muttock recognised first her old colleague Miss Mac-Donald and then Melanie. As if by magic, though more probably as a result of reading the same article in one of the Sunday colour magazines, Mac wore exactly the same gear that she sported herself, except that the swimsuit and hat were white instead of black. And white, it had to be acknowledged, suited her very well now that the muscular hardness of her athletic limbs, the fine smoothness of her back and her strong shoulders and arms shone with a deep tan. The two women grinned and kissed each other on the cheek.

Miss Muttock turned to embrace Melanie, who had been one of her most gifted students and whose literary talents had proved a gold-mine since the premature departure of both of them from the college. The smiling girl stood there in an outfit of pale blue cotton material as well suited to the bedroom as to the beach or pool: a bust-hugging little top with narrow shoulder straps and a trimming of scalloped white lace above the bare belly, and high-sided knickers, loose round the hips but snug at the crotch, with lace at the waist. Her long fair hair was tied back with a scarlet ribbon. 'You look enchanting, dear,' said Miss Muttock, and kissed her on the mouth.

But who was this other girl? She seemed to be about eighteen and was definitely familiar – yes, she too must be an old Cunlip girl. She was shortish and a bit lean and bony. But it was the dark eyes with those shadows under them, the long thin lips turning down at the corners and the crooked front teeth that really jogged the memory. Mary Muttock knew only one girl who managed to look pretty and seductive in spite of those disadvantages. Imagine away the small breasts and remember the hair as it used to be, all dark and greasy and without the present fringe, and this had to be that hot little bitch the ex-principal had always wanted but had never got round to possessing. What was her name? Ah yes – Helen Lascelles, whose mother . . . But never mind. Helen had evidently dressed to exploit and make the most of her little-girlish looks. Instead of swimwear she had on a short, candy-striped dress in white and mauve. Its bodice hugged her chest snugly, fitting neatly under the fluffy armpits and just covering the bumps of her breasts, which its tightness both flattened and made to seem more prominent in their refusal to disappear completely. Half-way down her narrow hips a loosely tied belt demarcated the boundary between the bodice and the flared, pleated skirt, generous in its fullness yet so skimpy in length that a most inviting expanse of those bare white thighs was exposed to view. And of course (could this be Mac's doing?) the final touch was there in the knee-length white socks and flat sandals. Miss Muttock patted the youngster on the head.

One of the pages came trotting from the direction of the office and shepherded the four visitors across the field and down the rather demanding steps to the beach. This, then, was why the pool had been so deserted: all the regular guests were already assembled on the foreshore. In a variety of costumes always falling short of complete nudity, they were sitting, standing, kneeling or lying in several rows forming a wide crescent. This gave them a good view of a table which had been placed at the water's edge; a rock on it served as a paperweight to prevent the light sea breeze from blowing away documents that must have been the register and marriage certificate. Beside the rock stood a battered megaphone. The young page conducted his charges to the front row, handing them each a towel to sit on.

A hush fell over the crowd and all heads turned to watch the progress of the three principal participants, who had followed down the steps a short way behind the visitors. Mary Muttock had no difficulty in recognising the Captain, bizarrely clad in nothing but a pin-striped waistcoat over which he wore scarlet braces supporting a pair of union jack shorts. He seemed to be offering himself in the guise of the ultimate yuppie yobbo. Beside him came Gloria Sweetbutts. She was being presented as a minimalist bride in flowery head-dress, white veil and lacy white G-string.

These two old friends were preceded by the bulky form of a man in floating druidic robes and an untamed red beard that gave off an overpowering reek of strong pipe tobacco even out here in the open air. This must be the freeloading archimandrite of whom the Captain had given Miss Muttock a diverting account in his letter. He carried a kind of crook or crozier, which he planted upright in the wet sand. Then he took the megaphone from the table. Turning to face the immodestly attired congregation, with the apprehensive couple standing on either side of him, he raised the megaphone and bellowed out his amplified message in a rich, west country burr that resounded back from the sandstone cliff.

'Greetings. Greetings and peace and love – peace and love

be among you, O ye my children. We are met here today to solemnise and celebrate the spiritual and carnal conjuncture of these two aspirants to Onehood, to the state that lieth beyond the ken of the profane. We shall conduct this ceremony in accordance with the pagan rite; yea, even as it is inscribed for those possessed of the hidden eye – inscribed in the runes and the stars and the ley lines and the pyramids and the crop circles and the mystic alignment of the henges. For thus were our pre-Adamic forebears united and so shall it be unto all eternity. So, verily, shall it be.' He placed his hefty right hand on the shaft of the crozier and continued. 'Behold here the iconic symbol of the staff of life, whence cometh all delight.'

Mary Muttock noticed his hand slide down to what appeared to be a rubber bulb attached to the shaft. Surreptitiously he squeezed it, causing the spiral whorl at the head (emblem, surely, of the rutting ram?) to unfurl and stand up straight. The tip was adorned with the representation of a large fir cone or acorn – or could it be the glans of a shining phallus? The voice boomed on.

'Behold this my mighty rod, which the ancients called the divine thyrsus. The ancients have passed away, my children in love, but this rod endureth and betokeneth the first great gift of the gods to women. It stands, I say unto you, as a token to point the way. Of what, then, is it the sign and symbol? Behold ye the *living* rod, the fountain-head of joy and generation!'

The congregation gasped as he lifted the front of his white robe and tucked it into the cord girding his ample waist. His own staff of flesh stood up at a steep angle, the purple acorn that bulged at its head far outstripping the symbolic one in size and impressiveness. Mary Muttock was conscious of the dampness seeping into the gusset of her swimsuit and was glad that she had chosen black. From what zoo had this ramping brute escaped? The beast, or priest, proceeded.

'And now, my children, make ye ready for the part vouch-safed even unto all of you to play in these our festive rites. Let the daughters of men kneel before me as I pass among you, their hands upon the fruitful members of their consorts. And as I stand before each of you, my daughters, receive ye my rod between the honeyed lips of your mouths. Thus shall your own unions be blessed. And thus shall this my priestly staff rise to ever greater heights of love, imbued with the fiery breath of our great mother, even the beloved Frigg of our Saxon forefathers, and vibrant with the energy of the outer cosmos. So shall it be.'

Noticing the Muttock, the MacDonald, Melanie and Helen, who were sitting almost at his feet, he improvised a procedure to meet their special case. 'Ladies without male partners to frig,' he said, 'should placate the goddess by finger-fucking their girlfriends.'

At this point a number of the older couples moved away from the semicircle and left the beach, the wives dragging husbands who looked back with some reluctance as they climbed the steep steps in the cliff-face. There was much murmuring and movement among those who remained. As Mary Muttock ran her eyes over the company, she had a general impression of women rising or sinking to their knees and laying bashful or brazen hands over the (mostly covered) privities of their partners. Some of these partners knelt on the same level as their wives, others lay back to let themselves be pampered and teased, while a fair number stood up in full view of anyone with attention to spare. Not far away a really attractive young blonde whose bikini bore a floral design in red, blue, yellow and white was administering the prescribed treatment to a thin man with the face of a rat – or was he (Miss Muttock shuddered at the thought) one of those mortuary rats which took over the pale corpses of men? The girl, whose rippling fair hair reached almost to her waist, had drawn something long and thin out of his red trunks. Could it, oh dear, could it be? What a relief – it was only a slender rod of human flesh. As the young lady's hand closed around it a stream of spunk jetted out and soaked the crotch of her bikini. At least there was now somebody else with a tell-tale stain between her legs.

The archimandrite waddled along the wet sand to the far end of the beach. From behind it was impossible to see that in front he was naked from the waist down. He moved among the throng bestowing his blessing as he passed his prick from mouth to mouth. As yet, however, the distance was too great for the somewhat myopic Miss Muttock to get a thrill from these activities. Instead, she concentrated on her immediate neighbours. She and Mac would have to pair off with Melanie and young Helen. Melanie, of course, she could have any time, but . . .

Too late. Miss MacDonald was already arranging the tired-eyed darling, Helen, on the towel; she had her on all fours with her head down and towards the sea. She lifted the hem of the girl's dress slowly, with a caressing movement. When it slid past the soft flesh of the upper thighs Mary Muttock caught her breath – the small, firm bottom was bare. Unfortunately, her ex-colleague's next move was swift and decisive, allowing no more than a momentary glimpse of the pink fruit pouting out between Helen's buttocks and thightops. A sun-tanned hand descended to cup the girlflesh, leaving the buttocks almost completely exposed. Slowly but relentlessly, the sinew running down to the knuckle of the middle finger began to work. Helen was being digitally penetrated.

There was no time for regrets or disappointment, however. Already Melanie, delightfully fresh in her blue cotton outfit with the white lace trimmings, was on her knees and pressing her tummy up against her old principal expectantly. Mary Muttock obliged. Running her fingertips round the edge of the pale blue panties where stray wisps of gingery hair peeped out, she found she could easily slip a hand inside the garment. With her index finger she felt along the parallel ridges of warm wet flesh and hooked up into the juicy love hole. Melanie smiled and squeezed the older woman's buttocks, divided but not covered by the shiny black fabric.

And now the priestly bulk of the archimandrite had almost reached the little group of visitors in his benedictory progress along the beach. His fleshy staff of life was stuffed into the mouth of a lean and apparently ravenous Chinese woman whose hand was leaping about inside the shorts of her stout partner. After bestowing a hasty blessing, the sacerdotal hands pushed her head away rather roughly and came to rest on the shoulders of Miss MacDonald.

Mac raised her lips from Helen's bottom, keeping her probing finger well sheathed. Her hat, with its wide brim, was forced to the back of her head and the wet lips were immediately

70

nudged apart by the bulbous cockhead. 'That's right,' the priest chuckled. 'You can bring her off now.'

Miss Muttock arranged her own hat neatly on the back of her head. She could see Mac's hand working furiously between the girl's legs. Helen was throwing her head about on the towel and groaning; suddenly she hurled herself flat on her stomach, clenching her buttocks and squeezing her thighs together as she hit her orgasmic peak. And in the same instant Mary Muttock found herself gagging on that mystic staff, which had been whipped in one deft movement from Mac's mouth to her own. The archimandrite's grizzled pubic hairs, the grey still streaked with rusty brown, were tickling her nose. They smelt of coarse, mellow shag. Her response to this forced fellatio was to agitate her finger furiously in Melanie's inwardly foaming cunt.

Once again the archimandrite spoke. 'OK, OK, take it easy,' he gasped. 'That's a cute chick you've got yourself there, but if you work us both as hard as this I'm going to come. Open wide and let me out.'

Mary Muttock complied with his wish. As soon as her stretched lips released the purple bulb, the whole ten inches of distended manhood sprang up from the horizontal to a near vertical angle, quivering in rapid but ever diminishing movements from the sudden release of tension. The great cock had already been an intimidating sight when first displayed to the congregation but by now it had been sucked up to dimensions that silenced their murmurs. And it still seemed to be growing.

Next the priest ushered the Captain and Gloria to the table. As soon as the Captain had produced from his waistcoat pocket a ring he had found on the beach a few weeks back, and slipped it on Gloria's finger, the archimandrite made them place their left hands on the prodigious staff of life while they used their right ones to sign the legal-looking documentation. A worried gentleman whose splutterings sounded like those of an indignant solicitor was trying to raise objections, and all those within earshot were relieved when his wife dragged him away from the front row.

Miss Muttock was no stranger to larky travesties of the marriage service, but this archimandrite, whatever an archimandrite might be in the eyes of the law, showed an inventive-

71

ness which staggered even her. He instructed the Captain, facing out to sea in the interests of decorum, to remove his shorts and waistcoat. Gloria, similarly orientated, was required to step out of her G-string. Standing between them, the bearded celebrant took their hands and led them out into the water.

The view from the beach was symmetrical and striking: to the left the muscular back, buttocks and hairy thighs of the bridegroom, then the priest, his white robes floating behind him on the waves, and to his right, adorned with the head-dress and veil that fell to just below her shoulders, the creamy smoothness and rounded contours of the bride. Mary Muttock remembered the pretty triangle of chestnut curls from last summer, when Gloria and the Captain had been her guests at Cunlip Hall, but so far today there had been no public display of this attractive ornament.

And now, all three of them flinching visibly as the coolness of the water grabbed their crotches, the trio had waded in up to what was seen when they turned to face the beach to be the level of Gloria's pebble-hard nipples. The breaking of the wavelets and their hiss on the wet sand drowned out the instructions uttered by the archimandrite. Gloria handed her head-dress to the priest. Bride and groom filled their lungs with air and dipped down beneath the surface. All eyes were fixed, for want of a better object, on that florid face with its great bush of a beard. At first, silence prevailed on the beach. This soon gave way to a babble of excited conjecture: the succession of expressions contorting those reverend features – the appearances of lust giving way to those of agony followed by effulgent rapture – bore eloquent testimony to the submarine activities of the newly-weds.

Gloria and the Captain broke the surface gasping and, in Gloria's case, spluttering. Her pretty head-dress was restored to her; its veil clung to the now dripping and darkened hair. And then, encouraged by their spiritual mentor, they embraced each other. Gloria clung round the Captain's neck, their mouths locked together. As he waded towards the beach it was soon obvious that they were also locked together genitally; Gloria's thighs were canted up around her new husband's hips and his hands supported her buttocks, taking more and more of the weight as they emerged from the buoyant water. The congregation was favoured with a glimpse of the archimandrite's limp but still fat member as he fumbled to let down his tucked-up robes.

One of the pages snatched the register and certificate from the table, just in time to save them from being soaked with the salty drops showering from the excited couple. The Captain deposited Gloria on the flat surface without breaking the carnal nexus. Her legs waved in the air and his glistening buttocks bounced lustily as he fucked her for all he was worth.

The visitors had been allowed to occupy the best places on the beach, right by the table. Of the four, Miss Muttock sat nearest, which was probably why it was she who was helped to her feet by the archimandrite and directed to act as witness first to the signatures on the documents held out by the page and then to the successful act of consummation. She was told to reach her hand carefully down round the Captain's testicles until her index and middle fingers were able to grip or at least apply pressure to the slippery prick as it thrust in and out. The point of contact was just where Gloria's pulpy cuntlips sucked against the manflesh.

Mary Muttock forced herself to concentrate on the joyful, life-enhancing aspects of the union at which she was assisting. She was terrified that her consciousness might be overtaken by a vision of, well, of what those *breeders* had to do in zoos. And she didn't even have rubber gloves or a face mask . . .

She was saved from these horrors by the bitter-sweet odour which wafted up from the mingling sex of the couple as they approached their climax. Her own cunt was awash with juices that now saturated her smart swimsuit – to all those seated or standing near at hand she must have looked by now as if she had been sitting in the water. She inhaled the familiar pungency. No longer were the bridal pair rutting beasts wallowing in the filth of their own corruption, but the beautiful bodies of two lovers coming together as one.

And coming together they surely were. The hairy ballsack twitched against her palm, Gloria was moaning deliriously and the hard, lubricated flesh between Mary Muttock's fingers swelled even thicker and stiffened to even greater rigidity. This was the moment of culmination. The whole congregation sensed it, but she had the tangible evidence there in her grasp. With a final thrust the cock went right in, so that her fingers were trapped between the man's damp pubis and his bride's clinging flesh. She closed her fingers tighter. She felt rippling movements in the hot shaft as the pent-up semen rushed up it in wave after wave. Finally the surplus poured out of the girl's cunt and Miss Muttock became aware of the warm mass flowing through her fingers to spread over the surface of the table.

She held up a sodden hand, smiled at the assembled throng and declared that the knot was well and truly tied.

FIVE

BED AND BARBIE

Although the no-nonsense wedding had been fun, the Captain viewed the prospect of bedding his bride that night with some trepidation. On the beach it had been different. Public performances always gave him a bit of edge. Perhaps this was because no conversation was required, no small talk; and no responsibilities towards one's partner except to arouse and satisfy her lust. He had really been able to forget his worries, if only for a short time. Old Jimbo had done a pretty decent job – if he was so inclined he was welcome to park his caravan on the field for a couple of weeks and enjoy the facilities of the motel. He could set himself up as some sort of resident guru or agony uncle. Maybe some of the guests who had checked in under false pretences could even be encouraged to come clean and submit themselves, for a small fee, to a similar wedding ceremony.

But now, as the fumes of sparkling and other wines began to clear, the old worries came flooding back again together with a new one. He had received an alarming letter from the local council. The planning department, it seemed, had been alerted to the possibility that the Captain's tame architect had not in every respect complied with building regulations. An early inspection was likely, and that could mean as early as Monday.

Although this was a serious threat, other less serious ones were rather more imminent. A number of motel guests had taken offence at the licentiousness in which they had been invited to participate on the beach. If the invitation had come from a young, pretty woman rather than from a fat and hairy man dressed up like some crazy druid it would surely have been accepted with alacrity. But this was not the case and the wives who had complained were threatening to terminate their honeymoons prematurely. What was more, the Captain had picked up a few hints at the poolside reception to the effect that Danvers Pelham, affronted by the idea that the dignity of the law had been brought into contempt by such a ceremony, was contemplating some kind of legal action against him. It would be prudent to arrange for Pelham to vent his ire on a pair of smooth young buttocks before it got out of control.

It was not even certain that the form of marriage gone through with Gloria would achieve one of its secondary aims, namely to allay the guilty feelings that had been inhibiting his sexual prowess with her. One good sign, though, was that he now felt as if he actually wanted her.

Locking up the reception suite and filling his lungs with invigorating night air, the Captain contemplated the stars. He recalled the first time he had had Gloria, more than a year ago in the library of Banesville University. He had spied on her as she pored in shocked excitement at an album of vintage erotic photographs and masturbated herself to orgasm there in his private office, his Palace of Fantasies. In view of her embarrassment when he burst into the room to surprise her, it had been a smart move of his to get her on the sofa and take her from behind rather than face to face. Once he had overcome her initial, puritanically conditioned reserve she had hardly managed to pass a day or night without him.

He crossed the courtyard to the luxurious quarters he had commandeered for their wedding night. So tightly was the front of his trousers stretched out by the erection these memories had conjured up that he was thankful to reach the door without encountering any stray guests.

He entered quietly in case his bride was sleeping after the day's exertions. The precaution was unnecessary. Propped on plump pillows, Gloria sprawled in the lake of soft light illuminating the bed. Her nakedness was displayed, in manifest readiness for love, upon a purple sheet bestrewn with rose petals. The purple made her creamy skin seem paler and this paleness in turn heightened the unbraided glory of her long chestnut curls and the appealing tuft at the base of her belly. Instead of masking her slit, this fluffy adornment seemed to have been carefully brushed to the sides tonight. She lay with her legs parted, her pink lovelips glistening wetly in the lamplight. This once-prudish bride was evidently lusting for a night of debauchery. The Captain felt somewhat confused. Was it mainly for his body she had married him after all, and not just for the passport?

She looked up with an affectionate smile, closing the album of specially selected photos the Captain had given her as a wedding present. The laying aside of the album brought into view the lovely, firm, pear-shaped breasts, their rosebud tips now bright red with expectancy.

'You gonna give me one, Doc?' she asked with a widening of her saucer eyes. 'Do you have something left for your new wife?'

His response was to strip at once to the buff. Then he turned to face her. Gloria drew in her breath when she saw the well-primed member with its swelling head which looked almost as if it had not been near cuntflesh for weeks. To demonstrate its viability he forced it down to the horizontal and released it so that it twanged up again, rebounded off his belly and wagged lewdly.

The young woman raised her knees and let them fall apart until her thighs were almost flat on the sheet. Her hands went to the waiting pussy and parted the lips for him. At this signal he flung himself between her legs and allowed his stiffness to find its own way into the soft trench. Once the head was enfolded in the fleshy leaves he gave a great shove and drove the whole length up her vagina. He straightened his arms to lift himself up and appreciate the look on her face before plunging down to suck her left nipple. She writhed beneath him and he began to thrust furiously.

Right on cue, their rhythm was disrupted by the buzzer of the phone. Gloria reached out for the remote control unit on her bedside table and flicked it in the direction of the TV screen. The Captain stopped screwing and felt himself growing even bigger inside his trembling wife. He twisted his head round just

77

as the screen lit up with the smiling images of Talbot and Yvonne Yglesias.

'Good *night* there,' said Talbot. 'Me and my good lady here just wanted to wish you two all the best on this truly happy occasion. And before I forget, let me tell you how chuffed I was to see tonight's in-house movie's one of my own – I've got my own little production company, you know. If you haven't seen it yet, take in an eyeful later when you need freshening up. First of all, though, it looks as if you guys have some unfinished business to take care of. We're going to be thinking of you in a minute when we get back on the job ourselves. Isn't that right, Yvonne?'

'Absolutely right,' replied the dark-haired Yvonne. 'And let me tell you, the view from here's so delightful I can't take my eyes off it and I want to sit on Talbot's lap with his dick stuck up me and watch you fuck while he frigs me out of my mind.'

Unusually for him, the Captain felt more than a little embarrassed. Surely the view was nothing special? She would have nothing but a foreshortened perspective of his legs, back, bum and bollocks humping away with Gloria's legs kicking out at the sides. The main item would be the butterfly tattooed on his bum and he wasn't too proud of that any more. Yet he had often found himself reflecting that the pleasure of voyeurism might be in inverse ratio to the completeness of the view. There was something to be said for leaving things to the imagination. All the same, he wasn't sorry that right now Yvonne was lowering her naked person on to her husband's erect penis in full view of the camera that brought the Yglesiases' pleasure in living colour to the screen in this room.

Reconciled for the duration to the painful awkwardness of lying on Gloria with his head twisted round to watch the Yglesiases, the Captain clenched his buttocks, withdrew a couple of inches from the tight sheath and plunged in again with all his force. This single thrust was enough to tip the balance. As his hairs ground into Gloria's and his balls bounced against her bottom, all the reserves of masculine pith that had been building up in him – all that thickening accumulation of hot seed which had seethed there ever since old Jimbo had made him have her on that table down on the beach – all this spunk gathered into a tight knot concentrated at the base of his belly. It took no more than a slight vaginal twitch from his bride, brought on by the sight of what Talbot's fingernails seemed to be doing to Yvonne's clitoris, to make him spill the lot in what felt like one great continuous spurt straight up into her womb.

When he had recovered sufficiently, the Captain rolled off her, wished the Yglesiases goodnight and flicked off the video phone. Gloria was not altogether happy with this abrupt termination of her own fun and seemed to be hankering after the satisfaction his bonking had failed to procure for her.

A quick rummage through the equipment cabinet produced a likely solution: he returned to the bed with a plastic device about the size of a gorilla's hand. Rather like a hand it had three curved fingers of varying lengths and thicknesses. Expertly he spread Gloria's thighs and clamped the device into position with the middle and largest finger plugging her cunt and a somewhat thinner one inserted into her anal entrance. The third finger, which was long, flexible and narrow with a kind of sucker on the end, he bent down until the sucker was cupped over her clitoral bud. A flick of the switch and she was hurtling down the highway to happiness, energetically massaging her own breasts as the technological wonder-worker buzzed away between her legs. Her orgasm washed through her in wave upon wave of muscular contractions which left her whimpering and exhausted. He removed the multiple vibrator and lay back sleepily.

Gloria, however, was ready for still more. She insisted on watching Talbot's movie. This must have been sent down from London by the Captain's contacts in the consignment for this week's after-hours entertainment. He took the remote control to see what it was like.

It was called *Teenage Sex Orgy 3* – quite an imaginative title considering the middle-aged faces of the actors. The action on the flickering screen was all mechanical bonking, sucking and frigging, with extended sequences showing close-ups of the pained faces of men and women bouncing up and down, and rare glimpses of cock and cunt. It altogether lacked the spontaneity of Talbot and Yvonne's recent performance. The Captain dozed off.

But his slumber was only shallow and it took no more than Gloria's hand lightly cupped over his genitals while one fingertip tickled his balls to bring him back to awareness of what was happening on the screen. This part of the movie seemed familiar. He had seen it, hadn't he, over in Banesville last year, that time he went to Dee Dee Burdle's motel room. Of course. That door on the set was about to open and a new character would enter to offer herself to the naked debauchees writhing on the cushioned floor.

Sure enough, the door opened. A lovely auburn-haired girl, a real teenager of eighteen or nineteen in blue jeans and a yellow sweater walked in, smiled and pulled the sweater over her head. Because of her heavy make-up he had been a little uncertain out there in the States whether the girl really was his old flame, the snobby Gina Wootton. Her breasts had seemed to be about the right size, and she had Gina's freckles in the tanned V between their white globes, yet so had many girls with auburn hair, and the same could be said of the chestnut-coloured triangle of fur briefly revealed when she pulled down her jeans and panties. But when the Captain had run into her again in London and asked her about her career since leaving Cunlip College, she had admitted to a bit of modelling and filming as well as her regular personnel management. So it was now with special interest that he watched his Gina's defilement at this ineptly directed but enthusiastic orgy.

The film presented her as an insatiable lesbian, her hands and tongue exploring every female orifice thrust in her direction. At the same time she was buggered, fucked and wanked over by all the men, simultaneously and in succession, until she lay back quivering, her coppery hair matted with spunk, spunk dribbling from her mouth to run down her chin and neck, spunk coating her shining breasts and forming a steaming puddle in the hollow of her navel and finally – the camera zoomed right in on this – spunk bubbling from her ravished cunt and oozing from her abused arsehole.

It had to be admitted that high production values were not a necessary ingredient of sexiness. The Captain's interest was thoroughly aroused by the time the film ended. He was as hard as a rubber truncheon. Snatching his wife's probing fingers away from her pussy, he jumped on top of her and plunged straight in without preliminaries. She responded savagely, seizing his hips with unsuspected strength and shaking his pelvis up and down like a dog playing with a dead rabbit until his semen jetted into her and he lay inert on her belly.

Almost asleep, he realised he was still as stiff as a bone inside her. When he pinched one of her nipples to see if she was awake, she gave a little quiver and opened her eyes. The muscles of her vagina contracted to tighten around the hardness of which she was now aware. Gloria brought her legs up and crossed them over his back, thrusting up with her loins to force him deep down into her. He pumped harder in response and they kept up the action for about ten minutes, until the sweat was dripping from his face on to hers. Just as his sluices opened to flood her yet again, she spoke.

'I'm gonna need some help,' she said. 'Guess I'm gonna need help filling out those papers for your Home Office.'

One activity not catered for in the Honeymoon Palace Motel was writing. The low tables and dressing tables in the guests' rooms were not designed for penmanship. For this reason, Melanie put off the chore of bringing her diary up to date for more than a week. It was only on the Sunday following the weekend of the wedding that she got round to writing it up. Mac had slipped out to join one of the couples she had become friendly with. As the sun was streaming in through the gap in the curtains, Melanie propped herself up in bed with her yellow notebook on her knees and wrote, heading the entry *Sun, August 2.* She began with an account of the wedding, after which she tried to jot down as many of the week's incidents as she could remember. But it was all a bit confusing, especially as she didn't know the names of half the people she had fucked. It was the events of the day before, still fresh in her mind, that she wanted to get to, so she crossed out a couple of pages of her scribbling, scratched her pussy and made a fresh start.

Sun, Aug 2 (Take two!)
That's better! Of course, now I've decided to get straight into describing yesterday's barbie I'm bound to want to digress

81

and write about things that happened in the week. Well, basically it was just doing the rounds, wasn't it? Like Mac and the Muttock and me kept taking it in turns to spend the night with each other, sometimes all three together and sometimes just two of us when one went off partying with motel guests or making love to Helen, who for some reason didn't want to do anything with me. Probably jealous. Oh, and I suppose it goes without saying that we all made sure we had plenty of time with the Captain and his Gloria, though for the first couple of days Gloria seemed to spend *most* of her time sitting with Mac in Reception and getting her to help with all those application forms – she's applying for a UK passport so she won't have to go back to America and won't get locked up if she does.

But no, I'm not going to get bogged down with all the comings and goings since that crazy wedding – not even with all the comings! I must say, though, that the Captain dropped down to earth with a bit of a bump on Monday. He's got this threat hanging over him of being inspected by the planning department or whatever it is. Rather like that funny play by Goggol (Gogol?), Mac says. Whenever any of the guests take a friendly interest in what's going on he jumps to the conclusion that they're inspectors posing as honeymooners and makes a right dickhead of himself. You'd think he could handle that kind of situation by now with all his experience of wriggling out of tight corners.

If he wasn't an old chum of Captain's, I'd say the most likely candidate for an inspector in disguise would be that archimandrake or whatever he calls himself, the bloke who did the wedding. Well, he seems to worm himself into everyone's confidence – as far as he can, that is. When he tried to worm himself into mine I let him know there were limits. One afternoon he came breathing his foul tobacco all over me and asked if I'd like him to do the I-Ching for me.

Not every day you get a chance to have a reading done by a guy in all those white robes and with that sort of saintly aura about him, so went with him to his caravan, parked over near edge of cliff. The mess inside it! Looked as if he'd just been driving at high speed over mountain roads with everything loose getting shaken up and thrown all over the place. What a dump! Grotsville. Anyway, he got me to move piles of washing-up and sit down on seat at end by big window with torn curtain pulled across it. Had my black silk bikini on. Stained seat cover meant to be velvet but felt all stiff and bristly against bare thighs. He got I-Ching things out, coins and dog-eared book. When I saw he wasn't doing it proper way I stopped him and said I'd changed my mind. He said, 'Let's do something else then,' and whipped up his robes so I could see 'staff of life' with tip sticking up above edge of table even though he was still sitting down. This bloke's crazy.

ARCHIMANDRAKE: Behold a rod for thy back.

ME: What've you got in mind, then?

ARCHIMANDRAKE: Let's not play games. I'll bet you've got a nice pair of tits inside that bikini top. Little pointed ones, aren't they?

ME: Look, grandad, my friends tell me they're just the right size. But if you think you're getting your hairy paws on them, forget it.

ARCHIMANDRAKE: My name's Jimbo, by the way. Just let me look at them and we'll call it quits. I'm showing you mine so you can show me yours.

Don't know what came over me but I reached up behind me, unclipped top and slipped it off. Sun coming through torn curtains spilt all over left boob. Skin sort of satiny as if with very thin film of gleaming sweat. Nipple soft and puffy – first that pink part (aureole? areola? – must ask Mac) round the actual teat got all pimply like it does when it gets cold or you're going to have sex, then teat started swelling and stiffening. Archimandrake stared at it hard and that made pimply part pucker up.

ARCHIMANDRAKE: You know, my dear, I find your – your armpits very exciting. That subtle hint of *odor di femina* draws my divining rod towards you as the moon draws the waters of the earth. Behold: the tide is already rising.

Sure enough, a blob of that clear sticky stuff had appeared from slot on tip of prick. It got bigger till it was too heavy to hold itself together, like a quivery bubble, then sort of collapsed and spread itself over side of purple knob.

He jumped up and came round to my side of table. Now I wasn't going to let an old phoney like that have me – no way – but on the other hand I didn't want to abuse Captain's hospitality. I certainly didn't want that hairy face anywhere too near mine. So I leaned back against pile of old magazines and just let him bring himself off over my tits and between them and then let him lick me clean. Well, I say lick but mostly it got spread around and mopped up by his prickly face fungus. Funnily enough that did something for me and I realised I was forcing damp gusset of bikini bottom against his thigh while he bent over me. Think he was so absorbed in absorbing all his fluids from my chest that he didn't notice when I twitched myself against him and came. Wanted me to stay so he could do Tarot with me but I ran off to tell Mac what had happened and have good laugh.

Every morning we've been busy helping Captain and Gloria 'do their rounds' of the guests, giving them advice and encouragement and sometimes a bit of a leg up (or over). At first all of us (that's to say me, Mac, the Muttock, Helen Lascelles and Gloria) just trailed along behind him and he used us like anatomically correct dolls to show the various possibilities. He soon realised this was going to be a bit hard on his cock, so by Wednesday we'd split up and were going round offering individual assistance, which meant much more ground was covered. I stopped wearing white coat and used blue playsuit instead, which was very popular – it's loose enough for the guys to get inside me without wasting any time undressing. There was this rather sexy fat man, though – Des, his name is – who made me take the top off. He's got too much of a gut on him to screw his Chinese wife from the front. She doesn't have much to say for herself, but when he whistles she bends down with her head on a chair while he sticks it in back entrance. Well, he said he was getting a bit pissed off with not being able to kiss her or even reach down to her boobs, so I stood beside him while he was buggering her and let him put his tongue in my mouth and tug my nipples. I was quite getting to like him until he started calling me Mel, which makes me see red, though I never complain about it.

Yesterday morning we all gave a hand carrying stuff down to the beach for the barbeque they have every Saturday when weather's good enough. It began about twelve. Nearly all the guests came down to join in, and the little army of maids and pages were allowed to have a slice of the action so long as they did their bit seeing everyone got enough to eat and drink. Actual cooking done mostly by Captain, helped by that paunchy Des and a smart-arsed know-all, name of Talbot Ecclesiastics or something like that.

Dress *very* informal. Beach-wear basically, with most of women topless. Some of them, and rather more of the men, wore those tiny black G-strings they sell in reception. Helen likes to stand out from crowd so she'd come in that stripey (spelling?) dress she had for the wedding, but with bare legs and feet this time. Also a floppy white sunhat and big round sunglasses.

I wasn't going to be upstaged by that little madam so I nipped back to room and changed into outfit I've got on in Captain's favourite photo, the one he always keeps in wallet. Hair in thick plait tied with red ribbon and nothing but my little white suntop, the one with narrow shoulder straps and buttons down front – I just fastened two top ones so all my tummy was bare. Looked down at myself when I got outside. Surprised to see how light and thin my gingery pussy hairs looked in strong sunshine – wondered how much of my slit showed from in front. Anyway, I felt pretty good as I skipped down steps to beach. Bottomless trumps topless any day and the way the men's little pouches swelled out and their wives looked away huffily proved the point.

Plenty to drink and lashings of lovely chops and sausages and chicken and burgers and all the trimmings. When people got greasy fingers they wiped them on partners' bodies (and perhaps not just partners'). Lots of waiting for meat to cook, of course, but time went quickly what with boozing and people oiling each other and splashing about on edge of water. After a time I noticed a few other women had taken their bottoms off. But I was still the one who got most of the winks from the blokes. Having that little cotton top on really works wonders.

When all the food was gone and the pages and maids were busy clearing things away most of the guests seemed pretty drowsy and just flopped about on beach or floated on inflatable mattresses. There were going to be some bad cases of sunburn after this, I thought. Captain took me and some of the others down to far end of beach behind some rocks and started playing reggae on ghetto-blaster he had with him. Quite a few of the younger couples made the effort to stagger over and join us when they heard this.

Captain stopped music and explained what we were going to do. He got us to join hands in two big rings with him in middle with the music. Blokes were on inside, facing out, and girls on outside facing in – had to be that way because me and Helen and Gloria and that Chinese Doris and a couple of other women didn't have partners so girls' ring was bigger. Captain was standing on wet sand where waves wash up and down, which meant half of us were on dry land and other half getting wet up to our thighs and occasionally bottoms.

Idea was for the two rings to dance round in opposite directions. When the music stopped girls had to pair off with nearest guy. They could go as far as they liked sexually but had to stop, link hands with their own sex and circle round as soon as music started up again. Rather like musical chairs. The four women who hadn't found partners would have to drop out. But it wasn't all that bad for them – after first bout of smooching their four husbands also had to retire to keep numbers uneven, so they'd be able to watch from sidelines and have whatever fun they wanted without bothering with rules and regulations.

I wanted to ask which men dropped out if any of us without partners weren't able to pair off, but Captain was already trying to make us grasp next bit. Doris looked really baffled, poor thing! We were starting off as twelve couples and the four extra girls. At some point, he said, it was possible there would be just couples (that was answer to question I hadn't been able to ask) paired off and all the extras eliminated. When we got that far, music would stop and there would be kind of race. First bloke to shoot his load would be out, leaving one girl too many. Then more dancing and another

86

girl would go, another race, another dance and so on till just one champion couple was left to entertain rest of crowd. Hard to see how long whole operation was likely to take . . .

Music blared out and round we went like a gang of kids at a birthday bash. Ones on beach able to move quicker than ones in sea so people kept stumbling and getting dragged through water. Helen was on my left and skirt of her mauve and white striped dress was soaked. I shouted to her that she ought to tuck it in her knickers when she got a chance.

I think Captain had his eye on the four of us, who were all together. Anyway, of the four girls who didn't get a guy first time music stopped, Gloria was the only one of our gang. I found myself grabbed by a thickset black dude who clamped his lips over my mouth like a great sucker and tickled my throat with his tongue while his fingers, surprisingly delicate in their touch, undid my top button. Couldn't help noticing his wife (she's black too – I've seen them both together) wasn't taking part. I shoved my crotch against his thigh but at that moment music began again. The three husbands of the eliminated married women left the circle and round and round we went.

In spite of all the confusion I still had Helen on my left. Her wet dress was tucked up now as I'd suggested. But not in her knickers – the little scamp wasn't wearing any! The whole week I hadn't had a chance to be alone with Helen and had never been anywhere near her when we were all doing rounds of rooms together, so I got a real shock when I saw that unlike two or three weeks ago at Mac's, the last time I saw her nude, she was hairless between her legs. When this registered with everyone I couldn't help noticing how the men's circle, which had seemed to slow down and drag its feet as they passed us, now tried to hold back even more.

Helen, me and Doris all got partners in this round. We seemed to be in demand, so we didn't have to make much effort to get paired. Mine was a red-headed guy this time. He was so preoccupied kissing and licking my ear as we stood in waves that his hands only got as far as undoing my second button and letting suntop fall right open on either side of my tits. While he did this I was looking over his shoulder. The black bloke had Doris and had ripped off her standard issue G-string, leaving her starkers. Another surprise! I'd only seen her from behind when we'd done the rounds (her Des was the one we had to concentrate on) so I hadn't realised she's got a shiny bare pussy too.

Just next to them Helen was being mauled by a mean-faced, mousy guy in ridiculous Hawaiian shorts. I think his name's Rob or Rod. He seemed to have tugged so much at the tight top of her dress that some of the buttons down the back had popped. He pulled the front down to just below her little white boobs. At the same moment I saw Doris's hand fetch the black guy's dong out of its pouch, but that was the Captain's cue to start music again. Three more lads dropped out, leaving six males and nine females, all pretty dishevelled by now.

The way things worked out this round, Doris was left out in cold. Three men made a grab at her, but they were caught by eager girls. I was landed with some bald-headed wimp who was too embarrassed to look me in the eyes and just stood there in the water stroking my bare bum. Helen's pert little boobs were slobbered all over by that awful Talbot, who forced her to put a hand on his pouch. And up on the beach I couldn't help noticing the big black guy enjoying himself with a really young and lovely girl with wavy blonde hair – I think she must be that Robbie's or Roddie's wife. She'd been wearing a shocking pink halter top which her naked black partner (or one of the earlier ones) had forced up to her chin. He'd pushed her high-sided pink briefs down over her buttocks – as far as I could see they still covered most of her sex at the front. You can imagine the contrast in colour as his huge hand rooted around between the cheeks of her arse.

When music started again there was a bit of confusion for Captain to sort out. Doris, of course, had been playing without a husband. But so had both of the other women eliminated in this round, which meant we were down to even numbers – five of each. So now the rules of combat had entered the second phase.

Round we danced with the wavelets washing over our feet.

'Dance' probably not the right word. Now that both circles were same size and so small Captain hardly had room to stand in middle with the music, girls could only just squeeze past boys. Just as well those lads had to hold hands with each other. Nobody was going to get left out when music stopped but we'd reached stage when it was pretty crucial to end up with suitable partner.

Well, the way it went was that I was landed with that mousy Rod (he put me right when I called him Rob). He stepped out of his shorts and I was able to ride on his long thin dick like on crossbar of bike. I slid backwards and forwards on it, wishing he'd do something to my tits as we stood there and hoping he wouldn't try to kiss me.

Helen was being manhandled by a big, muscular guy with sunburn. He had her dress pulled right down now so that it was all rolled round her waist and everything else was bare, though she still had her sunhat and dark glasses. He was stooping down and seemed to be kissing her bald snatch.

The black bloke had been lucky to get his big hands on Rod's young blonde again. In spite of her resistance he'd got the pink briefs down as far as her knees. I got the impression of his pink tongue licking all over her and the pink tip of his cock sticking out from one of her hands – she was trying to fight him off but was actually giving him an unintentional wank. Suddenly he got desperate. He grabbed her by the ears and forced her head down, wanting her to suck him off. But before he could force his cock into this girl's mouth he spunked all over her face and hair. That was the end of those two!

More music. Down to four couples now. When we stopped it was Talbot with his flashy medallion who had me and the red-headed one who got Helen. The other two guys still in the running were Rod and the sunburnt one whose peeling skin looked like flakes of dried sperm.

Funny situation. Having this race, but nobody really knew if they wanted to win. On the whole I reckon the girls wanted to stay in as long as possible to get the benefit of the variety, while the boys just wanted to get their rocks off. Well, that's what the lobster-coloured one succeeded in doing with the tall, thin brunette he'd thrown down on the wet sand, stripped naked and stuck his cock into. This happened so quickly that me and Helen were hardly touched by our partners.

With only three pairs left we couldn't make those concentric rings any more – it was just a sort of free for all and when music stopped I was being hugged by the red-headed gent while poor Helen had Rod and Talbot was with a petite girl whose black one-piece swimsuit was still intact. My guy actually had time to bend me over and get stuck into me from behind so I couldn't see what Rod was doing to Helen. Then I heard a scream and broke away from my partner. The petite girl was lying in the shallow water almost nude, her stretchy swimsuit ripped to rags and ribbons. Where the sperm had gone I don't know, but Talbot was holding his limp prick, still oozing white stuff, and acknowledging defeat.

To decide the final pairing we just sort of feinted about. I knew I didn't want Rod and I think Helen quite fancied him so we only made a token effort to open things up and when Captain stopped music it was me and carrot-hair again and Helen and Rod. My guy was stronger than he looked. He lifted me up and had me sitting on his shoulders with my belly against his face. By pressing my buttocks up really hard he was able to get my cuntlips in line with his mouth. Looking over his head I saw little Helen lie down on sand and arch her back right up so she was only supported on elbows and feet. As her feet were apart the shaven pussy was fully exposed. Rod knelt down and went straight for it with his slim tool. But just as the dark red tip touched her flesh he exploded and his stuff came jetting out. He fell back, deflated. Helen's tummy, thighs and cunt shone in the sunlight like wet jelly.

Redhead and I were cheered as the winners but I didn't want him up me and just wanked him off in front of all the eliminated competitors and other spectators. I thought the whole game was a bit pointless but the others didn't seem to think so.

No sooner had we finished than all hell broke loose. The crowd parted to make way – how my heart sank – for none other than Derrick, who had appeared out of the blue in his motorcycling leathers to take me back to Upchester. Well, it seemed he'd been watching all the fun from up on cliff and was furious. He stood there making the most godawful scene. Luckily the crowd were on my side, the women anyway. They all jumped on him so he was immediately buried under a heaving mound of mostly naked flesh. When at last they got off him he'd been stripped bare. Don't know exactly what they did to him – he didn't want to tell me afterwards – but there was no life left in his plonker and I've had no trouble from him since. We compromised and I said he could take me home tomorrow (Monday) as long as he promised to keep his hands off Helen. Mind you, even if he got his hands on her he wouldn't be able to fuck her, not in the state those women left him in.

SIX

CORRUPT PRACTICES

'And where nature fails us, art can come to the aid of nature,' the Captain declared, sniffing the rose-bud in the lapel of his white coat. The audience in the motel's small auditorium looked up expectantly and with as much alertness as could be mustered on a rather showery Monday morning. Some of them were still recovering from that highly successful barbecue. Others were simply fucked out after another night of happy honeymooning. Nevertheless, although a distaste for Monday mornings must be pretty universal, the Captain was usually able to draw quite an enthusiastic crowd when he began the week with one of his instructive lectures. Today, the first Monday of August, was no exception.

It was the practice on these occasions for those guests who had volunteered their services as guinea-pigs to appear nude but masked. In most cases, however, their identity was obvious to those present in spite of the disguise. The couple now standing beside the podium were unmistakably Des and his Doris, as could be seen from his paunch, the colour of her skin and, for those in the know, her smoothly shaven pubis.

The Captain continued his discourse. 'What we have just witnessed was a well-executed demonstration of penetration *a retro*, made that bit easier by the way this athletic young lady is able to bend right down and touch her toes. The main disadvantage, of course, is that although the male can enjoy an unusually deep sheathing this way, he is unable to kiss her. If he's a bit more athletic than our present subject he should be able to reach forward and fondle her breasts, but kissing's definitely out. From her point of view,' he added, as he always did at this juncture to raise a bit of a titter from the ladies, 'this may be a positive gain.

'For our male subject this morning, as you have seen, this is just about the only way he can achieve sexual intercourse, on account of his obesity. In fact, the case is even worse than I've led you to believe. What you saw just now was not sexual intercourse in the strict sense – our unfortunate friend here is unable to achieve that, even from behind. No, ladies and gentlemen, it was outright buggery. But, as I say, in such cases art or technology can be summoned to the aid of nature. You will have noticed that the gentleman's penis is still erect, because I instructed him to withdraw prior to ejaculation. We are fortunate today in having in him a subject lacking the kind or degree of sensitivity that would cause him to wilt under the concerted gaze of such an audience as you, ladies and gentlemen.

'You may be wondering why we have bothered to demonstrate what looks like such a commonplace mode of intercourse. No doubt all of you have had a bash at it from round the back, even if the lady wasn't able to bend right down like this one and even if you avoided the tradesman's entrance. Well, it was for two reasons: one, watching it is good fun and a bit of excitement for all of us, and two, it's also a bit of excitement for our heavyweight here who needs a good stiff hard-on for what's coming next.'

It was getting unnaturally dark in the auditorium and rain was pattering on the metal roof, so the Captain switched on the stage lights. He returned to his podium and produced a plain cardboard box about eighteen inches long, from which he removed a white object.

'This, ladies and gentlemen, is technology's answer to the problem we're considering. The manufacturers call it the Studmaster and offer a generous discount if you place your orders with us through Reception. Essentially it is what we call a penile extension. One end of the appliance, you observe, consists of a simple but effective artificial vulva not unlike those provided in your rooms for use when the female partner needs rest. But in the Studmaster the vulva is attached to a semi-flexible dildo. The upper part of the shaft, you will notice, is not smooth but ridged like the bellows of a concertina. This not only procures an agreeable sensation by its friction with the walls of the vagina – the ladies tell me it drives them crazy – but also has a crucial function if realism is important to you or you are anxious to start a family. The rim of the artificial vulva, here, forms an airtight seal with the root of the gentleman's penis. In fact, the whole sheath fits so snugly that there is no room for his seminal fluid to spill backwards and escape. Instead it is forced forward into a narrow capillary tube running through the shaft to the lifelike plastic glans. But halfway along the shaft the juices accumulate in a reservoir. The pumping motion of the act of copulation operates on the concertina-like part of the device to produce pressure which, at the critical moment, propels the accumulated semen in a succession of powerful spurts into the vagina.

'You can all imagine – indeed, we are about to observe it in action – how useful the Studmaster will be to anyone with this particular couple's disability. No offence, dear; it's Des I'm talking about, not you. But it can also offer endless fun to those of you blessed with more, hmm, let us say more modish proportions. Yes, gentlemen, you can now service your wives from a whole new range of angles and positions. The extension is so long you could almost dodge into the kitchen and make tea while waiting for her to come. And look: it's so flexible it can screw itself!'

Having bent the thing round until the tip was tucked into the artificial cunt, the Captain straightened it out again, smeared the inside of the female end and the outside of the male one with lubricating gel and handed it to Des for the demonstration everyone had been awaiting. As he drew the tight-fitting vulva up over his erect stem, those of the audience whose attention was not narrowly fixed on the process of insertion were struck by a curious effect at a higher level: the two openings in his black mask suddenly flashed white as Des rolled up his eyes in rapture.

Doris was made to lie on a clinical couch with her feet in stirrups while her husband lowered himself upon her in the basic matrimonial attitude. The Captain used a hand-held camcorder connected to a large screen to give the audience the closest possible view of the proceedings. With the man's stomach in contact with his partner's there would normally still have been a good six inches separating the tip of his prick from her vaginal opening. But using this impressive appliance he had no difficulty splitting her apart and screwing her so vigorously that she was soon waving her legs in the air and moaning without inhibition.

'You can all see,' said the Captain, 'how much better the view is when the female subject is hairless. Look how the labia minora are drawn right up out of the large outer lips on each outward stroke. I think we would all agree she's getting a very thorough rodding from him now.'

This turn of phrase brought a blush to the cheeks of Sally Nugent, who was sitting in the front row. She thought of the husband she had left snoring in bed. He had still not been able to get his thing into her before spilling his messy white stuff. Maybe he'd be more successful with one of these Studmasters or whatever they were called, because he wouldn't actually have to touch her. And that might be an advantage from her point of view, too.

As soon as they had both come, Des and Doris got up and crept rather sheepishly from the stage. There was time for one more demonstration. The masked couple who now entered the auditorium were even more unmistakable to those who knew them: Mr and Mrs Brown, whose dark skin gleamed with fragrant oil and whose short pubic hair was tightly curled like astrakhan. Mrs Brown's other hair was done up in thin beaded braids that must have taken hours to plait. Once more the Captain began to speak.

'We are all familiar with the delights of the classic sixty-nine and its major variants, I take it. Although this is one of the most intimate caresses, we will conclude today's lecture by showing how easy it is to admit an additional player to the game. Ladies and gentlemen, I would like you to welcome a visitor some of you will have met already in the last week. As an outsider she needs no mask. A big hand, please, for the very lovely Helen, who is doubly welcome for our purposes because she, too, has removed the hair that used to conceal her delightful quim.'

Judging from the way the men in the audience were crossing and uncrossing their legs it was not only a big hand that was produced in response to Helen's appearance. Part of the attraction, no doubt, was the contrast: the shining blackness of the Browns against Helen's fair skin, relieved only by a sparse scattering of moles; Helen's straight, light brown hair with its saucy fringe against their black curls; their well-built, mature, muscular frames against Helen's delicate, almost skinny body with its little boobs.

The Captain instructed Mr Brown to kneel on the couch with his knees apart and sit back on his heels. His wife then lay in front of him, face down, and began to fondle his genitals to prepare him to be fellated by her. The Captain lifted her hips and slid a quantity of cushions under her belly so that her gleaming rump was cocked up at an inviting angle. He then seized Helen and lifted her bodily in his arms. She squealed and kicked in pretended protest, struggling like a slippery eel.

Almost dropping her, the Captain turned her upside down and dangled her in front of Mr Brown. Then he draped her legs over the kneeling man's shoulders so that the white thighs and buttocks concealed the lower half of the black face buried between them. Helen's hands came to rest on the cushions and she angled her head until she was in a position to work her tongue freely up and down Mrs Brown's pink gash.

Now that the triple gamahuche was under way the Captain took up his camera and hovered around the threesome, seeking out revealing angles to show on the large screen. The tightness of the caresses made this difficult but he conveyed his wishes to the participants and they accommodated him as far as they were able. Mr Brown grasped Helen by her slim hips and lifted her slightly forward. On the screen his tongue could now be seen clearly as it flickered up and down the wet groove from her anus to her clitoris. The camera swept down. Mrs Brown withdrew her lips a few inches from her husband's pubic curls and ran her mouth back and forth over his magnificent organ while she fondled his testicles. Finally the view shifted to what the red-faced, inverted and backwards-bent Helen was achieving with tongue and fingers in the groove of the black woman's uplifted behind. So much moist pinkness was on show there that it almost looked as if she had sucked the vulva inside out.

The Captain interrupted his camerawork for a moment to address the audience once more. 'I can see from your faces, ladies and gentlemen,' he said, 'that you are wishing we had enough Helens to go round, or that she could stay here long enough for you all to have a turn with her. Well, there's only one Helen and she's going to be a busy girl. But let me remind you about our friendly and efficient room service. All our maids have been trained to undertake this kind of work and so have the page-boys. The service is absolutely free, though generous tips are always appreciated. And now I'm sure you are keen to see how our volunteers are going to manage their big moment.'

Before the lecture, the Captain had privately explained to the volunteering couple and their much smaller partner how they might go about aiming for simultaneous orgasm in this position, or at least for the delay of the man's release until both women were experiencing their own ecstasy. Everything depended on Mr Brown's signalling to Helen how close he was to climax; this was to be done by a pre-arranged code in which his tongue would communicate with her cunt. The code was quite logical and really no more than what nature would have prompted anyway – the faster his tonguing, the more imminent the crisis. In her turn and by the same method Helen passed on the information to Mrs Brown.

By applying this system and alternately either speeding up their licking and sucking or holding back, the trio seemed to have the inexorable progress of their pleasure well under control. It was only at the very last instant that something went wrong and even then the trouble was not that they failed to hit their peak all at the same time. Whether on account of her youth or because of a certain hypersensitivity in her private parts, Helen's body stiffened and straightened out in orgasm with the result that the lustful triangle was disrupted even as its constituent members writhed in lewd spasms. Helen lay stretched on her back, clawing madly at the swollen flesh of her cunt. Mrs Brown collapsed on her belly and moaned as she ground her sex into the pile of cushions. Her husband, knocked backwards by Helen's violent disengagement from his mouth, arched his pelvis up and the audience applauded as an intermittent fountain of creamy spunk jetted vertically into the air to rain down in great splats and dollops on his own taut stomach and his wife's tightly plaited hair.

After the lecture the Captain sat in his office, worrying. He was spending far too much time worrying these days. He ought to be enjoying the full fruits of his Palace of Honeymoons now that it was fully operational. But somehow there was always a snag. Just now he found it difficult to relax with this visit from the planning department hanging over him – there were cost-cutting irregularities in the design and structure of the motel that would take a great deal of ingenuity to explain away. And old Pelham's appetite for beatable bums seemed to be growing so uncontrollable that quite soon Gloria and a couple of willing 'maids' would no longer be able to satisfy it.

Yes, Gloria was proving to be quite useful in that department. Nevertheless, it was probably just as well that he had persuaded Mary Muttock to try to resume her carnal relationship with his new wife and run away with her. Now that she was helping Gloria with her passport application it really looked as if his freedom would soon be restored. Meanwhile he would just have to avail himself of enjoyable opportunities as and when they presented themselves.

The door opened and a potentially enjoyable opportunity presented itself in the mouth-watering form of young Sally Nugent. She must have come straight from the lecture, where he had noticed her sitting in the front row without her husband. She was wasted on that pasty-faced premature ejaculator. What a tempting dish! Her wavy blonde hair was looking even lighter these days against the honey tan her skin had acquired on the beach and beside the pool. Today she was wearing a two-piece outfit of faded denim, designer-frayed at the edges. This consisted of a top with narrow, non-functional shoulder straps, buttoning down the front and leaving bare a broad expanse of midriff, below which a pair of skimpy shorts didn't give much more cover than the leather belt slung low round her hips. A double string of red beads round her neck added a touch of colour.

Sally closed the door behind her and eased herself down into the chair the Captain indicated. She crossed her slim legs but before the manoeuvre was completed he couldn't help noticing that the seam of her crotch was giving.

'And what can I do for you, my dear Mrs Nugent?' he asked. 'Did you enjoy the lecture?'

'Oh yes. It really gave me some ideas. It's just a pity that all this is going to be over so soon.'

'How much longer have you got with us?'

Sally bit her plump lower lip. 'That's what I wanted to speak to you regarding. This is our last week – our month's up on Saturday. We're having such a lovely time – well, I am, anyway – that we wondered if . . . if there was any possibility of staying on a bit longer.'

'Well, let's see,' said the Captain, pretending to consult his computer. 'This is the busiest time of year and the most expensive, of course, but I'd like to help you if I can. How many more nights might you want?'

Sally blushed and fiddled with her beads. 'I'm afraid we can only afford a few – days. We can't really afford that, being as we're both on unemployment, see. Rod would murder me if he knew I was doing this. I thought maybe, if you'd got something for us that I could just manage to pay for out of my savings, like maybe you could sort of make out we had a lucky number or something on our booking form and we'd won the extra time.' She caught the Captain's eye for a moment and looked down again.

'Which suite are you in?'

'Eight.'

'I thought so. As a matter of fact it's going to be free for the whole of next week. Would that suit you?'

Sally fumbled with her beads. 'Well, yes, that's great. But . . . Well, how much will it be? I just hope I've got the necessary.'

'Oh, you've got the necessary all right, Mrs Nugent. You've got what any man would give his right arm for, except that he'd need both hands to make full use of what you've got for him.'

'I don't quite . . .'

'Not to worry, dear. It's not as if we were complete strangers. I've seen you in the altogether quite a few times, haven't I? And you remember that first morning when I touched you up before we tried to get Mr Nugent to perform?'

The youthful bride grinned shyly. 'Course I remember,' she giggled. 'You sort of squeezed me down there and stuck your finger in. Rod would've had a fit if he'd noticed.'

'No need for him to know anything about what happens today. Oh, and every other morning as long as you're here – if you want me to say it's a lucky prize for the two of you, that is. Just come through into my studio – this little room at the back. I call it my studio because I keep this studio couch in it.'

With one hand the Captain opened the couch into a small but serviceable double bed. He sat on the edge and beckoned Sally over to him; she was docile. As she stood there he rested his hand on the small of her back, lightly stroking the sensitive down and pressing the smoothness of her tummy, with its cutely dimpled navel, into his cheek. His free hand ran over her legs, relishing the backs of her thighs, their flesh soft but firm over the tautness of healthy young muscle. The shorts were so brief that he could feel and pinch the beginnings of her buttocks springing out from the thigh-tops. But they were also tight, so tight that he could get no more than the tip of a finger under the frayed edges.

Sally, meanwhile, seemed to be acting on the understanding that she had clinched a deal – she had unbuttoned her denim top and cast it aside. Glancing up, the Captain was struck by the almost obscene contrast between the golden tan of her belly, throat, face, arms and shoulders with the creamy pallor of her plump little pink-tipped breasts.

He unbuckled her broad belt, undid the button of the waistband and tugged the zipper down. The shorts were already slung low over her hips and needed no more than a little encouragement to clear her bottom and drop to the floor. Along with her sandals, she kicked them aside.

Sally's only garment now, apart from the beads, was a skimpy pair of black knickers fastened with bows at the sides. Over the pubic mound, which they hugged snugly, was embroidered in red the slogan 'Merry Xmas'. The Captain pushed her down on the bed, tore off his own clothes and extended his eager body beside hers. Her first reaction was to go rigid and yelp with pain as he accidentally applied his weight to an outlying hank of her rippling curls, tugging sharply at her scalp as they were forced into the yielding mattress. But as soon as he realised what was wrong (she seemed to expect him to know this without being told) she lay back and let him snuggle up to her. Her attitude was one of relaxation contradicted only by her rapid, shallow breathing and the way she was biting her lower lip. Her legs were just slightly apart. Her hands rested, palms upwards, on the pillow above her head, exposing the fragrant tufts of golden hair that adorned her armpits. The Captain plunged his nose into the nearest of these and ran his hand down, avoiding contact, between those pert breasts, over the flat belly and down to the knickers. He cupped the tight package in his hand. It was agreeably warm and, if he was not mistaken, fluids of arousal had already begun to seep through the thin fabric. Hungry for penetration, his cock stretched and stiffened against the girl's thigh.

After scrabbling a bit with his fingers he moved his head and took one of Sally's breasts into his mouth. Its silky softness delighted his lips, while the tip of his tongue stimulated the growing hardness of the nipple. But the real motive for doing this was to provide cover for a quick shift of his caressing hand, which slid up to her tummy and straight down again with the fingers slipping inside the knickers. The tips passed through the fine hair; the first and third fingers came to rest in the creases of Sally's thighs and the second one between the sticky leaves of her sex. She sighed and pressed her legs together.

The Captain withdrew his hand, sat up, placed the other hand over the wet breast and dipped his mouth and nose down to the knickers. The black triangle with its cheery if unseasonable greeting was so redolent of many happy occasions with untried young women that he knew he would have to hurry if he was to give her any more joy than that husband of hers was able to. Not that Sally was untried, strictly speaking, but she had never yet been properly broken in as a wife, had she? Catching the elastic with his upper teeth he dragged it downwards, letting the wispy blonde hair spring up as it was uncovered. Ah, yes – this was one of the things he liked about Sally: the way her pubic hair was fair and fine enough for the pink line bisecting her plump little pubis to show through clearly. On this occasion that pink line had darkened to purple and multiplied itself into an enticing array of puffy parallel grooves and ridges. He unfastened the bows on both sides. Sally was now completely bare, the double string of red beads serving only to emphasise her nudity.

He knelt between her thighs and smiled down at her. 'How would you like it, Mrs Nugent?' he asked.

'Oh, just a straight fuck, please, but really quick. I'm dying for it. I can't wait to be filled, properly filled, with something a bit more solid than my boyfr . . . my husband's thing when he's just squirted his stuff all over me. And a bit more lifelike than those plastic things we've got in the room.'

Even as she spoke the Captain was nudging his swollen organ against the juicy petals of her girlflesh and easing it inch by inch into the tight opening. No doubt about it, this young lady was responding to his thrusts with all the symptoms of overwhelming and rarely satisfied desire. The thought that she was probably fantasising about her less than satisfactory husband did nothing to diminish the Captain's enjoyment. On the contrary, it actually increased his ardour.

At first her lips remained closed to the probing of his eager tongue. But as his slow, steady stabbing into the hot depths of her belly began to accelerate and his manipulation of her tits became more urgent, her facial muscles relaxed and he found himself licking a double row of perfect teeth through which the girl's saliva was leaking like lovejuice. He tugged one of her nipples. Her jaw went slack and his tongue slipped in with the vigour of a rampant prick.

Young Sally writhed and scratched the Captain's back in the throes of sensual longing. These manifestations of her appreciation were becoming too much for him to sustain much longer. As if she could read his thoughts – although more probably she was merely remembering one of the points from the tuition provided on this unusual honeymoon – she reached behind him to fondle his bursting balls. It was the touch of her cool hand that triggered the outpouring of his lust. Great masses of seed welled up from the core of his being, trembled for a long, rapturous moment on the verge of expulsion and finally fountained into the innermost recesses of hot little Sally's cunt in surge after surge of boiling joy.

'Every morning for the rest of this week,' he panted. 'And then every morning after that, as long as you want to stay. You'll be very welcome, Mrs Nugent - you and that precocious husband of yours.'

Mary Muttock had missed the lecture, having frolicked through an arduous weekend. She had made the acquaintance of this charming old boy called Danvers Pelham, who had warmed to her on discovering she had wielded the rod of correction at an educational institution for young ladies. His attentions had grown warmer still when she told him about her less academic but even more punishing adventures working on the Raunch Ranch outside Las Vegas. The two of them ended up glowing rosily. Even the sickly Mrs Pelham, who was taking ages to recover from her wedding night, got quite worked up as a spectator of their efforts.

The Pelhams, however, had not claimed all Miss Muttock's time, or even most of it. She had been able to renew her close association with Miss MacDonald and the latter had generously allowed her a fairly free hand with her little protegée Helen Lascelles. Melanie Winspur, on the other hand, although she actually lived with the MacDonald, was now an adult young woman for the enjoyment of whose favours no permission was needed but her own. Melanie had made a point, in fact, of letting her former headmistress lick her cunt in the presence of that scruffy Derrick in open defiance of his opposition. No wonder Mary Muttock was tired.

Yet the energy she had expended with these companions was as nothing compared with the demands made on her by that larger-than-life archimandrite. Big Jimbo had run amuck with her until his caravan had rocked with their bucking and from every vent and window opening had issued steam mingled with incense. A succession of young wives and quite a number of couples had been sent away on the pretext that the Reverend

103

DeVayne had been too deeply engaged in his devotions to spare them the time of day. 'Go in peace and amity,' he had called to them without opening the door. 'Be fruitful and prodigal of your seed, for it shall be abundant.'

His own seed was certainly abundant and he had scattered it abroad with great prodigality. And not only abroad – a fair quantity of it had been sluiced into her various bodily openings in the course of their wild rutting. If the gin had not flowed even more freely than this potent elixir, more of the thick fluid might have finished up inside her than was in fact the case.

The man was an animal. So were most men in Mary Muttock's varied experience, but with some of them it was as if the sap that flowed up the stem of the evolutionary tree pulsed as strongly through their loins as it had done through those of their primitive ancestors. Often you could tell from their manes; the reddish, shaggy growth sprouting from the archimandrite's chops was a case in point, and then there were his ruddy-manged loin (or lion) chops down below. Well, she was a bit confused after all that – mainly all that humping. Maybe it was not so much their manes as their names that betrayed their bestial origins. *Jimbo* had to be straight out of the jungle. Her own name, *Muttock*, she had long since recognised as an etymological derivative of *Mammoth*. Viewed in this light, the tusking and coupling, the trampling and trumpeting, the clamping and clowning – the whole elephantine circus had clearly been inevitable and predestined.

When at last, replete with the passional liquor which had gushed forth from the loins of this shaggy brute, she staggered out of the caravan into the cool night air, she had been quite unable to find her way back to her room. Inexplicably she had wandered straight into the pool. To some extent the shock of the cold water had sobered her up and enabled her to keep her head above the surface. All the same, she would probably not have found the strength to drag herself out unaided. It was that lovely American girl, the Captain's new bride, who had come to her rescue.

Gloria had just locked the office and reception for the night when she had heard the splash and the confused cries for help. Casting aside the dressing-gown which was all she was wearing at this late hour, she had plunged unhesitatingly into the water, towed the floundering Muttock to the edge and somehow heaved her up on to the concrete surround. Then she stooped over the sodden form and applied the kiss of life.

One thing led to another. When she recovered her voice, Mary Muttock had begged the younger woman to help her back to her room. Gloria had undressed her, dried her, massaged her and cuddled her, first back to a state of comfort and then to something better than that.

Most of the Muttock's thinking this evening had been done by her fanny but now, at last, her head was beginning to operate again. She remembered that the Captain had attached great importance to the matter of persuading Gloria to go away with her. No point in trying to fathom the reasoning behind this: the Captain generally knew what he was about. All she had to do was arouse the blossoming Mrs Haggler's interest and get her to make some kind of commitment.

She had succeeded in whipping up this interest, first by sucking Gloria's tits and licking her sexlips until she came, over and over again. Then she had told the young American how she would love to see the States once more and how good it would be to make the trip in the company of a beautiful and compliant friend who would be able to ease her access to the best transatlantic society. In return for such favours, she hinted, she would be able to introduce Gloria to a select establishment in Nevada which surpassed even the Honeymoon Palace Motel in the luxuries and delights it offered.

The girl had expressed a real interest in this prospect but had then adopted an innocently naive look. She explained that due to a misunderstanding about the business they had all been involved in so profitably last year, there would be a strong likelihood of trouble if she returned to her native shores. 'Oh, but you'll be able to travel under your married name once we get you fixed up with your new passport,' Mary Muttock assured her. 'They'll never catch up with you, you silly girl.'

Gloria had accompanied Miss Muttock from the pool naked and dripping wet, but she had brought her discarded dressing-gown with her and also the large bag in which she carried things she thought she might need, and from this bag she now produced the Home Office documentation that included the endless and not yet completed application forms which would have to be sent with the marriage certificate. Mary Muttock had devoted the rest of the night, or that part of it in which she remained conscious, to once again helping her friend to negotiate the obscurities of Whitehall English. And even more usefully, she had appended her own name and address as a referee of professional standing to vouch for the applicant's moral probity.

Such were the recollections that came flooding back into Miss Muttock's awakening awareness as the excited voices of couples hurrying past her window after the Captain's lecture made her realise it was much later than the darkness had suggested. Gloria had disappeared from her bed – regretfully, as nothing much had passed between them after the initial rapture of the poolside resuscitation. At least she had done her a good turn, and the Captain too, by helping to finish off those forms for her. So what was it that was troubling her as she struggled to recall the fine detail?

Of course. Maybe it wouldn't really matter – they never checked on that kind of thing, did they? It might even help, lending credence to her professional status. When she signed her name, she remembered, she had given her address not as Cunlip Hall, far away in the East Midlands, but as Cunlip College, near Upchester, the scene of her disgrace.

That evening the Captain felt thoroughly disconsolate, in spite of record sales of the Studmaster. His hints had worked all too well and Miss Muttock had left with Gloria, only nine days after her marriage to him, for an extended visit to Cunlip Hall while waiting for him to receive and forward the passport that would make possible their proposed trip to the States.

Apart from anything else, it was bloody hard work running the motel without Gloria. She was very strong on the admin side and had made everything look so easy. Rather than face the embarrassment of having to offer excuses to disgruntled guests he locked the office, installed a 'maid' and page-boy in Reception and left it to them to sort things out.

As a distraction he prowled his secret passages and lurked in the rooms deliberately left empty, savouring through spyholes and two-way mirrors the activities of some of his honeymooners. Yet the sport held far less charm for him now than formerly. He felt too detached and preoccupied to get really hard while watching the unskilled conjoining of novices. And the second-timers all too often left him cold.

All the same, there was one couple he was always curious about: Mr and Mrs Roderick Larby Nugent. Not that Rod was anything special; far from it. No, it was young Sally who had taken his fancy in a big way. When he made a real effort to analyse his present feelings, he reached the conclusion that the sort of fun that might lift his spirits right now would be to share a ringside seat with Helen Lascelles next door to the Nugents.

Helen was game and Miss MacDonald was willing to spare her and make do with a 'maid' as Melanie had left the previous evening on the back of Derrick's noisy bike. Helen slipped into a standard black motel G-string, wrapped a towel round her shoulders and proceeeded with the Captain to the permanently unoccupied Suite Nine, which was specially equipped for viewing.

There was no need to switch on the light, as sufficient illumination spilled in through the mirror running most of the length of the wall which separated this room from the Nugents'. And now that the rain had stopped it was quite a warm evening, so the Captain immediately shed his bathrobe and slipped the towel from Helen's shoulders. He gave the pretty, brown-nippled breasts and the narrow white back with its array of moles no more than a passing glance at first, so eager was he for his first peep at whatever activities were taking place in Number Eight.

Sprawled on the bed, which was directly opposite the mirror, lay Ratface Rod, naked and propped up on a pile of pillows. With one hand he was playing with his testicles while the other one ran idly up and down his erected dick.

Slightly disappointed, the Captain sat down on the edge of the upholstered viewing bench and indicated to Helen that she should make herself comfortable astride his lap, also facing the mirror. He rested his chin on her shoulder and reached under her arms to squeeze her tits. Her back was deliciously smooth and cool against his chest and belly. His penis straightened out under her, its head pressing up against the soft cotton G-string. Feeling the immediate response of Helen's nipples, he let one of his hands drop to her lap and slid his fingers inside the little garment, where they nestled into the moist warmth of her crotch.

The scene in the adjoining room now became more interesting. Sally Nugent appeared from somewhere off at the side and stood at the end of the bed. 'Look,' Helen sniggered, 'she's wearing one of those frou-frous.'

'Tutus. It's called a tutu.'

Evidently Sally had been inspecting the contents of the fancy dress cupboard provided in all the apartments. Her choice, in the Captain's judgement, was a tasteful one. Her middle was just about covered by the scarlet ballet skirt, all layers of stiff net sticking out and leaving her legs bare to the very tops of her thighs. Well, not quite bare. Wrapped round her ankles were the crossed-over ribbons of the scarlet ballet shoes. Apart from the shoes and the tutu, all she had on was a matching silk scarf in which her hair was bundled up on the top of her head and the double string of red beads she had been wearing that morning. As a final touch, she had achieved a striking effect by painting her lips and nipples with lipstick of the same vivid red.

And now she started to dance, casting disdainful glances at her masturbating husband as she rose on her points with a skill she must have been taught at ballet classes as a little girl. Her hands met high above her head as she slowly turned, displaying the yellow tufts in her armpits, more noticeable now than when the Captain had first seen them. In this position the tutu was lifted a fraction. He could almost be sure she had no knickers on under it – almost but not quite. His imagination ran riot and he gave Helen's shaven pussy an excited squeeze. No traces of prickly stubble scratched his hand as he rubbed it round the fleshy pouch.

Just for a moment he removed his other hand from the girl's breasts to turn a knob which brought the sound system into play. The dreamy strains of Gluck's *Dance of the Blessed Spirits* flowed from the twin speakers, as well as some background grunts from Rod. Sally executed a neat pirouette. This time there was no ambiguity. The scarlet tutu flared out into a spinning disk and, as she twirled around, the optical illusion was created of a bare bottom with a triangle of yellow down superimposed on it. As she slowed down the two parts of this composite image were separated into rapidly alternating bum and twat. But her deceleration also allowed the hem of the tutu to fall the few inches that were sufficient to hide then again.

Sally flopped down to the floor, doing the splits with impressive ease. In this attitude her lower parts were completely covered but the rounded breasts looked more than usually tempting, their creamy whiteness contrasting with the bright red of their tips and the surrounding accessories. She stood up again, used one hand to steady herself against the wall and with the other one clasped the ankle of a leg she had raised until the toes pointed straight up at the ceiling. And now for the first time her sexual slit was exposed to the fascinated gaze of her husband and the two concealed watchers. The pink of the engorged lips grew richer in hue until it matched her costume. The Captain groped Helen more vigorously.

Such a pose could hardly be maintained for long. Gracefully Sally lowered her leg, did a few more turns round the floor and then, half-facing the mirror, parted her feet slightly and raised her arms. Her next move was to bend right back in a controlled movement in time with the music until the top of her head rested on the floor. Her body now formed a supple arch with her taut belly as its highest point.

In one direction, the arch curved back to the inverted face contorted in an expression of what was probably concentration. Once again the Captain stiffened even harder at the sight of the golden hair under her arms, now darkened with perspiration and sticking to her skin in little tangled skeins. Her breasts with their painted teats were so firm that their shape was only slightly modified by her backward-leaning posture, but their swelling undersides shone with an alabaster whiteness, forming curved highlights against the mellow ivory from which they jutted out. Eagerly the Captain tugged Helen's nipple as she squirmed on his lap.

In the next room the apex of the human arch was adorned with the stiff, multilayered tutu with its taffeta lining, standing out like a large halo; its lower circumference was crushed against the carpet. On the hither side of this blood-red halo were braced the strong, shapely legs terminating in the scarlet ballet slippers with their crossed red ribbons. Just free of the tutu, Sally's hips projected as little points sticking up from the skin stretched over them. And under the hips her buttocks were tensed into dimpled concavity.

But the central beauty of this attractive display was undoubtedly the wound-like rift that pouted its wet invitation between Sally's flexing thighs. As usual, the Captain found himself drawn to all the contrasting variety that constituted the unity of this picture. The slick, oily texture of those lewdly parted labia was offset by the surrounding blonde down of her bush, and the effect of this in its turn benefited from the way it sprouted out of such smooth, shining skin. Moreover, the variations in this skin were a source of delight, variations which depended on the underlying bone, muscle or internal organs. Thus, his glance ran caressingly from the tight flatness of her belly with its pretty navel, over the velvet-sheathed sharpness of a hip down to the dimpling of a buttock and then from the undercurve of the thigh to the thigh's tensed upper surface. Finally, his eyes came to rest once more on the flaunted pussy which seemed to be ever changing, ever more eager for action and satisfaction.

His erotic contemplation of the young girl's beauty was interrupted by her husband. Rod jumped impatiently down from the bed and placed himself on his knees between Sally's legs. He rested his elbows on the floor and let her lower her bottom a little to be supported by the upturned palms of his hands. He plunged his sharp features into the gaping cunt and slurped audibly at it, plundering the nectar at the centre of this great scarlet blossom.

The Captain could tell that Helen, too, was inflamed by the performance. He stood her up, kissed her lightly on the lips, wrapped her towel round his middle, took up his key-ring from the shelf and led her out into the warm evening air. His master key slipped easily into the lock of the adjoining apartment.

Sally and Rod were so engrossed in each other that at first they failed to notice the almost naked intruders. When they did so they seemed to be really pleased to see them. Rod looked up from his work and immediately found Helen's G-string thrust into his face, which was now smeared with Sally's juices. He pulled it down and began to tongue Helen's hairless snatch.

Helen, however, had other ideas. Putting her hands on Rod's shoulders she gave a shove so that he lost his balance and fell on his back. In no time at all his slim prick, which stood up vertically, was engulfed in her descending quim without spilling a drop. Helen rocked above him, gasping in her keenness to reach orgasm.

Meanwhile the Captain had been quick to offer Sally the satisfaction she never seemed to get from her husband. Reluctant to damage the splendid tutu, he seized her by the buttocks and hauled her up to a level at which he could spear her on his shaft. Her head still touched the floor, but the scarlet taffeta hid her face and breasts from his staring eyes. He shook her loins violently against his own until the hot flood spurted into her thirsty cunt. He had slaked that thirst some ten hours earlier and hoped to repeat the service the following morning; all the same, it showed every sign of being the kind of thirst that only grew stronger with slaking.

When both couples had finished and the males had withdrawn from their partners, the Captain kissed Sally and complimented Rod both on his performance with Helen and also on his choice of Sally as his bride. Helen, who now looked even more exhausted than usual, stepped into her messy G-string and pulled it up rather carelessly so that the top inch or so of her slit remained uncovered. Her little towel again served as a loin cloth for the Captain, who led her swiftly through the puddles and the gathering shades of evening to his office, hoping they would not encounter any of the guests on the way.

As they passed through Reception, the page on duty tried to say something but the Captain told him it could wait until later and dismissed him curtly. He drew Helen into his office with him and switched on the light. To his surprise, the room was not empty.

At ease in the Captain's leather-covered swivel chair sat a thin man with wrinkled, papery skin, thick black hair which had the appearance of being dyed, glasses with heavy black frames, a narrow black moustache and little pointed beard, a

111

navy blazer and silk cravat, grey flannels and suede shoes. To the Captain's experienced eye he looked like the sort of man who would wear driving gloves over his nicotine-stained fingers and keep a set of golf clubs in the boot of his car. The visitor looked up without surprise at the bare flesh that had just entered the room, and spoke.

'Captain Haggler? I'm from the planning department. Name's Brice. Do sit down, sir, you and the young lady. That's right, don't mind me, miss. I've been looking round this establishment following one or two complaints from patrons. Now I'm fairly easygoing myself, sir, but one of the letters we received at the town hall was from a solicitor chappie who's likely to throw the book at us. I must tell you, sir, for a start, that building regulations appear not to have been complied with in every respect. Not quite in *every* respect, you understand. This place can't expect a shelf life of more than fifteen years.'

The Captain shrugged. 'Well, maybe my contractors cut the odd corner, I wouldn't deny that. But before fifteen years are up the whole site will have fallen into the sea anyway. Great chunks of cliff break off every day.'

'And that's another thing, sir. You had no business building a public amenity like this on a dangerous site. Your clients and employees are sitting on a time bomb.'

'The point is . . .'

'The point, Captain Haggler, is that this is altogether a pretty rum joint, the kind that no self-respecting district council could be expected to put up with if they knew the half of it. Now while I was waiting for you I took the liberty of going round the place with one of these sets of master keys you've got. *You* might call it a motel but there are those who would have a different name for it, especially if they bumped into the likes of the young lady here. Sorry, dear, I don't mean it personal. Just doing my job.'

Helen, who was perching on a hard chair with her arms folded protectively over her little breasts, blushed and simpered in a way the Captain considered unhelpful. He tried to bluff his way out of this tight corner. 'Look,' he improvised, 'I can explain everything.'

'You don't need to explain anything, sir,' Brice replied. 'I've seen quite enough of the way you operate to put you seriously out of business. I'd only been waiting here a couple of minutes when you and your little friend came in, you know. I came straight over from the last room I inspected – Number Nine I think it was. Very nicely set up it is. But you know what they say about the grass being greener on the other side of the fence. You'll never guess what I saw in that two-way mirror.'

The Captain was horrified to realise he had been so well and truly caught. He felt as if his personal, private space had been encroached upon. On the other hand, unless Sally Nugent had lied to everyone about her age and married status it was hard to see anything criminal in the evening's engagement, which had been between consenting adults more or less in private. What was more, there was something in this Brice's tone of voice, something whiningly insinuating. Yes. Maybe he had the measure of this bespectacled carpet-creeper.

'Care for a drink, Mr Brice?' he offered. 'I wonder if we could come to some sort of, well, understanding.'

Brice stubbed out his cigarette and nodded his compliance. 'I'll have the young lady there for starters,' he said. 'Come and sit on my lap, dear.'

The Captain indicated to Helen that she should do as she was told. Then he poured the drinks and tried to relax while he ran through a list of facilities he was prepared to offer to secure the short-term future of his business. Negotiations were conducted smoothly and to the satisfaction of both parties while the corrupt planning inspector caressed and mauled Helen's slim body. Finally Brice dropped his grey flannel trousers, got her down on the floor and started to fuck her. The Captain slipped out of the room with a sigh of relief, realising how easy it was going to be to make a video recording of his persecutor's activities at an early opportunity. Just for insurance purposes, of course.

SEVEN

A JOLLY GOOD SHOW

Friday had come round quickly, all too quickly. The weather had improved and every day brought not only agreeable experiences that had made the hours flash past for the Captain but also a host of renewed problems and harassments. And so he was not exactly best pleased to have his early afternoon love-making disrupted by notice of yet another difficulty.

It was in the hope of getting away from the constant stream of queries and complaints that he had ventured forth for a stroll along the clifftop, and when he ran into the beautifully healthy figure of Miss MacDonald exercising in her tracksuit he had welcomed the encounter. Mac was a good sport and they were soon romping in a hidden grassy trough where part of the cliff had crumbled away. The muscular but well-proportioned length of her athletic body ticked over in his arms as they lay there naked after the shock of the initial discharge. The Captain could have easily fallen asleep but with his experience of women he was not surprised that she insisted on chatting and soliciting his views.

It seemed that Mac had worries of her own. Fearing that she might have outstayed her welcome when Melanie was carried off to Upchester by Derrick, she had offered to pay her keep and Helen's for a few more days at the motel by putting on a show for the guests. The Captain remembered productions she had mounted on previous occasions and had been happy to agree. The venue was to be the flimsy but opulent-looking structure that served as the motel ballroom and the date Friday the seventh. Tonight.

Mac was a great organiser and was now able to report that the final rehearsal was planned for that afternoon. Everything was well in hand for the performance, except for one rather major snag. On the Captain's suggestion she had phoned Upchester and engaged the services of Susie and Darcy O'Flammery to do one of their expressive dances. The O'Flammerys, who had now been married two years and had reached the ripe old age of eighteen, had accepted the offer with alacrity. With them, youth was the watchword, the keynote. For this reason Susie had announced that they would bring with them, as part of their act, an even younger couple: Tim, Darcy's brother, and Gail, a girl Tim had picked up in the town. These two, according to Susie, were well into their seventeenth year although they looked younger.

To the Captain this sounded like good news. He did not see what Mac was so upset about. The little quartet promised to provide the high spot of the show, surely. Mac concurred but explained this could only be the case if they actually turned up. She had expected them after breakfast and there was still no sign of them. However well they had planned and rehearsed their act at home, time would be needed to adapt it to the actual locale and to fit it into the evening's programme.

The Captain could see her point. On the other hand, his own concerns seemed so much more daunting that he was inclined to dismiss this problem as trivial. The MacDonald was such a perfectionist! But before he was able to calm her down or distract her by putting to use the second erection that was beginning to stretch out towards her slim form, they were rudely interrupted. A shadow fell across their intertwined limbs. Above them stood Mr Brice, the corrupt inspector from the planning department. He was fully dressed from suede shoes to panama hat. But he too was sporting an erection that stretched out from his open fly. He raised his hat in mock courtesy.

'Hallo there, old boy,' he began. 'Glad to see you can still find time for life's simpler pleasures. We've a lot in common, you and me. Take this lady, now – I could see myself becoming one of her biggest fans. I'm pretty big already, if you see what

I mean. Sort of *physical*, isn't she? Physical and receptive's what I'd call her. A real beaut. Think she'd mind if I just took advantage of her under the terms of our agreement? This cliff's a death trap, you know – I could have you closed down tomorrow, except that tomorrow's Saturday.'

Miss MacDonald was smiling vacantly. She actually seemed to be charmed by this unappealing intruder and now began to assess his gnarled cock with interest. Catching the Captain's eye she nodded. With mixed feelings of disgust and relief he got off her and rolled to one side while Brice dropped his trousers and pants.

'That's what I like to see,' the inspector remarked. 'Know the old rhyme? Goes something like this:

> I like my buns well buttered
> I've done so all my life;
> It makes the buns all runny,
> But tastier than the wife.

Come on then, old girl. Let's get stuck in.'

The MacDonald was actually one of the most attractive women the Captain knew. He found it quite sickening to see her being abused by a slimy toad like Brice, so he pulled his shorts on and headed back towards the motel. As he approached, one of the local taxis drew up outside Reception and four young people got out. He trotted across the lawn to greet them.

Yes, he was right – they were Mac's late arrivals, Susie, Darcy, Tim and Tim's girlfriend. Of the couple the Captain already knew, Darcy had changed the most since they last met a year ago. He and his wife must now be eighteen. The lad had grown taller and filled out slightly. His dark brown hair hung down to his shoulders. His legs were at last getting hairy and a line of down adorned his upper lip. Not an improvement, on the whole, the Captain thought.

Susie, on the other hand, had hardly altered at all. She had even kept the pair of golden plaits that had helped to make her such an adorable plaything. The only noticeable change since last year was that her breasts, which at seventeen had still been tiny in spite of the disproportionately developed nipples, had now plumped out into respectable little mounds. Like her husband she wore blue jeans and a tight-fitting black vest. The breasts jiggled firmly under this as she moved, the teats projecting prominently enough to cast little shadows in the early afternoon sunlight.

Darcy introduced his younger brother Tim, a cheeky imp in a shellsuit top and snug little white shorts. If he had met him alone, the Captain would have thought he had run into Darcy as he had been a couple of years ago, except that Tim's hair was cropped to a crew-cut and much fairer than Darcy's. The hair on his head, that is – like his brother's at sixteen, Tim O'Flammery's features were innocent of whiskery growth and the slim, sun-tanned arms and legs were equally hairless. When he spoke, his patrician accents emerged in a fluting contralto.

Tim's friend Gail was delightful, with green eyes, freckles and frizzy red hair. She wore a long, full skirt of floral design which reached from her narrow hips almost to her ankles. To compensate for the modesty of this garment she had merely tied a scarf of similar flowery design round her chest, although the chest appeared to be as flat as a boy's. She had rolled the scarf into a strip of silk so narrow that it barely covered whatever she could boast in the way of nipples. Her gleaming shoulders and freckled arms were slight and almost fragile-looking without being skinny, and her collar bones were certainly more noticeable than Susie's.

This newly arrived foursome inhaled the sea air and expressed a wish to go to the beach. As they had already eaten and the MacDonald was otherwise engaged, the Captain saw no harm in stowing their bags in Reception and leading them down to the water's edge.

Although most of the guests were away having or recovering from their lunch or otherwise enjoying themselves elsewhere, quite a few couples were splashing in the waves or sunbathing on the sand. The Captain conducted his little group to the far end of the cove, where they passed around some rocks uncovered at low tide, crossed the barbecue area and reached a smaller, deserted beach.

The young people turned out to be really keen paddlers. They stepped out of the sandals and trainers they were wearing. Tim took off his shellsuit jacket, exposing a smooth chest and trim tummy, golden-brown against the white of his skimpy shorts. Gail removed her skirt but kept on the tiny green panties that set off the freckled white of her girlish thighs most attractively.

Darcy and Susie were somewhat bolder, leaving only their black singlets on as a protection from the sun. The Captain always loved to see young people naked from the waist down. For a long moment he feasted his eyes on the married O'Flammerys. Even in its flaccid state, the lad's prick was much longer and fatter than when he had last seen it, and the tangle of brown curls from which it sprang had grown denser and spread up his lower belly towards the navel. The balls, too, seemed to hang more heavily. The male hormones must now be in full flood; Darcy had at last moved from delayed but randy adolescence to unambiguously virile youth.

But if Darcy looked rather less appetising than last year, this was more than made up for, as the Captain had already noticed, by the way his wife had blossomed in that time. It was not just that her breasts had grown more womanly, though still undeniably young-womanly. The golden tuft at the base of her belly was as soft and silky as ever. The difference was fractional, perhaps too slight to be measured, but it seemed to the Captain that the flesh on her limbs was just that marginal bit fuller. She had rounded out almost imperceptibly. He remembered her as a lovely, lively kid, but as he looked at her today he no longer found any incongruity in the idea of Susie as a desirable young wife.

Tempted though he was to let the sea breezes dry the salty leakage from his own genitals, the Captain judged it prudent to keep his shorts on. Frail Gail, on whom he was keeping at least one of his eyes, had appeared to shrink at her first close view of the black and grizzled mat of hairs on his chest. The sight of what he kept below his belt might frighten her off completely.

The four of them waded out up to their thighs. The brothers had Gail between them. She held their hands and gave a little squeal every time she trod on a pebble or shell. The Captain and Susie lagged somewhat behind. He laid his hand lightly on her soft bottom and spoke to her in discreetly low tones. 'How

118

are the two of you getting on, dear?' he asked. 'Does Darcy still make you happy?'

'Oh yes,' she replied. 'He's really good to me and things are better than ever now he's got so – well, so *big*. I often think of how nice you were on our wedding night and how simply ginormous you felt inside me after Darce had gone to sleep. Well, I get that sort of feeling nearly every night now.'

'Not quite every night, though?'

'We've got this sort of understanding. Every now and then Darce has a night out. I don't ask questions. It's best for both of us if he's having a good time. Now that he's finished growing – well, I hope he has – he seems to need an awful lot of it.'

The Captain hooked his hand under Susie's crotch from behind. Her buttocks tensed, then relaxed. The others were now well out of earshot. 'Ever cheat on him?' he enquired.

'Wouldn't call it cheating, not compared with his carryings-on. But yes. Sometimes I let Melanie's Derrick – remember him? – flirt with me. But nothing serious, not what I'd call serious.'

And now the Captain crooked his index finger, trailing the tip along the warm, hairy groove. Maybe as an effect of the tangy sea air, Susie was still dry, the bud of her sex tightly furled against intrusion. She stopped wading, rubbed a palm across the front of his shorts in a friendly way and addressed him with a fleeting smile.

'You don't have to be in such a rush, Captain. I'm sure there's going to be a chance for you to give me a bit of a poke later on.'

They linked arms and moved forward companionably, splashing and almost stumbling several times in the warm water as they hurried to rejoin the others. Gail had broken away from the boys and was untying the scarf that bound her chest. Picking her way along a submerged sandbank, she made sure that she was further out from the shore than the others and kept her back turned to them. The tops of the highest waves were wetting her knickers and making them a darker green where they had been splashed. On the left the Captain could see that the wet material had got caught in the rift of her bottom, leaving that white cheek bare and gleaming.

Susie gave the Captain's arm a squeeze and left him, cutting away towards her Darcy, who had rolled his vest up under his armpits and was just managing to keep it above the wavetops by bouncing up and down with them. She had waded up to the very tops of her thighs and was beginning to shudder as each incoming swell lapped against her pussy when suddenly she screamed out in alarm. Everyone, including the flat-chested Gail, turned to witness an extraordinary commotion. Susie rose like a latter-day Aphrodite from a tumult of foam, borne aloft by some dark-shagged monster of the deep.

When she stopped kicking and screaming it became easy to identify this sea beast as big Jimbo, who must have been lurking below the surface for longer than the Captain would have supposed possible. The hair that covered his body, both back and front, was slicked into a semblance of wet sealskin. Water streamed from the sodden pubic bush surrounding the upright sceptre of his lust. What could be seen of his facial growth looked like a crop of dark seaweed. But not much of it could be seen, because it was mostly buried in the fork of Susie's thighs as he held her sitting high on his shoulders.

'Greetings, friends,' the archimandrite spluttered, forcing his head back from the wriggling girl's crotch to make the utterance. 'You took me by surprise. I was just mortifying the flesh and sharpening my spiritual faculties through the discipline of oxygen deprivation, meditating on our marine origins in the warm slime of the ocean floor. And lo! The sun shone forth upon the waters and the breeze of heaven breathed fire into the loins of woman, and now behold! – in the stead of the warm slime of ocean, I pasture upon the warmer slime of those loins. Go in peace, I say unto you. Yea, go in peace even as I pierce her asunder with the gift of my tongue.'

Susie shrieked and kicked her feet against Jimbo's back as he head-butted her stomach and squeezed her buttocks, pulling her sex hard back against his mouth. After a few moments she quietened down and slumped forward over the top of his head, gasping.

The relative silence which made her gasps audible was broken by the shrill blast of a whistle sounding from the clifftop. All turned and looked up except Jimbo, whose eyes were masked by Susie's pubic mound and whose ears were sealed by the flesh of her thighs.

Silhouetted against the blue sky, the tracksuited figure of Miss MacDonald stood above the spot where the Captain had left her. She had recognised the new arrivals and was desperately signalling for them to join her for a belated rehearsal of their routine for the evening's show. Susie neatly and astonishingly detached herself from Jimbo's sucking lips by hanging backwards until she could clutch his hips. Then, with a leap like a salmon, she kicked her legs straight up into the air and flipped right over so that her feet landed in the water.

As the four young people splashed past the Captain, he was sorry to see that Gail had replaced her concealing scarf while he had first been looking up at Mac and then distracted by Susie's virtuoso display. He was curious about this new girl's small or non-existent tits.

Before the more formal part of the entertainment began, the motel guests were encouraged to get into the mood by the provision of a disco and cut-price bar. The Captain found the darkness, interrupted as it was by flashing strobes, and the head-splitting thumping of the music quite distasteful, but he had always been prepared to put up with the awfulness of such occasions for the sake of the pleasures they offered the practised voyeur and groper. Small tables and chairs had been set up all around the ballroom for the convenience of the guests when the show commenced, but at this early stage in the evening the presence of these items left the remaining floorspace extremely crowded with gyrating couples and cavorting individuals.

Although Miss MacDonald's show was to be the first such production the Captain had mounted, the Friday-night disco had become a regular event at the motel. The patrons regarded it as an occasion for dressing up (or down) in ways that let them feel they were doing something a bit special. He moved rather clumsily among them, enjoying the jerky flashes of female display revealed by the lights. His progress round the floor was something between a casual stroll to the bar on the other side of the room and a limb-shaking routine meant to suggest the motions of a dance.

Several of his favourite women were flaunting themselves. But the closer he got to them, the more determined they seemed to avoid eye contact. As for aural communication, the thudding beat of the disco music ruled that right out. He was dazzled and disorientated by a flickering succession of images: manes of hair cascading to the floor from heads thrown back in abandon; clapping hands raised high in the air to reveal shaven or furred armpits; plump white thigh-tops momentarily exposed above black silk stockings as the dancer twirled around and her skirt was lifted; the curve of a crimson-tipped breast visible through an upper garment of wide-meshed green net; a dimpled navel set in an expanse of sun-tanned belly. He picked out Doris, whose corpulent spouse was knocking back the beer on the sidelines and cheering her on. Doris was showing off acrobatically among the other dancers, attired in a diminutive but expensive-looking blue bikini – positively overdressed, the Captain thought, compared with the way he usually seemed to see her.

He moved to the side as she kicked out with a shapely leg. This movement brought him into contact with Sally Nugent, who was shaking her body energetically and bumping it against her Rod's. The Captain moved in to form a threesome, whereupon Rod made a gesture indicative of thirst and sloped off to the bar. Sally paused for a breather, resting both hands on the Captain's upper arms. She gazed expectantly into his eyes, the strobes making her look as if she was blinking.

He sized her up. The golden hair, held back from her brow by a red band, rippled down over her shoulders. How demure she looked in that snugly fitting black sweater with its high neck! But provocative, too – the sweater was thin and tight, so that her nipples, stiffened by friction with it during the dancing, stood out visibly. She had pushed the sleeves up to just below her elbows. As the coloured lights flashed, the Captain caught sharp, almost hallucinatory glimpses of the fine dusting of hair that fledged her forearms.

If the sweater was demure up to a point, her clothing below it was anything but, as he discovered when he drew back to let his appreciative eye run down her full length. She wore a shiny red PVC microskirt, split at the sides to facilitate dancing and, for that matter, walking. Her legs were sheathed in black fishnet tights.

Oh, yes – what attractive packaging! The Captain moved in and let his left cheek brush Sally's. He spread his left hand and pressed it firmly on her plastic-covered bottom, drawing her towards him so that she would feel the hardening erection inside his trousers. That she did indeed feel it was confirmed by the smile which lit up her face as she leaned back and away from him to plant a peck of a kiss on his lips. He now realised what it was about her, apart from the fact that she was fully dressed, that had seemed unusual: she was wearing make-up.

Although the other dancers had whipped themselves up, or allowed the music to whip them up, into a frenzy, the Captain elected to take his partner through the slow paces of a smoochie. His left hand still tight on her bum, he slid the right one up under the back of her sweater until it came to rest on the slightly oily skin between her shoulder blades. Straining his ears in the effort to perceive, behind the curious beat, some coherent rhythm conforming to his notions of waltz, foxtrot or quickstep, he steered Sally backwards through the leaping throng.

She stiffened and yelped as he trod on her foot and it occurred to him that this was not, perhaps, the best way of wooing a young lady in the nineties. In fact, his Terpsichorean talents had never reached the standard needed for this purpose. If in the past a turn on a ballroom floor had sometimes been followed by a turn with his partner between the sheets, it was probably because his intimate embraces had appealed to her as less uncomfortable and more private than the indignities she had suffered beneath the glittering chandeliers.

At least Sally was grinning and making the best of it. At a do like this, none of the other dancers could see how you were disgracing yourself and they wouldn't have cared if they could. 'Sorry, dear,' he shouted. 'That's the way we used to do it in the old days.'

She brought her lips to his ear so that he could just hear her reply: 'And that's the way you still do it now and always will do it, I'm afraid. Let's go and have a drink, shall we?'

But as they threaded their way towards the bar and the Captain was wondering how he was going to handle Rod, the main lights were switched on, the music stopped and an amplified female voice requested everyone's attention. On the dais at the far end of the room stood the tall figure of Miss MacDonald, impressively suave in a black sheath of a dress which emphasised her contours from the jutting shelf of her breasts down to her shapely calves. She was inviting the dancers and drinkers to return to their tables to watch the show she had been asked to devise for their entertainment.

The Captain was at a loose end because his regular ladies were away, Mac was involved with the cabaret and Helen was helping behind the bar. He drew up a chair to a table occupied by the Nugents and the Yglesiases. Sally seemed quite glad that he sat between her and Talbot, who looked like some fashionable American novelist in his well-pressed but poncy white suit.

The first number was a cancan zippily danced to canned Offenbach by the motel's fifteen 'maids'. Mac had got them up in plumed head-dresses and colourful knee-length skirts, all flounces and frilly petticoats, over green stockings. They wore gloves reaching to their elbows. Wide chokers adorned their necks, but between the chokers and the tops of their skirts they were bare, front and back. Not surprisingly, their appearance was greeted by a roar of approval, emitted mostly by the male spectators.

The girls formed a line across the upper end of the floor, their hands resting on each other's shoulders. As soon as they began their high-kicking and bum-flashing routine, the line wheeling through three hundred and sixty degrees to give everyone a fair whack, it became clear that they had on no other garments but red girdles and suspenders. Fifteen twats of varied growth and hue winked at the enchanted onlookers as the heady music blared out: *DA dadadada DA dadadada DA* . . . Every now and then the dancers unlinked their arms to execute all-revealing cartwheels or to lift their skirts and shake their pelvises vigorously, thrusting them out as if inviting the spectators to sample their hot quims.

At the final climax of this corybantic extravaganza the girls flopped to the floor, doing the splits like old troupers. For a moment they all took one of their hands from their neighbour's neck to pull up their petticoats and make sure their cunts were exposed. The hands were then replaced and the girls let their heads hang down, as if exhausted.

Mac, who looked and behaved as if she had been knocking back the cocktails, stepped forward in her role as mistress of ceremonies. She coughed ineffectually, fiddled with the microphone and coughed again, sending the audience diving under the tables for cover. Once the volume was properly adjusted she made an announcement.

'Did you like that, you naughty boys? Now listen – you can all have one of these young lovelies for your very own. Yes! But only one of them between all of you and only for half a minute each. You probably know most of them from the excellent room service they provide, and no doubt you have your own special favourites. They like a generous tip, don't they, these girls? You all know that. And you all know they're worth every penny – every fifty pence.'

She signalled to the dancers to rise to their feet, unclasp their waistbands and let their skirts drop to the floor. 'See what I mean?' she said. 'In a moment these young damsels are going to circulate round the tables. They haven't got much on, so I'm asking the ladies present to see to it that your husbands don't take advantage – not at this stage. If you feel like it, boys, you can stick a tip – no, not the tip of *that* sir! – into their – wait for it, lads – into their clothing, or what there is of it. We'll count the loot during the next number. Then the most popular girl will come out and let you have your money's worth. Give them a big – hold it; no, don't hold *those*! – a big hand!'

It took some time for all fifteen girls to make their rounds; they were offered drinks as well as the five, ten and twenty pound notes that were tucked into their girdles and the tops of their stockings. As far as the Captain could see, the cash was fairly evenly distributed. Some of the punters were hedging their bets by putting money on more than one filly or even on all of them. He himself, though, was really keen on one particular girl. He decided to back her so heavily that she would have to be the outright favourite.

His choice was the petite Swedish blonde Astrid, whose sexy body he had never got round to enjoying in the ten days or so she had been working at the motel. When she came to their table he patted her bottom and winked at her, though she seemed to be more interested in Talbot. That white-suited poseur laid his cigarette carefully in an ashtray, took out his wallet and tucked a tenner into her choker. As she stooped to let him do this, Astrid's breasts dangled down like little udders. Then she perched on the table, drew up a knee and hugged it so that Talbot had a good view of her silvery pubic mound and the pink lips of her pussy.

It was now Rod's turn. Sally glared at him as he prepared to outbid Talbot with a twenty, thought better of it and stuck a measly fiver into her stocking. Astrid gave him a curt nod and accepted a drink from Talbot. She dipped a finger into the glass and ran it round one of her nipples, winking wickedly.

The Captain did not intend to let Yglesias get away with this exclusive flirtation. Moreover, he was determined that this perky little Astrid should be the outright winner. He peeled off a fifty and three tens from the wad he kept in the pocket of his denim jacket and slipped them into the front of her crimson girdle so that the lower edges of the notes were hanging over the upper reaches of her blonde thatch. Her response was to swivel round on her bottom so that she faced her major benefactor (who also happened to be her employer) and then to proffer the wine-wet nipple for him to lick. As he savoured the stiffening teat he let the back of his middle finger press for a moment, as if by accident, against the puffy petals of her cuntflesh.

After Astrid's visit to their table the cattle auction was over pretty quickly. Talbot was still lavishing banknotes on the remaining girls as if to prove his manhood. He must have spent more altogether than the Captain, yet the latter felt sure that he had laid out his eighty sovs more judiciously. The only thing that rankled was that if his bid proved successful, Talbot would still be able to claim an equal share of the Scandinavian's body.

Miss MacDonald was announcing the next act. 'And now for something completely – well, to some extent – different,' she began. 'Most of you will have met the Reverend James DeVayne, the popular – sorry, titular – Archimandrite of Durdle Door, if you'd believe it. Well, tonight the reverend is going to amaze us with a little of his New Age magic. A warm welcome now for Mr DeVayne!'

Jimbo waddled white-robed into the spotlight. He wasted no time on patter but ran briskly through a routine that left the audience feeling first astonished and then relieved. He invited gentlemen volunteers to approach him one by one. This, he explained, was for his blessing to be administered by the laying on of hands in order to ensure the efficacy of his magic, which, he swore, was whiter than virgin snow. About a dozen men accepted this invitation. When they had all returned to their places, Jimbo asked them to check whether any of their possessions were missing. A gasp went up. Every one of them held up a hand, shouting indignantly that wallets, combs, cigarettes and lighters, handkerchiefs, watches, condoms and in one case a set of dentures had disappeared from about their persons.

These disgruntled guests were asked to return to the floor, this time all together and bringing their wives with them. The Captain guessed exactly what was going to happen next. Standing in line, these ladies were required to raise their skirts and ease down any underwear that veiled their secret loveliness. To spare their blushes at this public humiliation the spotlight was lowered and adjusted so that they were illuminated only from the waist down by a small but intense circle of light that first raked along from one end of the row to the other and then settled on the first lady's pussy. Jimbo stood behind her, made a few passes with his hairy hands and then, to everyone's surprise (except the Captain's) appeared to ransack her fanny and produce a watch from it. What was really surprising, the Captain thought, was that Jimbo knew which object had been lifted from which husband. He moved rapidly along the row of spotlit quims until all the missing property had been restored, along with a measure of decency as the wives rearranged their clothing.

This demonstration of paranormal powers was followed by another announcement from the mistress of ceremonies. 'And now something for the ladies,' Mac began. 'Those among you who share my feminist sympathies may be thinking yourselves hard done by. Well, if you really want to be done by something hard, this next number's what you've been waiting for. As you all know, the Honeymoon Palace Motel has a team of young male employees at your disposal as well as those cheery maids who entertained us earlier. Some of these pages are dancers of near professional standard, but not enough of them, I'm afraid, to justify mounting a performance like the cancan we all enjoyed so much. As a conscientious showperson, all I'm prepared to do is show them off to you. Come on, boys!'

One of the husbands who had been drinking too hard to follow the exact drift of her words – probably Des, the Captain thought – shouted out, 'Get 'em off then, darling! Show 'em off to us – don't just say it but do it!' Mac paid no attention but stood back to make way for the fifteen handsome young men and youths who filed into the ballroom and paraded across the floor. Unless they had been limbering up by engaging in very strenuous physical activity they must have oiled their bodies, which gleamed like those of racehorses just past the winning post. Apart from the oil, they wore nothing but black leather pouches just big enough to contain their mostly quite bulky genital equipment.

While they flaunted their supple, muscular grace, Mac explained that these lads would pass from table to table as the girls had done, and for the same purpose: the ladies were invited to mark the degree of their appreciation by sticking tips in the pouches of their favourites. Later in the evening the boy who had collected most would be at the ladies' disposal, half a minute of him for each of them, while their husbands were having his female counterpart. As Mac pointed out quite frankly, this female exercise would be slightly different from the male one. Once Mr Popular had spouted, the game would be over as far as the wives were concerned. But if he lasted more than one round, she promised, they could go on and on until his climax came. Viewed in this light, the half-minute time limit ought to seem no bad thing. The motel management, she was sure, did their best to avoid employing useless Johnny-come-quicklies, and with luck they would be able to keep their chosen stud up all night.

The actual 'bidding' was carried out more briskly and with less flirtatious dalliance than when the girls had made their rounds of the tables. Most of the wives were emancipated enough to carry their own cash but those who had entrusted themselves to the financial protection of their husbands were in a strong position to plead for assistance. The Captain got the impression that this was rarely refused, although some of the men had already surrendered all their folding money to the 'maids'. He was interested to see Sally Nugent slip a rather furtive tenner into the jock-strap waistband of Ricardo, the biggest and hairiest of these gigolos, over the smooth flesh of his right flank. Yvonne preferred a much younger-looking one called Helmut. It was impossible to see the number or denominations of the notes she was contributing, as she had squeezed them into a tight ball. Beckoning the lad close to her, she rubbed her nose against his leather pouch, an action which summoned forth the metallic chink of coins. Then she shoved her hand right down inside the pouch, scrabbled about a bit and withdrew it, leaving his bulge plumper with money and lust than before the operation. Soon these preliminaries were over and the young men pranced out of the room to count their takings.

And now, as Mac announced somewhat nervously, it was the turn of Susie, Darcy, Gail and Tim to perform. While a large white screen was set up in front of the dais and a low couch covered with a blue sheet was carried by pages to the middle of the dance floor, she gave the briefest of introductions.

'They call their act Family Bedtime,' she said. 'In case you think some or even all of them are too young to be in a public exhibition of this kind, let me assure you that I insisted on checking their birth certificates and – hmm – *things*,' she paused as a chuckle rippled round the audience, 'to see that everything was going to be more or less legal. Here they come, ladies and gentlemen.'

First the two eighteen-year-olds trooped in and took a bow. Darcy, his hair tied back in a tight pigtail, sported a black and gold silk dressing-gown, the sophistication of which was matched by Susie's black lace negligé. They closed with each other in a tight clinch, fondling each other's bottoms as they kissed. Then they broke apart and slipped out of their boudoir attire. So quickly that the spectators got no more than a glimpse of their nudity, they now jumped into bed and drew the sheet up to their throats.

No sooner were they covered than the younger couple entered. Tim wore striped pyjamas and Gail a white cotton night-dress. Her frizzy red hair was done up redundantly in curlers, one of her thumbs was stuck in her mouth and she dangled a teddy bear upside down by its foot. The audience held their breath as strains of dreamy, romantic music were heard over the sound system.

Gail stooped over Susie and Darcy and kissed them both goodnight; she was followed by Tim, who kissed only Susie. Hand in hand, the two youngsters then withdrew behind the screen. The Captain was aware of Yvonne squeezing his thigh under the table.

Susie reached out a hand to mime switching off the bedside lamp. For an instant everything was lost in darkness vibrant with the seductive music. Then the white screen was illuminated and the spectators turned their attention to the sharply defined shadows of Gail and Tim who were concealed behind it.

They were seen in profile, facing each other at a distance with most of the white expanse separating them. Gail was the first to move. People shifted in their seats and Yvonne's grasp tightened on the Captain's thigh as the nightie was pulled up over the girl's head and cast aside. At last the Captain's curiosity regarding her build was satisfied, at least as far as it could be satisfied on the basis of a stark silhouette. That chest, he saw, was not quite as flat and boyish as he had supposed. Flattish, yes. But the almost straight downward curve of her bosom was interrupted by a tiny hillock. This would have risen to a sharp point except that it was capped with a blunt, tiered protuberance easily recognisable as the outline of a puffy areola surmounted by a prominent nipple.

When Gail shifted her stance this outline of the profiled breast doubled itself, leaving only the colouring and three dimensional appearance to the imagination of the onlookers. Her hands ran luxuriously down her body and busied themselves at the level of her crotch. Meanwhile, Tim's interest seemed hardly to have been attracted: he picked his nose and yawned before scratching his head and then his bum.

Gail's hands were withdrawn from her loins and it could clearly be seen, since she stood sideways-on to the spectators, that she had been fluffing up her pubic hair so that a little wispy spike of it stood out at the base of her belly. She stooped to retrieve the teddy bear from the floor where it had fallen. Cradling it in her arms like a baby, she made a lewd show of pulling her nipple right forward and applying the bear's snout to it.

For a few moments the watchers' attention was distracted from the screen. A spotlight stabbed down on the couch to reveal Susie, who had turned down the sheet to her waist. She was caressing one of her white breasts, rounder and more developed than the shadows of the pert cones on the screen. Susie licked a finger repeatedly, transferring the spittle to her nipple, which she stimulated into hardness by running the fingertip round and over it and then pinching the pink bud until it had grown dark and fully engorged. Then the spotlight went out and all eyes returned to the shadow show.

Tim fumbled with the front of his pyjama bottoms and drew out a limp tool which he flicked up and down with busy fingers. It straightened and stretched out horizontally. Gail went on suckling her teddy but appeared to be twitching her loins for the benefit of the masturbating Tim, who still kept his distance from her. He untied the cord of his trousers and let them drop to the floor. The erection he now brandished, though slender, was surprisingly long.

Once more the spotlight stabbed down to illuminate part of the couch, this time Darcy's side of it. Darcy too had pulled the sheet down, uncovering a purple-headed hard-on quite as long as his brother's and twice as thick. He had certainly come on since marrying Susie at the age of sixteen, the Captain reflected, taking advantage of Talbot's concentration on the show to throw a casual leg over Yvonne's thigh. Darcy began to frig himself slowly. Suddenly the spotlight was extinguished.

Tim now discarded his pyjama jacket and began a little dance as the music assumed a livelier rhythm. He always kept his left side turned towards the screen so that the spectators never lost sight of his prancing prick – indeed, the dance was designed to display it to them as well as to Gail. The latter dropped her teddy and moved in time to the music and the boy's cavortings.

Gradually the couple moved closer but always leaving a gap of white screen between their shadows.

After a while Gail dropped to her knees right in front of him and sank back on her heels. The Captain's cock leapt up in his trousers in the expectation that Tim was about to be fellated. But no contact was made between the youngsters, even at this stage of their arousal. Instead, Gail bent backwards so that her breasts were pointing up. Tim took a pace forward and the overlapping of their shadows showed that he must have planted his feet on either side of the girl's thighs. He now stood over her, rapidly stroking his prick and forcing it down from the horizontal. Gail's hands went to her little tits; she appeared to be trying to squeeze them together, although there was obviously no chance of getting them to touch each other. Yes – she was offering them to Tim's cock.

Tim thrust it nearer but still no touching took place. Clearly visible on the screen, a copious and almost uninterrupted stream of semen squirted from the swollen tip to coat the proffered targets. It looked as if strings of beads were being tossed in rapid succession from the boy to the girl. So sharp were the details of the shadows that the Captain was sure he could make out the outlines of blobs of spunk slowly sliding down the slopes of those conical breasts. His right hand came to rest on Sally Nugent's knee.

Suddenly the screen went dark and the couch in the middle of the floor was brightly lit. The sheet had been stripped right off. Darcy and Susie were already well into their love-making, Darcy flat on his back with his wife straddling his hips and bouncing up and down on him. She took care to prolong each upstroke sufficiently for everyone present to get a good view of the shining wet cock slipping in and out of her as she held the petals of her girlflesh open.

The onlookers were so intent on this performance that most of them failed to notice Gail and Tim until they emerged stark naked from the surrounding darkness to join the older couple on the couch. They lost no time in assuming the positions Mac must have worked out for them. Tim got astride Darcy's belly so that he was facing Susie and almost in contact with her – in fact, her nipples could hardly be prevented from brushing against his chest as she bounced up and down. Gail placed herself with her front to Tim's back, kneeling slightly awkwardly so as not to crush Darcy's face but just letting the lips of her pussy kiss those of his mouth.

As she mounted the couch she had given everyone a clear view of these cuntlips. Under the spotlight the contrast between the freckled pallor of this slight girl's skin with the vivid dark red of the rather sparse pubic hairs she had brushed upwards behind the screen had been striking. Even more striking, though, was the pale pink of the enlarged inner lips that hung down moistly beneath that ruddy growth. To the Captain's not-inexperienced eye they had seemed disproportionate to the narrowness of her hips and the smallness of her loins. Unless she had been born like that, they seemed to supply unequivocal evidence that Gail had crossed the threshold of womanhood.

All four performers were evidently in a hurry. Darcy's tongue lashed so eagerly into those engorged and protruding lips and his hands played so passionately with the puffy nipples that Gail had to screw up her face in an expression of the most intense concentration as she struggled with the task in hand. And in hand it was, quite literally. She had reached forward round the fair-haired Tim's hips to cradle his testicles in one hand while she frigged his cock with the other. The concentration was needed in order to keep this slim implement aimed at least roughly in the right direction, slightly downwards, when its natural inclination was to raise its head at a steep angle approaching the vertical.

The Captain hooked his hand up under Sally's tiny skirt, feeling for the gusset of her tights. 'How are you enjoying this?' he whispered.

'Well,' she replied, 'it's a bit rude, isn't it? But yes, I think it's great. Just love the one on his back.'

If Rod heard any of this exchange from the other side of the table he gave no sign of it. His eyes, turned to the couch, were popping out of their sockets. He wiped his forehead and loosened his striped tie.

As if they had been putting on this rather hastily botched-up act for years, all the entertainers hit their climax at exactly the same moment. Susie, who had been rubbing her own clitoris with abandon, now suddenly tore the petals of her vulva apart as she threw her head back and arched her body so that her husband's thick member nearly slipped out of its sheath. Little Gail, dribbling and spluttering as the lust exploded inside her, delivered the final jerk to Tim's cock. He ejaculated convulsively. His first creamy load splashed Susie's belly and soaked the blonde fluff at its base. The second spurt landed accurately on the unhooded clitoris, while the most substantial spendings gushed all over the shining flesh she was stretching open to receive it and over Darcy's angry stem which was now pumping its own charge into Susie's womb. As Tim's dick lost its rigidity it dribbled the sticky residue over his brother's chestnut bush.

Gail's efforts had been heroic indeed. But now, writhing in the throes of seemingly endless waves of ecstasy, she rolled over on her side. Darcy's head was clamped so firmly between her thighs that he must have been in some danger of suffocation. Tim fell forward on Susie, forcing her right back and off Darcy's still-spouting cock. Then, utterly spent from their exertions, the four dragged themselves to their feet to take their bow and acknowledge the applause, delayed at first but rising to a crescendo as the spectators recovered from the shock of this powerful spectacle. 'That was a jolly good show,' Talbot opined.

A five minute break now followed to allow everyone to calm down, have a drink and fondle their partners to prime them for the final event. Miss MacDonald stepped into the centre of the floor to announce the winners of the 'cattle auction'. The lucky male was a Latin-looking type who rather implausibly called himself Eric. His female counterpart, to the Captain's relief, was Astrid from Uppsala. These two pranced out, unashamedly nude, and lay down side by side on the couch, where the MacDonald told them to engage in some heavy foreplay to get themselves ready for action.

When she judged their petting to have gone far enough, Mac pulled them apart and made them stretch out on their backs to await the onslaught of their admirers. Eric's horn stood up straight; Astrid drew up her feet and let her knees fall open until they almost rested on the mattress. To avoid long queues, those of the spectators - nearly all of them - who wished to participate were invited to step forward table by table. There were some calls from guests he had got on well with for the Captain to take his table up first as proprietor of the establishment. He declined with a gracious wave and his little party waited for their turn.

They were in fact the fifth table. By the time he and his four companions stood at the foot of the couch, the sheet on which the human prizes lay was wet and rumpled. Most of the moisture had spilt and was still spilling from Astrid's dark, pouting opening – quite a few of the husbands who had already humped her must have been able to get their rocks off within the thirty second limit monitored by Mac with a stopwatch. Eric was still erect, very wet and glossy from the juices of the wives who must now be praying that he would be able to keep it up for at least one more round.

Following the example set by the earlier tables, the Captain's lot had already divested themselves of their nether garments before coming out on to the floor. Talbot looked silly in his white linen jacket, especially as his maroon socks were held up by elastic suspenders round his calves. Rod was hardly more impressive in his mauve shirt and that striped tie which hinted with obvious vagueness at a wished-for minor public school background. As for the Captain himself, he would not have presumed to pass judgement on his own appearance; he felt comfortable enough in his denim jacket and the coarse dark curls that shagged his private parts.

In any case, he felt sure that the ladies were attracting more attention from all quarters. Yvonne Yglesias had peeled off her silver sheath of a dress and stood there in nothing but a little black bra which left her nipples exposed. Being blonde, Sally supplied a pretty contrast. When she struggled out of her skirt, shoes, tights and panties, she had left her upper body and arms covered by her closely fitting black sweater.

Astrid and Eric, both of them rather bleary-eyed, looked up at these newcomers. The Yglesiases were busily feeling each other up in preparation for business. Now they separated and advanced on the waiting servants. Yvonne lowered herself until she was fully speared on Eric's prick. She massaged her breasts while rocking up and down. At the same time her husband plunged into the petite Swede. From the spasmodic clenching of his buttocks it was plain that he was discharging on the very first thrust, so great was his state of readiness and so urgent his desire. He withdrew and pulled back to enjoy the sight of his spunk bubbling out of Astrid's already flooded vessel. Yvonne too had already been on the verge of climax as she sank down on Eric. A look of bliss spread over her features as he stretched up inside her. She touched her clitoris with the tip of a finger, gasped aloud and collapsed on his chest.

Next it was the turn of the Nugents, although the Captain felt he could hardly wait and was tempted to cut in ahead of Rod. Instead, he gritted his teeth, gently lifted Yvonne off Eric and helped to guide the freshly lubricated shaft into Sally's narrow alley. The girl closed her eyes and bit her lower lip as she slid slowly down until at last she felt Eric's balls between her buttocks. She seemed to be lost in her own dreams. Eric did his best to make up for her inertia by heaving his hips up and down.

On previous occasions when the Captain had been present, Rod had often been able to penetrate other women successfully if without finesse; usually it was only the approach to Sally's quim that triggered his premature ejaculation. But probably because of a certain physical resemblance between the two blonde girls, or perhaps in emulation of the example set earlier by young Tim O'Flammery, he now disgraced himself in the all too familiar way. As he lunged down towards Astrid's proffered sex he was shaking so uncontrollably that his liberal though rather thin spendings were showered over an area of her body extending from hip to hip and from navel to mid-thigh. Naturally, however, most of the come was concentrated on and around her snatch, plastering the closely trimmed curls on which earlier layers of sperm had already dried.

Rod straightened up at once. Unlike the others, who were keen to see their friends' performance through to the end, he skulked back to the table to hide his shame. The Captain lost no time in taking the place Ratface had failed to occupy.

The feeling as he drove his prick deep into Astrid's cunt, brim-full as it was with the spunk of the men who had just enjoyed her, was quite remarkable. The sheath, as he had expected, was superbly slippery. He had not reckoned, though, on the tightness with which she was still able to grip and squeeze him in spite of all that juice.

He lay there in her cunt's close embrace, meaning to count twenty seconds and wait until the last ten seconds for ten decisive thrusts. But he had counted only as far as five when muscular contractions began to ripple along the walls of that clinging vagina, communicating waves of lust to his bursting cock. Even as his seed flooded through the tube of rigid cockflesh he began to ram rapidly and violently into the quaking girl's innermost core. The sensation in the tip of his cock was almost unbearable as the slit was forced against her cervix, which obstructed the outpouring of semen like a finger pressed against the opening of a running tap. He could feel the hot fluid being forced out by his own orgasmic spasms and rushing back between his tight skin and the membrane that lined the girl's cunt. And then, as his last drainings were still pulsing into her, he felt the wet warmth sloshing out over his balls, into the channels of his groins and into his pubic hair. He lay there wiped out, awash and drowning in a sea of lechery.

EIGHT

JUST LIKE OLD TIMES

The Captain sat, naked and tense, on the edge of his chair. Susie and Darcy lay on the covers of their bed, equally naked but relaxed in sleep after their recent exertions.

The rest of the prize-taking, and indeed of the evening, had rushed by in a whirl. He remembered that poor Sally had been pulled off Eric's prick without reaching her climax when her thirty seconds were up. Eric had survived into a second round and lasted long enough to yield up his accumulated fluids into the ecstatic cunt of Hong Kong Doris. That was it. As Doris (Des had already retired drunk) belonged to the fourth table, Sally would have to rely on Rod or her own devices to relieve her aches and longings tonight. Maybe she would have a wet dream.

The Captain's chair was pulled up close to the wall and his eye was applied to one of the spyholes normally hidden behind sliding panels in these apartments. In the adjoining room Tim and Gail were certainly taking their time. After the show they had dressed in the things they had turned up in that morning, probably the only clothes they had with them – Gail's long, flowery skirt and scarf and Tim's brief white shorts and shellsuit top. Pressing his eye against the hole the Captain could see that Tim, rather pretty with his cropped yellow hair, was still wearing the shorts. Gail had untied the scarf, which now hung loosely round her neck, its ends covering her nipples as long she did not move about much or raise her arms. At the moment she was removing those ridiculous curlers from

138

her hair, so the white cones with their pink caps were fully visible.

Why were they taking so long about getting into bed? The sound was switched off, so nothing could be heard of their conversation, but both of them, especially Gail, appeared to be hovering about, finding endless excuses for delay. This lack of eagerness seemed curious in view of their lively enactment of that 'Family Bedtime'.

Darcy cried out in his sleep and reached out for Susie. They both opened their eyes, momentarily bewildered by the unfamiliar surroundings of the motel room. The Captain handed them a couple of cans of cold Coke and invited them to have a quick peep at the younger couple. How could they explain this show of reluctance?

'Oh well,' Susie began, 'they've never actually slept together, you see. They often watch me and Darce doing it and they like to wank each other a bit without actually coming. But this show we did was probably the first time they'd seen each other with nothing on. They're shy, both of them.'

Darcy agreed. 'That's why it was such a great idea of yours to put them in that room together for the night and let us watch them at it,' he told the Captain. 'Did you say there were holes for all of us?'

'I certainly hope there's going to be one for me,' he replied. 'Down on the beach your Susie promised me a bit of a poke later on, if you don't mind – oh, you mean holes to look through.'

He opened another couple of sliding panels and placed chairs for Susie and Darcy before switching on the one-way sound system and resuming his own viewing position.

'Go on,' Tim was saying. 'Why won't you let me take these shorts off? I'm all hard inside them.'

Gail tried to pull a brush through her frizzy red hair. 'If you lie down,' she said, 'I might just come and put my hand on it for a bit. But only if you keep quiet and don't let that stuff squirt out like it did in the show.'

'Look at that, Darce,' gasped Susie. 'Your Timmy's got quite a hard-on. Those shorts are so tight he must be in agony.'

The Captain glanced sideways and noticed that Darcy, too,

had a sizeable erection, in his case not constricted by clothing. He hoped the young man would not insist on claiming Susie with it before he was allowed to shove his own rising prick up her. His eye returned to the hole in the wall.

Gail unhooked the fastening of her skirt, stepped out of it and dimmed the lights. Her skimpy green knickers were too small to confine the straggling red hairs at the edge of her pubic triangle, sparse though these hairs were. Because of the vivid green of the cotton knickers and the whiteness of her thighs and belly, the coarse orange-red had a strangely exciting effect, an effect which caused Tim to groan and clutch his bulging crotch. Sitting on the bed beside him, Gail pulled his hands away and replaced them with one of her own. With the other she fondled her mound through the knickers.

These activities seemed to have lost their allure for Darcy, who snorted in disgust. 'I'm keen on that Gail,' he remarked. 'Wouldn't mind sitting up all night peeping at her. But now I'm actually watching the two of them together like this I'm not so sure. There's got to be something creepy about a guy watching his own kid brother doing it for the first time.' With these words Darcy, who seemed oddly unaffected by the scene they had acted out in the ballroom, returned to the bed and was soon snoring. He had definitely coarsened, the Captain thought. His sexuality, like his body, had turned into something quite commonplace, almost loutish.

Darcy's peephole was just to the right of Susie's, so the Captain shifted over into his abandoned chair, from which he could enjoy the leisurely proceedings in the next room while slipping an arm round the girl to stroke and pinch her left side, hip and thigh. She responded by squirming her bottom and crossing her left leg over her right one so that he could just reach underneath her and feel the damp hairs brushing his knuckles. His erection was standing up straight but she made no attempt to touch it and kept her eye pressed against the hole in front of her.

In the next room Gail sighed and shifted her hand from the outside of her knickers to the inside. A dark green stain was now seen to have spread over the front of the garment. The Captain marvelled at the power of his imagination as he seemed to smell her female heat. When he mentioned this to Susie, however, she pointed out that it was the smell of her own juices, which had now begun to gush in anticipation of the scene they hoped was about to be enacted. He pushed up a little with the backs of his fingers and discovered that she was right.

Meanwhile, Gail's other hand had worked its way into the waistband of Tim's shorts and the youth was throwing his limbs about in all directions, quite out of control. At least he had more staying power than Rod Nugent! Perhaps that was because the juices of his maturity had only recently begun to flow, or perhaps it was simply a reflection of the variety of human nature, and its capability. Suddenly the lad lifted himself on his elbows and gazed at Gail intently as she frigged both him and herself.

'You've got to let me do it,' he panted. 'We mayn't get a chance like this again. Just the place for it, a motel for honeymooners. Let's pretend we've just got married.'

Gail's eyes lit up as if she found the suggestion really dirty. 'All right, then,' she said. 'But you've got to be gentle with me. It's no good trying to stuff it in all at once, the way Darce does with Susie.'

The Captain gulped as she slid the green panties down over her thighs and kicked them off. For a moment he had a tantalising glimpse of the moist gash in its nest of red fur, the straggly edges of which were plastered darkly against the tender white skin around it. The pretty sight was soon denied him as Tim, who had ripped his shorts in his haste to get them off, lowered himself over her. She raised her knees on either side of him to admit the pointed tip of his prick.

A bird in the hand, etcetera, the Captain told himself. He drew back from his spyhole to turn his attention to Susie, who was still eagerly watching the novices. 'Tell me what's happening,' he said. 'Look, you can get an even better view from over here.'

Leading her to yet another sliding panel a few feet along, a rather larger one, he bent her forwards so that both her eyes were pressed to a small glass window. With her hands she supported herself against the wall, her bottom stuck out and her legs parted. From her giggling it was obvious that she knew what was coming.

The Captain's hands juggled with her breasts. 'Ooh,' she cried. 'I think he must be sticking it into her – I can tell from that screwed-up look on her face.' Susie's cuntlips fell open of their own accord and folded themselves around the nudging cockhead, which then drove forward into her vagina with one smooth thrust.

A stifled cry came through the intercom. 'That must've really hurt her,' commented Susie. 'My own wedding night wasn't so bad because my mate Nikki had already cleared the way with her fingers. Ah, Gail's beginning to relax, now that he's properly in. That's quite funny – he looks like a rabbit or something, bobbing his pink little bum up and down.'

Taking his cue from this observation, the Captain commenced his pumping – not a bobbing action, but slow, regular sweeps in and out. One of his hands was still tweaking and lightly scratching Susie's nipple. The other one had slipped down to forage through her silky hairs until a finger found her swollen clitoris.

Susie wriggled in response, thrusting her bottom back against his loins and forcing him even deeper into her. When she spoke again, her utterance was broken by his shoves and her squirmings as his finger worked her into a regular rhythm. 'Ah – ah – ah,' she gasped. 'Her – legs – are – kicking – in – the – air. He's – he's – hooked – them over – his – shoulders. Oh! – *fuck* me!'

The Captain doubled his rate of thrusting and shifted both his hands to Susie's smooth flanks, steadying and caressing her as he drove both her and himself towards orgasm. Her grunts and moans had now degenerated into an inarticulate, dribbling stream of obscenities. Over this babble the Captain was aware of Gail's amplified words of encouragement to Tim before they too were reduced to a mere continuous gurgle.

'Ow – ow – ow,' Gail whimpered. 'That – hur – hurt. But it's – bet – better now. Pretend you're – my – my – husband. Pretend – you're – Darce – and I'm – I'm – Susie. Fuck me – like Darce – fucks – Susie! Ow!'

The sounds of their screwing and the creaking bed stopped for a moment while Tim interjected a comment: 'Bet she's not half as tight as you. She's a married woman. He's really opened her up now she's his wife – he told me. And anyway, she's older.'

Their copulation resumed and now jumped into overdrive. It seemed to the Captain that the eighteen-year-old girl in whose cunt his own cock was embedded could hardly have sheathed him more tightly if she too had been a freshly broached virgin. But then he, of course, was of an altogether bigger build than Darcy.

Suddenly Susie shuddered in his hands and almost broke away from him as her climax hit her. Her head flopped down towards the floor but he dug his fingers into the creases between her thightops and her pubic triangle and hugged her bum back firmly so that his spear could go on lancing into her limp body. Now that Susie was folded double, it was possible for him to gain stability by resting his forehead against the wall. In this position he had a clear view of the couple in the next room and could go on fucking Susie at the same time.

But the excitement could hardly last much longer. Although most of Gail's body was covered by the nakedness of her bucking boyfriend, the Captain could see enough of her face and torso to recognise the tell-tale flush that had raced down from her brow to her loins. He fixed his gaze on Tim's tight pink scrotum as the lad drew back for a moment, exposing a length of wet prick. The Captain followed suit and waited. Tim thrust forward and collapsed on the girl, hammering the bed with his fists as he poured his young lust into her. As his own spunk began to shoot up his bursting yard the Captain nearly forgot to make his own final lunge into Susie. Some of his juice was already splashing back from the petals of her flesh enfolding his glans as he dragged her hard back towards him and skewered into her hot depths.

Darcy stirred impatiently on the bed behind them. 'Come on, Suze,' he said. 'This is supposed to be our second honeymoon, isn't it? I'm dying to get it into you.'

Miss MacDonald's fat tomcat flopped down from one of the apple trees in the garden of her cottage. The points of its claws were already digging into Melanie's belly but had not quite broken the skin when the angry girl lifted it bodily and chucked it into a bed of nettles. Why, she wondered, did the fucking tom go for her like that whenever she came out to sunbathe in the nude? She stretched out again on the lounger, adjusted her sunglasses and began to write.

She's a fast worker, the Muttock! Derrick brought me back here a week ago yesterday. A couple of days later I got a note from her saying she'd got the Captain's Gloria staying with her at Cunlip Hall and inviting me and Mac to a sort of reunion party of old Cunlip girls with boyfriends and husbands she was giving on Saturday. Well, Mac was still at the motel getting ready for that show she was organising, so I got her on the phone and we agreed to go to this do separately and meet up there. Although she wouldn't admit it in so many words, I got the impression she'd still got that Helen with her and planned to take her along with her, as well as the O'Flammerys with Darcy's brother Tim and Tim's little friend Gail.

Me and Derrick zipped ourselves into leathers and I jumped up behind him on bike. Covered the forty-six miles in half an hour, and got there quite early on Saturday afternoon. Cunlip Hall even more overgrown and dilapidated (spelling?) than last summer. What's she been spending all those lovely dollars on? Toyboys?

Next to arrive was snobby Gina Wootton with yobby boyfriend Joker Jennings in tow. Muttock was upstairs for a 'rest' with Gloria but sent us out to cut lots of laurel from those rather depressing bushes that grow right up against windows of house. Quite dark in shrubbery – Derrick swore he got glimpse through bushes of Gina giving Joker blow job. I thought idea was just to let sunshine into windows but when we'd been at it for a time (and I'm not really sure what Gina and Joker had been at but that auburn hair of hers was all over place) manic Muttock came out and told us to take all the stuff we'd cut off into house. Then she gave us job of trimming it and making it into laurel wreaths, would you believe it, enough wreaths for everyone expected at party. I soon twigged what she had in mind of course – a Roman orgy.

While we were doing our best to get these fiddly wreaths

right the others turned up. First came Mac. Yes, she did have Helen with her, as well as Darcy, Susie, Tim and Gail. They'd all squeezed into the Morris Minor, taking it in turns to cool off in front seat. No wonder they looked rumpled. Tim's little shorts had got ripped and everything was showing.

Then came various unexpected arrivals – unexpected for me, that is. Alexandra Fellowes with her long black hair and even longer legs. In our sixth-form days everyone had thought she was a virgin but she had told me she was faithful to her brother and only fucked in the hols, with him. By the time I left, of course, she was really one of the girls. Anyway, Alexandra showed up with this famous brother of hers, called Dick. He's in the Guards or something, tall and upright with a black moustache. Found myself wondering if Romans ever had moustaches.

A bit later our redheaded, ham-fisted German Romeo from the college play, Heini Hintenburger, rolled up with big-busted Cathy. Wasn't just his head that had that red hair, of course – no one who knew him as well as we all did would claim his head was his most distinguishing feature, outside or in. But the two of them had certainly made a lovely Romeo and Juliet.

So there were sixteen of us altogether, including four females without partners of the opposite sex – Helen Lascelles and the three 'grown-ups': Gloria, Mac and Muttock. The Muttock was very insistent, of course, that everyone should 'socialise' so that we didn't have six couples and four wallflowers, not that there was much chance of them getting left out of the fun, what with their attractions and their tastes.

Well, it was still quite sunny when the evening's activities started and some of the sun was sloping in through the tops of the windows above level of encroaching vegetation. We had all dressed up in the laurel wreaths and white sheets or specially adapted pillowcases. The Muttock took us through into the library, where she'd arranged lots of low tables and couches and rugs for us to sprawl on. I recognised that moth-eaten old leopard skin she used to have in her study at the college – Dick Fellowes draped it over his toga and looked like a colonial district commissioner gone native.

Plenty of wine flowed from jugs and vases and there were great piles of grapes and other fruit as well as lots of bread and cheese and cold chicken. After a while the Muttock apologised for having to break in on the Roman illusion. Said she had a special treat for us that wouldn't take too long. Our old friend the Captain, who was sorry he was too busy to be there himself, had sent a video that had gone down well in motel. The M said she was just going to show us part of it and wheeled anachrinostic (spelling?) TV into room.

After the usual fuzzy scribble on screen when she first switched on, we found ourselves watching rather crudely done orgy – not a Roman one, though. Suddenly we all caught our breaths except Joker, who swore. Who should be filling the picture but our very own Gina, heavily made-up and wearing jeans and a yellow sweater. At least, that was what she was wearing at first but she soon pulled them off with encouragement and assistance from the awful middle-aged men who were screwing all round her. Yes, no one could possibly mistake that triangular patch of coppery fur – you could say it was Gina's hallmark. Well, the 'real' Gina blushed dark pink as we cheered on the character she was playing on the video. This character went for the women in the movie, who all wanted her to lick and suck their mouths and pussies. But while she was doing that the men had her every which way and made a real whore of her. At the end she lay back all wet and spermy and camera zoomed in on her open cunt.

After the video we time-warped back two thousand years and got on with our own orgy. No good trying to remember all the combinations and permutations we got into. As I said, the Muttock had insisted we shouldn't stick with our own partners. But the O'Flammery gang partly got round this for a while by Darcy taking Gail and Susie taking Tim and staying with them as long as they could. The four spare women, by which I mean the ones left over at any particular moment when all the cunts were filled, were never unoccupied but had hands and tongues working on them and used their own on whatever sexy parts were in reach as they were frigged. And all the time partners kept changing (except O'Flammerys) till men were starting to flag – even Heini, who screws like a horse and prefers bumholes to cunts. Then it was girl on girl. But not just a straight lez binge, if straight's the right word. At least half of what was done was for benefit of the blokes, who stiffened up again pretty quick, especially when little Helen stripped off tunic and pranced about library, really cute with fringe showing under laurel wreath and tiny silvery-yellow bush fluffy and dampish when she rubbed it on everyone's faces.

While all this was going on I thought I heard hammering on front door. Too tied up with Alexandra's Dick (or do I mean Alexandra's Dick's dick?) to take much notice, and if Muttock heard she didn't want to know as she was in sixty-nine with Gloria. Five minutes or so later French windows burst open to let in part of overgrown shrubbery and these two figures who must have been watching us from it. One of them switched on a desk lamp and pointed it into our eyes. When we'd been well and truly dazzled he turned it away from us. We were face to face with forces of law and order!

I recognised them – they were the sergeant and WPC who stopped me in car last year that time I was taking Captain with Susie and Darcy for picnic on river. Must have come over from Upchester.

SERGEANT: 'Allo, 'allo, 'allo. I won't say *what's going on there*, being as it's (a) obvious and (b) not actually illegal. Leastways (*bending down to look at Tim and Gail*), not such an open and shut case we'd have no option except to take the lot of you in, you randy buggers. Consenting adults and that. What d'you say, Jives?

WPC: I seen them two at it down Hoggin Bottom, sarge. With each other that is, not with these two older ones we've run across already if you remember. Can't vouch for the youngsters' legality, mind you, not strict like, but one thing I can say: they ain't no innocent beginners. Don't mean to say he actually *done* it to her, of course. I never seen it go right up her. But a nod's as good as a wink if you know what I mean, sarge.

SERGEANT: Thought you was going to say it's as good as a wank, Jives. Want to watch your lip when you're dealing with Joe Public. But then again (*winking at all us partying 'Romans'*), we don't really want to go public with this little business, do we, gents? You want to keep it private, what you gets up to with these good ladies. Live and let live's what I say, know what I mean? Ain't that right, Jives?

WPC: Never known you say different, Albert Raddle, not in Upchester and not anywhere else you taken me.

SERGEANT: (*straightening up and glaring round room*): Now then, boys and girls. We're looking for a Miss Mary Muttock of this address, the owner of the, er, establishment, I do believe. It's regarding a certain lady's application for British nationality. A Mrs Haggler, with a H and two Gs. Mrs Gloria Haggler. Maiden name, er, Sweetbutts. An American lady, it would appear. She wouldn't happen to be here too, would she, this Mrs Haggler? – Ah, right. Maybe there's somewhere private we could give you two good ladies a doing over – ask a few questions, like.

Poor Gloria and a defiant-looking Muttock wrapped torn sheets round themselves and the four of them left the library. This visit had rather taken the wind out of our sails and the lead out of the blokes' pencils. We just lounged about drinking and stuffing our faces till Helen, the only one who didn't seem upset and hadn't bothered to cover herself up, sat down bold as brass in middle of floor and very slowly started masturbating.

She started off in a sitting position, working away at clit till we could see it sticking up out of its hood – she must have a really big one when it gets excited. Her sex lips got all red and puffy and I saw sticky whitish cream there as she pulled them apart. Flesh on inside looked really appetising, all wet and pink. Then she lay back on a cushion, opened legs even wider and started sliding fingers in and out. Dick Fellowes – quite a crude bastard I think he must be – gave her an empty bottle and she shoved it up as far as it would go. Well, I hope it was empty. Just then the plods came back with Gloria and the Muttock so she rolled over on tummy and kept legs together till they'd gone.

Between the two of them, M and G tried to explain what it was all about. Rather complicated – can't be sure I've got it right. What seems to have happened is something like this, though. Nerds in Home Office have found something wrong with Gloria's marriage certificate which was sent off with application for British nationality. She gave address as motel, obviously, but when Muttock signed form as character reference she was a bit pissed and wrote Cunlip College instead of Cunlip Hall. Now the college is quite well known to authorities and they must have found stuff about the Muttock on computer. That's why they contacted Upchester and got local constabulary to go looking for her. When they drove up to college first person they saw was my Derrick doing one of his odd-job days there like he still does in the summer. Well, this sergeant didn't say so but Derrick admitted to us he couldn't see anything wrong telling them Muttock was miles away, up here at Cunlip Hall. Muttock and Gloria say they didn't give much away under grilling – what was there to give away? – and concentrated on trying to distract sergeant with a bit of flashing and flirting. The Muttock seems quite concerned that they'll be after Captain next, but I can't see what he's got to do with it. If that certificate's a bit dodgy maybe it's the archimandrake they need to talk to. None of my business, anyway.

Party/orgy went on all night and I got my turn with everyone. Even the O'Flammery clique got broken up in the end and I had or was had by all four of them. So worn out I slept most of yesterday and so did the others. Quite late in afternoon people started going home. The Muttock was too hung-over to come downstairs and see them off.

Imagine how I felt when I discovered Derrick had disappeared! Mac tried to calm me down. She said he'd asked her to tell me Susie was so keen for ride on motorbike he'd let her dress up in my leathers and helmet and had given her lift back to Upchester. I had to go in car with Mac, Helen and the three others. Poor Darcy seemed a bit peeved. Very quiet and sulky. He sat in back, between Helen and me (Tim had Gail on his lap in front seat).

Without saying anything and without even looking at him

I pulled down zip of Darcy's jeans, pulled out his prick and just held it in my fist. At first all except tip of foreskin snugly in my grasp. But rattling of the old Morris Minor did the necessary – that car's a motorised wanking wagon. As we sat there still as statues but jigging up and down on the bumpy road he thickened in my hand and stretched up into a regular Nelson's Column with its one eye winking wetly. Helen watched what was happening. Just as Darcy groaned and tried to stretch his legs, down went her head and she had the big fat tip in her mouth. I could actually feel the sperm as it rushed up through the thick, fleshy tube in my hand.

He pulled my hand away and tucked the limp, wet plonker back in his jeans. Helen rested with her head leaning on back of seat. On her face she had dreamy smile. Her mouth was open and shiny curtain of spunk made sort of membrane between top and bottom teeth, spilling down over lower lip and accumulating on her chin. How could I resist? I leaned across Darcy, opened wide and kissed her, sucking all that lovely juice into my own mouth and gulping it down. Well, it must have been surplus to Susie's requirements, surely.

When we got back to Upchester Mac drove straight to the O'Flammerys' cosy little flat (paid for by parents) just off Market Street. There it was outside – Derrick's Yamaha. I hurried upstairs with Darcy and he let us in. Both of us raced to bedroom. I got there first.

Just as I'd expected, there was Derrick, his bare bum bouncing up and down on top of Susie, whose jeans were still caught round one of her ankles. He was asking for it, wasn't he? I raised my hand and brought it down with a resounding thwack on his hairy buttocks. Then again and again and again till his backside was blushing like an old-fashioned bride on her wedding night.

This treatment was too much for the dirty bastard, who knows what I feel about him two-timing with Susie. His legs stiffened out between hers, those buttocks clenched and he poured his stuff into her uncontrollably. I pulled him off the girl angrily – being so close to edge of bed he rolled on to floor and hurt shoulder.

Darcy was angry too. While I was dealing with Derrick

he'd stripped off and was waiting on red alert, stiff and upright. He plunged hard into Susie's cunt and started to show her who she was supposed to enjoy herself with – what they call exercising his conjugal rights (or is it rites?). But I didn't stay to see him finish. Just dragged Derrick downstairs and made him give me lift home on bike. No conjugals for him for a while!

The tomcat had slunk back to the side of the lounger and was purring and rubbing its tail against Melanie's naked flank. She closed her diary with a smile of satisfaction, got up, stretched and strolled through the sunshine towards the open kitchen door. She had just heard the Morris Minor pull up in front of the cottage. Dear old Mac was back.

NINE

THE SUCCESSFUL APPLICANT

Even as this happy reunion between Melanie and her mistress took place, the Captain sat frowning in his office. He had not expected the slap in the face from that last girl. Once again he scanned the advert he had placed in the local paper.

> RECEPTIONIST/ESCORT DUTIES – Attractive, fun-loving young woman required for general and 'specialised' work at motel catering exclusively for honeymoon couples. Professional experience not essential but the successful applicant must be prepared to move easily among newly-weds, relating well to clients of both sexes, and to partici-pate in all our activities. In-service training provided. Please note that great importance will be attached in the selection process to physical appearance as well as to personality and charm. Write with photograph (utmost discretion guaran-teed).

The recession being what it was and the economy showing no signs of being kick-started into recovery in spite of the fact that all the indicators were supposedly in place for a modest boom, the Captain was not surprised that this attempt to find a replacement for Gloria had met with such a keen response. Well, the purpose of the ad was not really to find a replacement. Or rather, that had been the original idea, but he had already hit on Gloria's successor before the *Courier* came out. He had looked forward to interviewing the short-listed applicants and putting them through their paces as a sheer luxury, one of the perks of operating a joint like this.

Three hundred and eighty-seven females of various ages had sent in their applications. Hard work though it was, keeping him busy for the last three days, it had been easy to eliminate most of these. Many of them were far too old or ugly, at least for the Captain's taste. Some of the photos were real horrors and many of the applicants had failed to understand that it was nude pictures he was after. In one case that nearly had him suckered the picture was nude and the girl beautiful (and vice versa). But the black-and-white photography, the hairstyle, the bomb-site setting, the hoarding advertising *Picture Post* and the ancient tram in the background alerted him to the strong possibility that it had been taken at least forty years ago. Another hopeful would have been ruled out on account of gross illiteracy if there had been any real question of considering her for the front-of-house job. She had written: 'I lik wiming as well as men and hop to please you'. Others had mistaken the gist of the advert altogether and clearly thought he was just after a legit receptionist.

Eventually the Captain had been left with about twenty girls he liked the look of and who seemed to appreciate at least part of what the job might entail. He noted the names, addresses and phone numbers of all of these but drew up a shortlist of just six to be called for interview. He had run through the first four before lunch, although literally so with only two of them, back there on the studio couch. With the other two he had husbanded his resources, allowing them to suck him to stiffness and even penetrating one of them and bringing her to orgasm but without himself ejaculating.

The morning's work had been enjoyable and relaxing. Any unpleasantness had been avoided by telling the applicants they would be informed of the outcome by post. Half a dozen letters of rejection were already signed and sealed, their harsh message softened by the charm of the Captain's epistolary style and the offer of casual work at busy times.

But the afternoon had been a real bitch. His first interviewee was a lovely young woman who quickly dropped the skirt of her striped business suit to reveal the classic erotic vista of a knickerless slit shaded by dark, silky hairs. The white skin in which this pussy was set had been framed by black suspenders and stockings, as in the photograph she had submitted. Just as he was on the point of slipping a couple of fingers into her moistness, the door, which he had forgotten to lock, burst open. In stormed an irate Danvers Pelham, mad for a bum to flog now that Gloria was no longer available. The lady offered herself with an alacrity not altogether pleasing to the Captain, who found her very tasty but had harboured no intentions of putting her on his payroll. Pelham was running an appraising palm over her buttocks when a second intruder had entered – Brice, the man from the planning department, in search of spare cunt. At first it had looked as if a regular row was about to flare up between the two ramping males. But realising that even if they had set their sights on slightly different objects of desire they still had something in common, they reached a rapid accommodation and marched off with the willing victim between them. Maybe she thought this behaviour would enhance her chances of employment.

And then *she* had offered herself for interview. She walked in with an air of not being reassured by what she had just witnessed as she waited in the outer office through which these three passed. This was to be the treat of his day: the tall, sizzling blonde the Captain had deliberately left until last on the strength of the captivating photo she had sent with her application. In the picture she posed with rouged nipples and shaven cunt. These features were not visible as she stepped into the office. Not directly, that is, but the contours of both (or all three) points of interest showed clearly through her tight clothing. She wore a pink boob-tube kind of affair which left a wide expanse of beautifully tanned belly extending down to the low-slung belt of her white hotpants. 'Good afternoon, Miss Jones,' he said.

He took her shoulders and spun her round so that the stiffness in the front of his jeans jabbed into her bottom. One of his hands went to a breast and the other to the tightly packaged cunt. Although he seemed to have the woman at his mercy, he had in fact placed himself in a vulnerable position. She butted hard back into his crotch, slipped out of his grasp and let fly at him with a blow that sent him staggering against his desk.

His cheek was bruised and his lip bleeding. As he pulled himself together he was dazzled by the flash of a camera this crazy cow had produced from the bag she was carrying. And now she was going on about him just waiting till he saw his name in the papers.

So that was it, was it? She had sent in that provocative picture of herself just to trap him, to make a fool of him and humiliate him in the public prints. Being somewhat strapped for cash, the Captain took out his cheque-book. Under the blonde's cool gaze he wrote the date, then 'Eight hundred pounds only' followed by the amount in figures and added his signature. 'Payable to "Kirstie Jones"?' he enquired sceptically.

'Of course not. Dodie Farquhar, if you don't mind.'

He handed her the cheque and she made for the door. Just as she was about to close it behind her a thought occurred to the Captain and he called her back. 'How do I know that name?' he demanded.

She stared at him. 'Read the *Courier*, don't you? I'm their chief reporter. I won the Young Investigative Journalist of the Year award. Wapping, here I come!'

After this the Captain had sat there for the last half hour nursing his wounded self-esteem. The final applicant, the one whose success was assured although this was not known to her, was late.

When she did arrive, Helen Lascelles looked more than usually washed out, having spent several hours making the awkward journey by train and taxi from Cunlip Hall, where she had not slept much after Miss Muttock's party. But there was something about Helen, the Captain had often thought, that actually enhanced her air of sullen sexiness when she was tired. You got the impression she had such an insatiable appetite for lechery that it kept her busy right round the clock. She was so devoted to the rites of Venus, he reflected, that he had been lucky indeed in his dealings with her. His first fuck with her, on the occasion of Melanie's famous dorm feast, had happened only a few days after Helen had lost her virginity. At the time she had boasted of her newly opened tightness. His recent exploration of her pubic region with his finger as she sat on his lap watching the Nugents at it indicated that nothing had changed in that department, however much Helen had been screwed in the last couple of years. Thanks to Brice's intervention the Captain had not been able to try the effect of this narrow canal on his own member – this was one reason, maybe the main one, why he had phoned Miss Muttock and suggested that her little protegée Helen should present herself for interview.

She stood before him now with her head cocked on one side and her features slightly displaced in something between a frown and a smile. Quizzical, he told himself, a quizzical expression. Well, if Helen felt quizzical, he felt physical. He moved his hand in his pocket so that she could see what he was doing. She reacted by starting to unbutton her coat.

Helen had been wearing a lightweight black summer coat and a black beret beneath which her light brown fringe hung neatly to her eyebrows. A touch of colour was added by a pair of dangling orange earrings and a silk scarf or handkerchief of the same vivid orange tied at her throat. Her slim legs were bare above the simple black shoes and white ankle socks.

The Captain stood behind her and helped her off with the coat. The dress she wore was of a slate-black cotton material, reaching to mid-thigh. It had a high elasticated waistband above which her back and shoulders were bare. A sprinkling of moles set off the whiteness of the back. With the removal of the coat an agreeable natural fragrance was released from under her bare arms. A hint of fine but luxuriant blonde hair was evident when she raised those thin arms to adjust the points of her scarf.

Helen turned to face the Captain. If he had not already seen her back he would have supposed she was wearing the dress the wrong way round. Its bodice consisted of no more than a sort of black frill forming an inverted arch that ran from shoulder to shoulder, dipping right down to the waistband and slightly lifting the two small breasts it left uncovered.

Declining his offer of a seat but accepting a cigarette which she dangled between her long, thin lips, Helen perched on the edge of his desk just to the side of his own chair. When she crossed her legs, a smooth calf brushed against his sleeve. 'Well, Helen, how very nice to see you again so soon,' he beamed ingratiatingly. 'And what is it you reckon an attractive girl like you could get out of a job like this?'

Helen took the fag from her lips and exhaled smoke towards him. 'Two things,' she said. 'Hard cash and hard cock. I need the cash because I've been living on benefit and dribs and drabs from Mummy's measly royalties. Miss Muttock gave me a nice present but it won't last long – most of it went on this dress. They call it empire line, you know. Yes, I need cash all right. And hard cock I need because I can never get enough of it.'

'How old are you now?'

'I'm eighteen. At my age some kids want nothing but hard rock. My scene's hard cock, though. And good and long too, if possible. Thickness doesn't matter – well, not all that much – but it's got to be rock-hard to stir me up and do anything for me. Ought to be a good selection here. And there's always you, isn't there, Captain? Yes, I still remember being had by you in the old Cunlip College days, you know. Maybe we could . . . But of course you were younger then . . .'

To prove how little difference was made by the mere two years that had elapsed since the event she referred to, he slowly eased down the zip of his jeans without taking his eyes off the nipples so shamelessly displayed by the daring creation she wore. His rigid organ leapt out, the shaft netted with blue veins and the head a shining purple. Helen touched it with her foot and the engorged tip began to weep clear fluid.

Dropping her cigarette into a cup from which the Captain had been drinking coffee earlier, she lifted the hem of her dress up above her navel and tucked it into the broad band that ran round beneath her bosom. Then she uncrossed her legs and splayed them wide to show off the clean lines of a knickerless fanny from which every trace of hair had been meticulously and professionally removed. 'Like the contrast?' she asked as she raised both arms. Sunlight streaming in through the Venetian blinds touched the thick, damp tufts in her armpits into yellow flame.

His heart pounded. Instead of uttering a verbal response the Captain leaned forward to kiss the smooth V which had now started to pout and gape pinkly. The smell of girlflesh enraged his nostrils but before he was able to dart out his tongue Helen slid down from the desk, stood astride his thighs, took his cock in one hand and ran a finger of the other one up her slit. The folds of her sex now hung wide open. She lowered herself carefully and let them kiss his hot knob.

He moaned softly at this stimulus to his sensitivity. Where another woman would simply have dropped down to his lap, spearing herself, Helen let the muscles of her slender thighs take the strain as she took him into her slowly, inch by inch. Her channel was well lubricated but even tighter than he remembered. This process of gradual intromission felt almost like boring into a virgin cunt, but without the inconvenience of bleeding and complaints. He licked the hard white expanse of skin over her breastbone before shifting his mouth to the soft, silky swelling to the left and clamping it on a tight pink nipple.

Helen leaned back, resting her elbows on the desk to support herself. The Captain now had an unobstructed view of her front. His eyes lingered caressingly for a moment on the cute fringe peeping out under her beret, ran down to the uptilted breasts, the points of the orange scarf between them making their nipples look almost as pale as the surrounding flesh from which they sprang, then down to the shiny smoothness of her thighs and knees. He glanced once more at the exposed bosom with its pert little breastlets and then ran his eyes over the white expanse below the raised skirt of her dress.

Perhaps it was simply the effect of the smallness of the girl's waist, the narrowness of her hips and the arching back of her body, but there was no doubt that her navel looked slightly larger than one might have expected. It formed an attractive feature set there in the taut skin of her tummy. Pretty though it was, however, it did not detain the Captain's attention for long. The gaze of any spectator of this scene, even one whose prick was not buried within Helen as his was, would have been drawn inescapably to the lewd nakedness of the plump split fruit between her thighs. The hairless outer labia shone polished white on either side of the wet pink trench dividing them. The sensitive inner petals had been forced apart by her partner's thick cleaver, the root of which could be seen clasped by those fleshy lips. Defying the tightness of the grip, her juices oozed from the sealing flesh to run down into his bush of hair.

The Captain was highly aroused, not least by the angle into which his cock was forced by Helen's backward-leaning posture. So powerful was his tumescence that it felt as if he was striving to lift her back to the vertical by the sheer strength of his erection. Helen smiled lustfully at him, winked and looked down significantly.

Placing the tips of his fingers on her bony but soft-skinned hips, he was easily able to reach the top of her slit with his thumbs. With one of these he sought out and activated the clitoris, which had already started to peep out from its pink hood. With the other thumb he caressed the gleaming stickiness of her opened sex, running the pad up and down the groove between the root of his own cock and her clit in time with the rhythm he had imposed upon that swelling bud.

Helen closed her eyes and responded with a ripple of contractions running up and down the length of her cunt. Her abdominal muscles tensed as a pink flush, already glowing on her throat and in the space between her breasts, flooded down to her crotch. The grip on the Captain's penis relaxed for a moment, but only slightly, and then another ripple followed. Another pause, another ripple. Helen had to be already experiencing a succession of multiple orgasms and their effect on the Captain was electrifying. He gasped as he felt the mass of semen gathering at the core of his loins, ready to boil forth. Reaching up under her tufted armpits he pulled her upright and towards him so that her cheek was scratched by his stubble and her bare breasts were crushed against his denim jacket. This new position opened up new depths inside her and his cock stretched up to fill them with its tumidity. Once more the waves of rippling contractions stroked his now upright stanchion, inflaming it to its final peak.

He came. He came in surge after surge of thick, hot sperm that rushed up the tightly confined prick to fountain from its bursting knob. He moaned into her ear as he emptied himself with enormous satisfaction into the secret, constricted place up there somewhere behind that sensual-looking belly-button.

Helen slumped against his chest, both her weight and his supported by the back of his comfortable office chair. As they sat recovering their wits and something of their strength, the Captain felt the familiar sliding flow of spunk as his cock slackened to an easier size and Helen's gripping cunt muscles went limp. He would be needing a change of underwear after this soaking.

'Right,' he said. 'You can start this evening.'

The rest of the afternoon had been devoted to some advice and basic training – hardly necessary, as Helen was clearly a natural. Between six and eight o'clock Helen sat beside the Captain, taking everything in as he operated the intercoupling service. On Mondays the demand was always heavy, mainly because of new arrivals who had checked in at the weekend and were just beginning to find their way around.

He sent her off to have a bath, instructing her to slip into something suitable for doing the rounds and introducing herself to the guests. When she presented herself for his inspection she looked quite enchanting in a tiny baby doll nightie. It was black, but so transparent that the whiteness of her body shining through it made the thin material look more like a shimmering smoky grey.

One small point the Captain felt he had to correct. As he gazed at Helen standing before him he could just make out the bare triangle at the base of her tummy with its slit running down between her thighs. But the provocative effect would surely be lost on anyone unaware that the hairs had been removed – the line of the cunt could easily be mistaken for nothing more exciting than a fold in the night-dress. After a moment's thought the Captain took from a drawer a tiny G-string in bright red. When she pulled this up over her thighs and fitted her sex into it snugly, Helen's appearance was transformed. He patted her bottom by way of approval and encouragement, and sent her off for her first night on duty.

He poured himself a beer from the fridge and sat down to monitor her progress on the array of screens in the inner office. Her progress was pretty swift. None of the couples she visited in their rooms could resist her attractions. Some of them already knew her from her attendance at the wedding and barbecue, and some had actually been serviced by her when she had been helping out as part of the Captain's therapeutic team. Other guests had arrived more recently and were delighted to make her acquaintance for the first time.

In most cases the wives got just as involved with Helen as their husbands, except in those activities for which they were physically unqualified. She was fondled, kissed, licked, ejaculated over, sodomised, made to suck cock and fucked so vigorously and repeatedly that the Captain feared she would not last more than an hour or so. But this remarkable young lady, who always looked as if she had stayed up most of the night before anyway, seemed to be whipped up to fresh heights of lascivious frenzy by all the attention lavished on her. She was going to be far more popular in this role than Gloria had ever been. The only advantage Gloria could claim was that the puritanical upbringing she had never entirely overcome made her a desirable object for clients with a thing about the seduction and violation of coy maidens. Still, Helen, with her small breasts and bare pussy, would be able to play the virgin even better than the real thing. Perhaps he might even get round to laying on a wedding for her.

Although he was exhausted, he was keen to see how she got on with the Nugents. It was well past midnight when she opened their door with her master key and slipped into the room. Because of his special interest in this couple, the Captain had got the engineers to conceal extra cameras in the suite and to enhance the sound system. He stretched his limbs and settled back to enjoy the sport.

By this time Helen was looking a little bit bedraggled. Her shortish hair stuck up in spikes and her nightie was slightly torn. When she raised her hem to scratch her belly button, the red triangle that made a show of guarding her sex like some prohibitive traffic sign could be seen to be polluted with a dark, spreading stain from the sperm that seeped into it and would have flowed down the insides of her thighs if the Captain had not thought of dressing her in that handy item.

Sally and Rod were lying naked on their backs, side by side. Rod was snoring. His limp prick rested on his thigh, long and wet. He must have worn himself out trying to please his wife. Sally had the appearance of someone trying desperately to relax after being over-stimulated and left in a state of suspense. At first the Captain was unable to make out any signs of love-making on her but then his practised eye noticed that the

161

upper edge of the fine yellow fur decorating her mound was darker than usual, matted and stuck down against the skin where Rod had spilt himself on her.

Helen moved over to the bed. Sally's eyes lit up as she saw her standing there. 'Who are you?' she asked, puzzled.

'My name's Helen,' came the reply. 'I'm your new receptionist and assistant manager. Don't you remember that game we all played on the beach after the barbie?'

A grin of recognition flickered over Sally's features. 'Oh yes,' she acknowledged. 'And I saw you at the Captain's wedding, too.' If she remembered, as she must have done, that Rod had fucked Helen in the course of that post-barbecue game, she was keeping quiet about it.

Helen smiled back at her. 'Yes,' she said thoughtfully. 'Yes, I enjoyed that wedding. Anything I can do for you, Mrs Nugent?'

'Well, you can call me Sally for a start. And this is Rod. Wake up, Rod, and meet Helen – remember her? Wants to know what she can do for us.'

Rod stirred and yawned, pulling himself together when he became aware of Helen's presence at the bedside. 'Don't know what she can do for you, Sal,' he murmured, 'but she's already doing it for me.'

The shiny pipe of flesh on Rod's thigh straightened itself out and began to lift its head in recognition and anticipation.

'Maybe you can help us, Helen,' said Sally. 'You see, Rod's got a bit of a problem . . .'

'Come on, Sal, it's not really a problem,' Rod interjected. 'More like a bit too much of a good thing – that's how I look at it.' While uttering these words he was gazing closely at the red triangle so close to him and sniffing lecherously.

Helen's face lit up with a flash of understanding. She bent down and stared at Rod's straightening prick. 'I know exactly what you mean, Mr Nugent. You mean you come before you can get it into her.'

'Well . . .'

'That's right,' Sally chipped in. 'I'm a bit desperate. The only fucks I'm getting round here are from other men. I need my husband to do it to me properly. Think you could distract him somehow, so he hardly notices when we put his thing in mine?'

162

Helen reckoned she had the solution. She climbed on the bed and got astride Rod, facing his feet (and indeed everything from his waist down). Her knees were placed just below his armpits, now fragrant with the heady scent of male arousal. Rod's upper arms rested on the backs of her calves and his hands reached round to fondle up the front and insides of her slender thighs.

In response to a gesture from Helen, Sally took up her position kneeling over her husband's legs, just below the cock which was standing stiffly and pointing back towards the girl on his chest. Helen now stooped forward, hitching the hem of her night-dress up as she did so and pushing her pale, lean bottom back so that it was even closer to Rod's face. Unable to resist this provocation, he slipped a finger under the red band that disappeared between her buttocks. He ran the finger right down until it was hooked round the inverted triangle of her G-string. Then he eased the damp material to one side, releasing the plump, bare pussy that pouted back and fell open at the touch of his tongue.

Meanwhile, Helen had been fluffing up Sally's pubic curls into something like the blonde silkiness that had been partially ruined by Rod's most recent premature spending on her. She caressed Sally's bottom and sucked her breasts to get her in the mood, at the same time running a fingertip up and down the young wife's slit. At the top of each stroke she paused to tap the clitoris before sliding down to probe the first inch or so of cunt. Then the finger would emerge with a fresh charge of juice to smear over the clitoris. Sally could hardly wait.

Rod, unable to see any of this titillation, was thoroughly engrossed in sorting out the dripping intricacies of Helen's sex with his hands and tongue. Her knees had moved even farther apart so that her private parts were stretched open. He buried his pointed nose between the gaping cheeks of her bottom, cupped the smooth pubis in one hand and lashed into the silky wetness of her cunt with a tongue as stiff as his cock. The index finger of his free hand homed in on the hard bud of flesh at the top of her slit.

Up until this moment Helen had been in complete control. But now she went wild. In a flash, Rod's rigid tool was in her mouth. She still had a finger up Sally's vagina. The pad of her thumb had been rubbing the young woman's clitoris and she now squeezed finger and thumb together. The effect of this pinching, combined with the spectacle of her husband being fellated right under her nose, was too much for Sally. Reaching down and under with both her hands she lifted Helen by her little breasts, tweaking the nipples really hard as she did so. The wet cock was released with a popping sound and Sally clamped her mouth over Helen's lips, giving the girl a tongue to suck on now she was deprived of male comfort at that end.

Sally lifted her buttocks and let the muscles of her well-formed thighs take the strain as she positioned herself in readiness to plunge down on the throbbing hardness she held upright between the finger and thumb of one dainty hand while with the other she held herself open. Everything was ready for the longed-for consummation.

Little Helen had always loved cock. She could not recall a time when her life had not been dominated by these wonderful instruments and the fantasies and realities they generated. Yet now, in this moment of deprivation, she suddenly found herself obsessed with the delights of tongue. Sally's tongue darting about in her mouth established a fast, exciting rhythm which communicated itself to her cunt. Her cunt flickered with little waves of tightness, forcing Rod's tongue to stab in and out in time with them. The thought of these two synchronised tongues, the tongues of partners about to be linked in copulation, working away at the inside of her mouth and at her sex, brought Helen to orgasm.

Her spasms overwhelmed Rod, whose face was masked with a pulpy convulsing vulva, in the juices of which he almost drowned. As those salty-sweet fluids flooded his mouth, his own freight of spunk shot up the pipe of flesh and forced its way in great hot wads from the tight slot at the tip. Some of it splashed into the entrance of Sally's gaping cunt. Some leapt as high as her navel and slid down in a slithery curtain to soak the silky hairs for a second time that night. Stray drops fell on the insides of her thighs and the surplus poured down the outside of the prick from which it had been pumped, flattening and soaking the crisp hairs and coating the tight ball-sack with the seed Sally had longed to receive in her womb.

The Captain's profound enjoyment of this scene was shattered by a man's voice behind his shoulder. 'You can see what she wants, can't you sir? Can't hardly wait for it. Well, she's not going to get it from that rat-faced runt. Think I'll, you know, take her aside tomorrow and offer my services. Of if you happen to run into her yourself, sir, just tell her old Bricey's got something for her.'

TEN

HELPING WITH ENQUIRIES

'Tell you what we'll do,' said Sally as they struggled up the steps from the beach the next morning. 'I'll toss you off to get rid of the pressure. Then we'll try to make you hard again right away and see if we can stick it in me before your balls have had time to fill up with more spunk.'

The Nugents wore bathrobes of white towelling and carried their wet bathing things after an invigorating swim. Although she had wrung the surplus water out of it, Sally's long hair looked much darker than its natural blonde and its dripping ends had soaked her robe at the level of her shoulder blades behind and her bosom in front.

The unmown meadow at the top of the steps was deserted, unless the long grass was sheltering couples who did not wish to be seen. Once more it was private enough for the use of lovers. The Reverend James DeVayne, harassed by Brice and no longer the almost universal darling of the honeymooning wives, had hitched his wagon and lumbered off in the direction of Glastonbury or wherever the next rave was going to be. Rod led Sally over to where the caravan and Transit van had been parked, thinking that the flattened grass might furnish a suitable bed, but the damp rectangular depressions were yellow, alive with creepy-crawlies and littered with beer cans and empty crisp packets.

They returned to the edge of the cliff and followed its line to the far end of the meadow, well away from the motel buildings. The relentless process of erosion had not affected this part of the clifftop in recent years; a wind-swept hawthorn hedge still marked the treacherous edge and provided a shield from the light breeze wafting in from the sea. Rod trampled a circular area of grass just large enough to spread one of their towels. They got down and lay for a moment side by side, looking up at the blue sky with a few wispy puffs of vapour suspended on its domed surface. Everyone at the motel had certainly been lucky with their honeymoon weather, being just far enough south to be spared the great swathes of cloud which had been sweeping in from the Atlantic and deluging most of the country with torrential rain for most of the summer. For a brief instant Sally wished that the Yglesiases were still with them. It was a pity that they had left at the weekend so that Talbot could start work on a new movie.

As soon as the couple had recovered their breath after the climb up from the beach, they turned to each other and started kissing. Sally reached into the front of Rod's robe and found his genitals.

'You *are* small,' she observed. 'It's all shrivelled up from the sea and feels really cold and wet.'

Rod pulled back slightly and looked at her. 'You can put that right, Sal,' he said. 'Tell me about one of your experiences when you were still, you know, a virgin. Before you left school.'

After thinking for a bit, Sally, her hand still clasping his limp dick and tight, shrunken scrotum, came up with a recollection from about a year ago, although now that she was a newly married woman it seemed a much more distant memory. 'Remember how that first night here you told me about doing things with boys?' she began. 'Well, that reminded me of this girlfriend I used to have. Claire, her name was. I had a real crush on her. A year older than me but a bit backward and didn't have mates her own age. Still flat-chested when I was getting quite pointed. Used to meet in the girls' toilets to compare ourselves and have a bit of a feel. Claire wanted us to do the same with our hair – you know, our hair down there. Mine was fully grown and lovely and silky in those days, but I wouldn't let her see it. Thought that sort of stuff was dirty. Well, it was, wasn't it, with another girl? Anyway, she insisted on showing me hers, not that there was much to show. She even made me touch it once.

'After school I used to go to the recreation ground with her. We'd walk past courting couples, giggling and making remarks, and hang round the boys who went there to play. Well, one sunny afternoon just after the summer holidays we found these two lads in football gear practising at one of the goals that had been set up for the new season. Claire and me sat down under a big tree to watch them. Think they were a bit younger than us but one of them was quite a big lad – he was in goal. They knew we were there but pretended not to notice and started showing off for our benefit. Couldn't really hear what they were saying but I'm sure it was smutty. Looked to me as if the one in goal was getting all big inside the front of his shorts. Then they changed round so we could see his mate from the front. As he stood there in the goal he hitched his shorts, loose red ones, right up at the sides and tucked the bottoms of the legs into his waistband so he just had his naughty bit covered. And then he rolled his shirt up to make it like a sort of bra. His friend got the idea and gathered the back of his own shorts into a narrow strip he pulled into the crack of his bum. The two of them ponced about, dribbling the ball and jiggling their hips like dancing girls.

'Suddenly they stopped and the big one whispered something to his mate. They came over to us and knelt down. The big one asked Claire if she wanted it. The silly cow said yes, not knowing what he was getting at. He pulled her dress up and her knickers down, got his thing out and stuck it in her there and then. You should have heard her yelp! When he pulled out I saw blood on her legs and on his thing. The younger lad wanted to do the same to me but I wasn't so keen. His big friend ripped my pants off and held me down with my legs open. But the other one couldn't get hard and they ran off and left us when they saw a couple of old ladies walking up the hill towards us. Hey, Rod, you're starting to get longer. Your turn now – you never got round to telling me about *your* first time.'

During Sally's narration Rod had pulled the front of her robe open above the waist and was now reluctant to interrupt his nibbling of one of her sea-hardened nipples. But her attempt to draw back his foreskin, which was still too tight to slip over the slowly expanding cockhead, concentrated his mind.

'When my brother Grant was still living at home . . .'

'I didn't ask about your brother. It's you I want to hear about. I love you, Rod.'

Rod looked somewhat exasperated. 'But this really sticks in my mind,' he insisted. 'Grant used to tell me everything he got up to, see. Anyway, one night just before he went off to work on the oil rigs he came into my room with some cans of lager and practically told me his life history. I'd heard most of it before, dozens of times, but this time he seemed to be much, well, much franker about everything. Didn't mind letting me know what a late developer he'd been. Seems incredible, but he was nearly eighteen when this thing happened I'm going to tell you about.

'Remember that Marilyn Lister, the TV news-reader? Well, Grant really had the hots for her. Thought he was in love, he said. When he was alone in the house he'd switch on the box, draw the curtains and drop his pants. Then he'd stand there over the screen, stroking his thing and waving it at her face while she was going on about the Falklands. Sometimes he'd get all worked up just when they cut from Marilyn to that "I speak your weight" guy who used to make out the bad news wasn't so bad after all. Grant said that gave him these awful guilty feelings and he'd panic in case I was about to walk in or, even worse, our mum. But mostly he'd got it worked out so he just went through his little fantasy in the time it took Marilyn Lister to say her piece and flash that gorgeous smile at him.

'Then one day he was at it as usual and she had an item about a girl being sexually assaulted. Before Grant knew what was happening his dick got even bigger in his hand and all this white stuff came shooting out of the end. It made a sort of fizzing sound – probably from the static electricity on the screen, I reckon – when it hit Marilyn right in the face and ran down over her cleavage.

'And what do you think? At that very moment in comes Mum, back from the shops early because the Co-op was closed.

Luckily that was the end of the news. Grant wasn't sure if she'd glanced at the telly but what she would have seen was the weather forecast, with a thick cloudy mass running from Inverness down to Exeter. "Do finish dressing, Grant," was all she said. "And make sure you have a proper wash – you'll never meet a nice girl till you learn to keep yourself smelling really fresh." '

This story had done nothing at all for Sally. Rod, though, had stiffened up remarkably during the telling. She wondered how difficult it would be to poke his tool up into her now that her cunt felt all tight after its soaking in the salt water. But no – better stick to the original plan. Wank him off first and then see about getting it in before it had lost all its stiffness.

She started masturbating him. In spite of the engorging blood which pulsed through it, the skin still felt cold in her hand. This must be why the foreskin refused to stretch and slip down over the purple plum, she told herself. Ah, well, there was one way she could probably loosen him up. Curling round beside him in their nest of long grass she dipped her head into the front of his robe and proceeded to lick and suck, making liberal use of her saliva to help ease the tight skin back until it was clear of the hard, shining rim. With her fingers she played with his testicles, stroking the wrinkled sac while she gently prodded and squeezed the balls to make him moan with pleasure at the care she was bestowing on this tender part.

While Sally wondered whether she could bear to let him come in her mouth like they did in those videos he was always making her watch with him, and like Talbot had done that first time they had spied on him making love to Yvonne, a sensation like a tongue of flame leapt up through her body. In fact it was not a tongue of flame but Rod's tongue, which was busily trying to undo the hard knot her fanny had contracted into as a result of its recent immersion. 'You're all salty, darling,' he observed before resuming these attentions to her sex with renewed vigour.

'So are you,' she replied, savouring the droplet of clear juice that had just welled up from the little opening on the tip of his penis.

At this point their sport was interrupted by approaching

voices, one male and one female, and a rather self-conscious clearing of throats. 'This seems to be about the right spot, don't it?' said the man.

Rod and Sally tried to disengage before the intruders were right on top of them. They succeeded in extricating their heads from each other's robes and partially closing the fronts of those garments but were still in a suspiciously sixty-nine-ish position when a double shadow fell across their bodies. Sally looked up in dismay. A bluff man of about forty grinned down at her. He wore an evidently uncomfortable brown striped suit, the jacket of which was slung over his arm. He had loosened his tie and his pink cheeks were shiny with perspiration. Thinning hair and a little brown moustache immediately convinced her he was nothing like her type. Nor was his female companion much more to her taste. Well, she could probably be classed as pretty in a round-faced sort of way but her shortish body looked – well, too *voluptuous* under that flowery dress.

'Excuse us, sir – miss,' the man began. 'We seem to be a little bit lost, if you know what I mean. Wandered from the old straight and narrow, as they say. Would that there,' he indicated the low building on the far side of the meadow, 'be the Honeymoon Hotel we've heard so much about?'

'Motel,' Rod replied. 'The Honeymoon Palace Motel.'

'Oh, so you two must be staying there then, seeing as . . .' His voice trailed off as he caught the disapproving eye of his companion. Loosening his tie still further and wiping his brow with the back of his hand, he resumed. 'Mind if me and the missis just sit down for a bit? We're that worn out. Walked all the way from the station, didn't we?'

'Well . . .'

The tactless newcomer lowered himself to sit on the edge of the Nugents' towel; his wife shrugged and eased herself down beside him. 'Now, we can't be hanging around, Albert,' she said. 'Just you get your breath back, like, and then let's up and be seeing about booking in.'

Sally, who had wriggled herself into an innocent sitting position and was unaware that one of her pretty breasts was visible in the opening of her robe, found herself speaking to the young woman rather than to the middle-aged husband. 'Well actually you can't just walk in like that and check in. It's not an ordinary motel. You have to book in advance and even then they're very fussy about who they take – sorry, I didn't mean to be rude. But it could be embarrassing if you wandered in and got turned down just because they didn't like your faces – not that they'd . . . Oh, sorry. You see, you've got to send in photos and all sorts of stuff. Even your marriage certificate. Are you actually on your honeymoon?'

Sally's eye had fallen rather obviously on the woman's hand, bringing a fleeting blush to the plump cheeks. 'Married on Saturday,' she confided. 'The ring my Albert give me was too big, see. Fell off and dropped down a drain while we was waiting for a bus.'

The rather breathless bridegroom chipped in. 'I'm Mr Smith,' he said, 'and this here's the missis – isn't that right, dear? I think we'll just be getting on over to see if they haven't got a cosy little room for us after all. What did you say he was called, the fellow what runs the place?'

Rod's sharpish business sense had alerted him to something fishy about this unlikely honeymoon couple. He put a hand on Sally's wrist and tried to warn her to keep her mouth shut.

'Haggler,' she replied. 'Calls himself Captain Haggler.' Too late she got the message. 'But he really doesn't like people just walking in off the street. I'm sure that's not the best way to go about it.'

'And he's very down on trespassers,' added Rod. 'The guests in a place like this want to be left alone.'

'Oh, I catch your meaning, sir,' said Mr Smith with a wink at his wife. 'A bit of the old consenting adults in private stuff, is it, and not too fussy about public decency down on the beach, eh? Sounds like what we're looking for, don't it, Ji . . . Joan? Haggler, you said, madam. Funny thing that – only the other day I ran into a Mrs Haggler. But that was miles and miles from here, up in the Midlands somewhere. Or maybe it was *Aggler*. Not exactly a common name, is it? Don't recall coming across any Hagglers or Agglers in the phone book, not even the London one, do you, Jean?'

Mrs Smith was looking increasingly embarrassed by the drift of her husband's discourse. 'Let's be going, Albert,' she said.

'I'm sure these young folks have better things to be up to than passing the time of day with the likes of you and me.'

She rose and pulled him to his feet. They took their leave of the Nugents and moved off, not directly across to Reception but along the hedge until they reached the crumbling part of the cliff, where they paused and had a good long look down at the beach. Then they strode purposefully across the meadow towards the motel. Instead of walking arm in arm or at least hand in hand like a pair of *bona fide* newly-weds they stayed apart, Mr Smith marching a couple of paces ahead of his wife.

'I'm still stiff,' groaned Rod. 'It's no good – I've just got to try and put it into you.'

He pushed Sally down on her back, got between her thighs and laid open her white robe. There was no need to loosen his own garment – seven inches of purple-tipped manhood had found their way into the open air, stretching out eagerly towards her at the sight of her splayed cuntlips.

'Wait a mo,' she objected. 'Remember how we said we were going to do it?'

Rod, however, was in no mood for waiting. He had waited long enough already. He threw his whole length down on top of Sally and buried his mouth in the softness of the side of her neck. At the very instant of genital contact and just before their bodies touched from groin to face, a straight line of sperm shot up her belly. It started at the upper edge of her maidenhair, streaked across the dimpled well of her navel, wetted the pale valley between her breasts and finally spent its force against her throat. Rod subsided on his wife; the hot fluid spread and was squeezed out to run down her sides. She giggled and he sighed. Then they slept.

The Captain was just finishing a cup of coffee and a fag and trying not to think about the multiplying pressures which threatened to undermine his seaside paradise. The least urgent of these by a long way was the irreversible advance of the sea. That he could live with. What really bugged him was the menace posed by malignant human agencies. He was harassed by Pelham, who had been so active with the motel's 'maids' that some of them could hardly walk. Then that bloody Brice was making life a misery. At least Gloria, whose gentle leaning on him seemed in retrospect more like pleasure than pain, had been taken off his back. And what he had lost there in the way of sexual gratification he had more than made up for by acquiring the lewd Helen, who was at this moment doing her morning rounds. But now he was faced with the likelihood that unless some royal scandal broke in the nick of time or another Cabinet minister got caught with his trousers down he was about to be hounded by the press. These insistent, intrusive thoughts were interrupted when a couple who rather lacked the appearance of honeymooners barged into Reception. They both established a disconcerting eye-to-eye contact with the Captain before he was able to look down and stub out his fag-end.

The man consulted a small notebook before speaking. 'Looking for – for Captain Haggler,' he began.

'What would it be regarding, sir?' enquired the Captain, doing his best to appear small and subservient, and to suppress those acquired attributes of the officer class he normally affected.

'Was just hoping, er, just hoping to renew an old acquaintance, see. That's it – what they call auld lang syne. We're friends of his wife's, you might say. In the back somewhere, is he?'

Tossing the brown jacket of his suit on the counter, the stocky visitor made to push past and enter the inner office. The Captain blocked his way, edged him back into the room and lowered the flap of the counter. 'If you don't mind, sir,' he said. 'There's a colleague of mine, a young lady colleague, trying to get a bit of shut-eye in there. Now, what can I do for you? You can take a copy of our brochure if you like and then get in touch through the usual channels. If you want to make a booking you have to do that in writing. It's policy.'

'Well, it's like this, see. I don't reckon we got the time to be bothering with letters and that, have we, Jane? Oh, by the way, this here is my fiancée Jane. Me, I'm Mr Smith, Mr J. Smith. See, we got this little problem . . .'

'Hold on, sir,' the Captain interrupted. 'Are you telling me you're not actually married?'

'Well, you know, not as such. Leastways, not yet. But we heard – yes, that's it, this Captain Haggler's old lady told us, didn't she, Jen? – we heard as how you do your own weddings here, short notice, like. Must be what they used to call special licence or something.'

As these words were spoken the Captain felt himself being torn between two opposing urges, each of them growing stronger as he contemplated his dilemma. On the one hand this Mr Smith and his fiancée seemed to be decidedly tricky characters, the man especially so. He carried an air of menace with him and was applying an uncomfortable pressure to get what he wanted. Gloria, if he had really met Gloria, must have been less than discreet – how else would he know about their 'wedding' on the beach? The safest option, surely, would be to get shot of Smith and his lady friend without more ado.

On the other hand, marrying this couple could be a nice little earner. He still had those spare certificates and knew that Jimbo, who had promised to give him a bell from his next location, would be only too pleased to come back to repeat his performance and make the acquaintance of new guests. What was more, the Captain had on occasion found appeasement to be the best policy in cases like this. Get your trouble-makers implicated in whatever funny business they were making trouble over and you had them eating out of your hand. Well, sometimes. Not, perhaps, if they were as persistently bloody-minded as Danvers Pelham, or old Brice.

As he pondered these nicely balanced imponderables, the lady friend made up his mind for him. She had thrown herself into a low bentwood chair beside the door and was fanning her brow with one of the motel brochures. And now, as if deliberately, unobserved by her fiancée, she was wriggling her bottom forward in the seat to let her flowery dress ride up over her thighs until the white flesh above her stockings was exposed. Still fanning herself and avoiding the Captain's eye, she allowed her knees to fall open and reveal the white triangle of her knickers, too small to contain the proud, luxuriant bush of black curls. Shamelessly she reached down and scratched herself.

'It's quite against the management's policy, sir,' the Captain said. 'I don't know what our shareholders would have to say about it. That wedding you heard about – that was a one-off thing, you understand. It's not offered as a commercial service. Wouldn't do at all if our other guests got to hear about it. I'm thinking of something rather discreet in the middle of the night, just you and your good lady, the officiating clergyman and me. It'll cost you, of course. And I must trouble you not to let on that you're still only engaged. Mr and Mrs Smith for the duration, isn't it?'

He conducted the 'Smiths' to an empty suite at the back of the motel compound. Best to give them time to settle in before satisfying himself as to the degree of their intimacy. Right now he was more interested in the Nugents, who had gone down to the beach earlier in the morning after he had excused Sally from her regular session with him, which could come later. Instead of returning to Reception he made straight for Number Eight and tapped on the door.

Rod and Sally seemed not to have returned from their dip. The Captain let himself in with his master key and searched carefully through the chest of drawers until he found the lacy knickers he wanted to borrow and make Helen wear for him.

The chest of drawers was situated right under the window. As he closed the drawer he happened to glance out through the net curtain just in time to spot the occupants of the room crossing the grass outside. Rod already had the key in his hand.

For a moment, the Captain, who had stuffed the knickers into his pocket, considered making out that he had just dropped in to check the light bulbs. But a hunch told him this might be a wasted opportunity, so he slipped into the capacious wardrobe and eased his way along past the hanging clothes until he reached the far end. Here he would be less likely to be discovered if Rod or Sally opened the doors.

These doors had been constructed with such a situation in mind. Not only was there ample ventilation through the louvres but the angle of one of the slats up at one end was adjustable to give anyone concealed in the wardrobe an unobstructed view of whatever part of the room interested them.

The honeymooners entered. 'Lovely and warm in here,' Sally remarked, letting her towelling robe drop to the floor. 'Look, Rod, my cunt's just aching for a good stretch. For some reason I really seem to need it this morning.' The Captain flattered himself that the reason would be the deferment of her daily cleaving by his own weapon. 'Look, I've been thinking. Maybe I could try to let you do it in my mouth. But that's not going to do much for my cunt, is it? I want you to get one of those thingies from the cabinet over there and do me with it while I suck you.'

Rod slipped off his own robe and fetched a dildo of realistic shape but unrealistic dimensions. Sally took it from him, rubbed the length of it between her legs, turning it as she did so to lubricate it in her juices, and handed it back to him. Then she threw herself on the bed and drew up her knees. Her husband knelt above her and let his half-erect prick dangle down to be seized between her lips. Once imprisoned by them it stiffened rapidly, its angle obliging him to keep his head right down between Sally's thighs which he had forced apart. Fortunately the lovers were slightly skewed across the bed so that the Captain's view was not dominated by the young man's bum. Although the opening of Sally's cunt was not visible he could see her squirming as the fat dildo was rammed into her. While Rod administered the artificial fucking she had craved, he was licking her clit in time with her suction on his dick.

The Captain's bollocks were heavy with desire and his penis already stuck out of his fly. He could not wait much longer for release. But just as he was on the point of emerging from the wardrobe the door of the room opened and in marched Helen with two aides.

Helen's outfit was the conventional white coat used for these morning rounds but she had heightened the effect by wearing red stockings and a red band over her hair. She was accompanied by a page and a 'maid'; they too, probably on Helen's direction, had dispensed with their usual uniform. The petite blonde Astrid (for she it was) wore a white vest and tiny white shorts, while the page, a young Korean everyone called Kim, was identically attired.

Helen ripped the artificial phallus out of Sally, ordered the smooth-skinned Kim to strip and in no time had him driving a prick as big as the dildo hard into the deprived cunt. Kim seemed to know what to do without being told. Once he was completely engulfed he rolled over on his back, holding Sally tightly to him. Helen and Astrid then helped the girl to bring up her knees until she was able to raise herself into a squatting position above him and ease herself up and down in her own time while he ran his hands over her belly and breasts.

Rod, of course, was still rampant and unsatisfied. Helen pushed him down on his back alongside his wife and Kim. Astrid, who had torn off her shorts and looked really sexy in nothing but the white vest that did not quite reach down to the triangle of silvery fluff, leapt up on the bed and dropped down on Rod's slender, well-greased stiffness. Astrid astride, the Captain mused. So swiftly had the carnal connection been established that Rod had no time to disgrace himself as he had on the other occasion when the delicate Swede offered herself to him and to all the other men present.

Not content with the role of enabler or ringmistress, Helen took off her clinical coat. The stockings were self-supporting and the Captain found the effect even sexier than if she had been wearing a suspender belt. Red formed the ideal contrast with the pallor of Helen's skin, and its blatant suggestion of the scarlet woman furnished an admirable foil to the connotations of untouched innocence conveyed by her hairless snatch.

She moved round to the Captain's side of the bed, her back to the wardrobe. Placing her hands on either side of the reclining males she leaned forward until she was licking at the juicy point of connection between Kim and Sally. It was hardly necessary for her to move her tongue: as the young woman rocked up and down, up and down, everything from her clitoris down to the root of the lad's prick was lapped by the eager tip. After a few thrusts Helen transferred these attentions to Rod and Astrid.

While she alternated between the two couples, the hands of the young men were all over her rear quarters, probing between the cheeks of her bottom and scrabbling at the smooth quim that now gaped and dripped above their faces. As they did so, they strained to lift their heads and get at her with their mouths. She was a shade too high for them, although every now and then the tip of a tongue just flicked the hanging labia and caused her to twitch up out of reach.

This was just too much for the Captain. He stepped out of the wardrobe, his jeans already down round his ankles, and seized Helen's soft little bottom. Straight through the lads' spidering fingers flew his prick and up into the already quivering cunt. He bored into her tight hole and fucked her with a kind of wild corkscrew action.

The sight of the two pussies in front of him, lightly furred with blonde curls, urging themselves up and down on the two stiff rods that shafted them, brought him to a frenzy. But Astrid and Sally would have to wait until he had finished with the lustful Helen. In no time at all, overheated as he was by the show he had witnessed from the wardrobe as well as by the present entertainment, he was on the point of shooting. He threw back his head, his eyes wide and staring blindly as the great gushes sluiced from his loins and splashed back out of Helen's tight receptacle to soak his pubic hair. As the waves of his passion gradually subsided, his eyes clenched back into focus.

What they were focused on, up there on the ceiling, was a slight movement in the fire sprinkler concealing one of the spy cameras that bugged the room. Now that Gloria had left, only he and Helen shared the secret of this surveillance system – and yet someone must be in the inner office at this very moment operating it. Brice? Of course, the smooth-talking snooper. The Captain withdrew from Helen's tight grip. He had shrunk to shrimp-like proportions and was unable to participate in the joy of the lads on the bed as they heaved up their hips simultaneously to unload their hot fountains into the blondes who had ridden them so valiantly.

ELEVEN

A BRUSH WITH THE LAW

But when he returned to the office there was hardly any trace of the intruder. Whoever had been monitoring the activities in Number Eight had even put the cover back over the main keyboard that operated the console. Only the fact that this cover was now upside down betrayed the violation of privacy.

The next afternoon the Captain sat behind the reception desk with Helen on his lap, confiding in her and at the same time trying to soothe her anxieties as well as his own by fondling a breast with one hand through her clothing while teasing away at her knickers with the other.

She jumped to her feet in alarm as the Smiths barged into the room and did her best to sidle round to the door without being noticed. Before slipping out she gave the Captain a signal behind the backs of the guests. First she pointed at the wall behind him and then at herself. Finally she held up the fingers of both hands and indicated her watch. *Give me ten* was what she seemed to be saying. She was out of the room just before Mr Smith swung round as if to hold her back.

'I recognise that one,' he declared. 'I seen her twice, you know – misbehaving herself yesterday morning and one other time. Where were that, now?'

'Don't you remember?' his fiancée prompted. 'It were last weekend, at . . .'

'Never mind where. Yes, you're quite right, my dear.'

The Captain, of course knew perfectly well where Helen had spent the weekend. On Monday she had come to him direct from Miss Muttock's bash at Cunlip Hall, pretty much the worse for wear. Something underhand was going on here. He was about to challenge Smith when the latter got in first.

'Nice little number you got here, Haggler. Yes, we know you're Haggler – a little bird told us, didn't she? Things not quite what they seem to be, if you take my meaning. What you might call irregularities.'

The Captain affected an obsequious smile. 'We do our best for our guests, sir. Not a bad little number for them, either. If sir is interested – oh, and madam too – it would be possible for you to, well, to share in some of the benefits.'

'Some of the profits, you mean?'

'Well, I don't know about profits.' He coughed and used the tip of a finger to remove a scrap of pubic hair which must have been lodged at the back of his throat since his early morning encounter with Sally. ' "Benefits" is what I said. I think sir has already had a chance to sample some of those benefits at what you might call one remove. Technology's a wonderful thing, wouldn't you say, but when it comes down to it you can't beat the old one-on-one.'

'What we seen yesterday were more like three-on-three if I remember rightly.'

'Tell you what we can do. If sir and madam would care to be my personal guests and enjoy all the privileges of the house as well as the special midnight wedding package, I think we might find it possible to waive all charges.'

For a moment Mr Smith's stony and rather damp countenance lit up with a grudging smile. 'Any waiving of charges you can leave to me, sunshine,' was his reply. He produced a card in a plastic wallet and held it out perfunctorily. 'Sergeant Albert Raddle of the Upchester constabulary, that's me, see. And this here's WPC Jives. What they call a fair cop, you might say.'

The Captain moved round to the front of the counter and invited the fair cop and her stocky colleague to sit in the easy chairs and join him in a small brandy. To his surprise they accepted; Raddle even asked for a large one. WPC Jives looked slightly embarrassed and overheated in her pleated grey skirt and woolly cardigan as she sipped her drink but there was something about her, the Captain told himself, that could grow on one. Pity about this godawful cock-up . . .

'It's quite clear to us, Haggler,' the sergeant continued, 'that these irregularities what I alluded to go far beyond what's allowable.'

The Captain grinned and raised his glass. 'A little bit ahead of public opinion. We cater to the liberal and broad-minded, officer.'

'That's as may be. But don't you be underestimating Joe Public's influence. Wants his pound of flesh, don't he, Jives? Wants it bad.'

'Pounds and pounds of flesh, sarge. And pounds and pounds of money if he can get it.'

The Captain sucked his cheeks in audibly. 'You're a man of the world, sergeant,' he ventured. 'It shows. I'm sure you can see your way to overlooking a little bit of high-spirited over-indulgence. We're not talking about anything you and your colleague wouldn't enjoy yourselves.'

'Well now – that's where you're mistaken, see. Them irregularities of a purely moral nature . . .'

WPC Jives corrected him. 'Immoral, sarge. Lewd and immoral.'

'Thank you, Jives. Yes, them purely immoral irregularities – if "purely immoral" don't be a downright contradiction – them kind of shenanigans would be within our discretion to overlook with a caution at the most, specially if we got a slice of the action ourselves, eh, Jives? But downright *criminal* misdemeanours, now them's another matter. Well out of order.'

'We already made two arrests,' said Jives.

'That's right. Well no, not quite right – we got the local uniformed lads to take them in for us.'

The Captain was horrified. 'Who do you mean?' he asked.

'Well, let's see, now. There was that solicitor chappie. Pelman or something. Had him on a charge of assault – he was really taking things a bit too far with some of these here young ladies what works for you. But that weren't the worst of it. We found some letters on him. Letters to you, Captain Haggler. Seems like he was thinking of extorting money and favours in kind. With menaces. There's a name for that kind of behaviour . . .'

'*Misbehaviour*,' Jives interrupted.

'Misbehaviour. And it ain't very nice. Reckon we've saved you a load of worry there.'

'And a load of money,' added Jives.

'If you catch our drift. Now the other bloke we run in, he was working for the district council. Highly respected, he was. A Mr Rice from the planning department. Seems he give way to temptation, like. Same kind of thing as that bent lawyer, almost.'

'Almost?'

WPC Jives explained. 'The other one went for bums, see. But Rice was more interested in – fronts of botties.'

The Captain heaved a sigh of relief and refilled the glasses. His burden of worries was melting away like morning dew; there was justice in the world after all. On the other hand, he shuddered at the thought of what might emerge in open court if these two villains were made to answer for their sins – assuming, that is, that their cases were not dismissed because they had been wrongly named in the indictment. But Sergeant Raddle had not yet finished.

'One other little matter, Captain, while we're talking illegalities. It's what we come here to investigate really. Home Office business, you know.'

Maybe they were targeting the 'maids' and pages, most of whom were foreigners without work permits. The Captain tried to look co-operative.

'Quite clever forgeries,' Raddle went on. 'Your wife, Haggler, if we can call her that. She recently sent in her marriage certificate in support of an application for British nationality. That certificate were dodgy, see. And now we've found a whole bundle in your desk, all out of the same stable. A Dutch stable if we're not mistaken.'

Throughout this uncomfortable interview the Captain had been glancing at his watch. Ten minutes had elapsed since Helen left the room. She was his only lifeline – what could she come up with? He rose, feeling somewhat weak in the knees, locked the door, pulled down the Venetian blinds and walked round behind the reception counter. The wall was draped with a blue velvet curtain, which parted and swung to the sides when he pulled the cord.

What was revealed was a long window of plain glass, looking into a bedroom furnished more spartanly than the regular guest rooms. In fact, it was a bedroom only in the sense that it was a room containing a bed. Raddle and Jives had followed him through the gap in the counter; he indicated that they should draw up a couple of bar stools and sit with him to watch whatever was about to materialise, if anything.

They had hardly settled on their stools when a door on the other side of the bedroom opened and three figures entered. First came Helen, radiant and only just recognisable in a magnificent full bridal outfit of shimmering ivory satin and tulle. Every detail of this creation was expensively correct, from the veil to the little satin shoes. She even held a bouquet of scarlet rose-buds, emblematic of the rites of Hymen. Nobody could have called this young bride voluptuous, but there was something about the way her rich apparel set off her slight figure that was inexpressibly and lewdly inviting. *Cock-stiffening* was the adjective that sprang to the Captain's lips; denied the liberty of utterance it translated itself into an erection.

Helen was followed by the servants Astrid and Kim, who were holding the splendid train that fanned out behind her. Both bridesmaid and page-boy wore pink; Astrid's pretty dress reached to just above her white-stockinged knees, while Kim looked rather selfconscious attired as an eighteenth-century flunky in knee breeches, stiff brocades and powdered wig.

Helen approached the window. She leaned right forward, as if peering through, causing the representatives of law and order to flinch back. 'Not to worry – it's a two-way mirror,' the Captain lied.

The bride was pretending to admire herself in the supposed mirror, raising her eyebrows and pouting her lips. Skilful application of make-up had transformed her usual washed-out appearance into a picture of blushing nubility.

Astrid and Kim stood behind her, side by side and impassive. Laying her bouquet on the little shelf the spectators could just see beneath the window, Helen stepped back a few paces so that her full length was visible. She pressed the palms of her hands together and looked upwards for a moment as if awaiting the blessing of heaven. Then she cast her eyes earthwards once more and let her hands, still joined, fall to her lap.

Astrid and Kim knelt down on either side of her, like heraldic supporters, lioness and unicorn or something. The comparison was not entirely inept, the Captain thought, as the profile of Kim's satin breeches was distorted by a great horn which threatened to burst the buttons securing the front flap. He and Astrid reached down to grasp the hem of the bridal gown on either side. Their next move made Sergeant Raddle pant distractingly. The Captain edged his stool away from him and towards WPC Jives as Helen's attendants began, slowly at first but with an accelerating eagerness of their hands, to lift the sides of her dress.

Inch by inch the white silk stockings were uncovered until at last creamy white flesh flecked with little moles came into sight above them. The upward progress continued. Helen's lean loins were now seen to be adorned with a lacy white suspender belt supporting the stockings. Of knickers, however, there was no sign.

Nevertheless, a modicum of decency was still preserved at this stage. It was only at the sides that the dress and petticoat had been drawn right up to her hips. In front they looped down between the great bunches of gathered material just sufficiently to hide the part reserved for the special use of whatever bridegroom she would be lucky enough to secure on this occasion. Her hands were lightly clasped over this hanging loop.

Kim and Astrid now took safety pins from the shelf below the 'mirror' and used them to fix the skirts in their elevated position. They then withdrew a couple of steps and stood patiently, as if contemplating the bride's reflection in the mirror in front of them.

Helen parted her legs slightly. One hand reached out to take another pin from the shelf. The other one raised the flounces of taffeta and lace to pin them up just under what, in a fuller figure, would have been the bust.

The hairless state of Helen's pussy came as no surprise to the three spectators, of course. But Raddle and Jives had never been so close to its smooth succulence. The sergeant commented on its neatness and on the way the outer labia shone, entirely free of stubble or the tell-tale soreness sometimes produced by razors on unaccustomed skin. 'Probably uses one of them creams,' Jives explained.

They all held their breath as with agile fingers Helen delved maddeningly into her cunt. She bent her knees and pulled the upper part of her body back so that her pelvis was thrust forward and tilted back and up. It looked as if she was turning her female flower inside out, such a profusion of pink, wet petals of flesh was splayed there between the creases of her thighs. Three fingers of one hand had been plunged in right up to the knuckles. The index finger of the other had found the clitoris and was teasing it out into prominence by means of alternating rubs and taps.

While the bride masturbated herself in this shameless way (doubly shameless in the eyes of the Captain, who knew that she knew she was being observed not just by her own attendants but by him and the plods on either side of him), Kim undid his buttons to take the strain off the satin flap in the front of his breeches. Out flew the proud lance of his manhood. Without romantic preliminaries he immediately grabbed Astrid by the hips and forced her to stand with her back to him, sideways-on to the 'mirror'. He pushed her head down and made her support herself with her hands on her knees. Up went the pink dress, down came the white knickers and in stabbed the young Korean's prick in a gesture that could be taken to symbolise either international harmony or ethnic aggression. Well, perhaps not, the Captain reflected – traditionally it had been the West that fucked the East, though that too was changing.

The well-lubricated prick was fully visible as it pistoned in and out of the girl's quim. Kim in the quim. In fact Kim was not thrusting in and out of Astrid but using his hands on her soft hips to shake her backwards and forwards so that he was using her as a tight, silky implement to void his lust into.

If the members of the little bridal party were in a state of incipient crisis, the trio watching them from the other side of the sheet of glass were not far behind. All three of them found it hard to know where to feast their eyes. The spectacle of the bridesmaid being fucked by the page was arousing in the extreme, and yet Helen's ever more wanton display and abuse

186

of her girlish parts, now streaming with lovejuice, was so close to their popping eyes that it was impossible to overlook.

Suddenly Sergeant Raddle's heavy breathing stopped and he spoke, his voice a dry rattle. 'Don't know as I can take no more of this. She's a right little whore, that bride. But you know what, Jives? She reminds me of my Ginny.'

'That's his teenage daughter,' Jives informed the Captain.

'It's much later than I thought,' Raddle continued. 'Promised the wife I'd be home for tea. Well, Haggler, you'll be hearing from us or from the local nick about them certificates. And now we really must be . . . Cor! Look at that! We didn't ought to let her get away with that, not without so much as a caution.'

The Captain raised an eyebrow. 'If you insist,' he said, 'why not slip in through that door and give her a piece of your, er, mind?'

The sergeant's features brightened. 'Let's be having it, then, Jives,' he panted.

'Meaning what, sarge?'

'Your hairbrush, of course.'

Jives produced a heavy-looking wooden brush from her bag and Raddle barged into the bedroom with it. The first reaction that registered on his face was one of surprise as he realised that the 'mirror' was actually a window of clear glass and that his caution would be administered under the scrutiny of Jives and the Captain. But justice, backed by the promptings of nature, would not be denied. Ignored by Kim and Astrid, who went on with their serene and long-drawn-out copulation, and unseen by Helen, who had only been pretending to have a reflection of the proceedings in front of her, he drew her heavy train to one side, laying it over the back of a handy chair. Then, even as she frigged herself to orgasm, he rained a succession of blows on her clenched and forward-arching buttocks.

The bride's features contorted with surprised horror and pain. Her hands flew from her cunt to the shelf before her, on which she supported herself as she instinctively thrust her bottom back to meet the belabouring brush. Tears began to streak her make-up.

Sergeant Raddle soon seemed satisfied that he had broken Helen's lustful spirit, although it was evident that he had done so at the cost of provoking his own to an unstoppable pitch. He dropped the brush. He dropped his trousers. For a moment the Captain and Jives had a fleeting glimpse of his daunting truncheon – not a weapon one would care to encounter up a dark alley or in the glare of a white-tiled cell. Then he was on her.

Such a strange look spread over Helen's face, no more than six inches from the watchers on the other side of the window, that the Captain was quite prepared to see the cocktip emerge from her mouth. Indeed, it was obvious that Raddle had entered her by a route that would have led him out that way if his penis had been long enough or if the rest of his body had been slim enough to force its way in after the penis. As it was, Helen was visibly recovering from the initial shock and actually winked at the onlookers.

Dedicated voyeur though he was, the Captain rarely felt happy with an entirely passive role. He got off his stool and made Jives do the same. 'Imagine it really is a mirror,' he ordered her (for her colleague's reaction had given away the secret). She placed her hands on the little ledge just opposite Helen's white knuckles and lowered her face until their mouths almost touched and a small area of the glass was fogged with her breath.

The Captain assumed a station corresponding to that of Raddle, who grinned back at him, vastly amused at this turn of events. But when he drove his civilian prick smoothly up into Jives, he made sure he was penetrating the regulation constabulary cunt rather than the dark and narrow dungeon favoured by the sergeant. That Raddle had indeed been lavishing attention on her rear quarters was suggested by something the Captain had noticed as he hiked up her pleated skirt and tore her panties down: the plump cushions of her bum were black and blue, and the bruises were of the same size and oval shape as the hairbrush.

Jives was a smooth, juicy fuck but a bit on the hefty side for the Captain's taste, as he confirmed when he reached forward and squeezed her boobs through her cardigan and bra. He waved a hand vigorously to attract the attention of Kim, who had still not finished servicing Astrid, and beckoned him to bring her through to Reception.

When the Korean lad withdrew his prick, the pale, glistening shaft stood out stiffly from the pink satin of his breeches. Astrid's face was now as pink as her clothes. Kim led her round to the Captain's side of the window, understanding without verbal instructions what was required of both of them.

The boy forced Astrid down into the same position as Jives, right next to her and the Captain. Then he lifted the pretty bridesmaid's dress (both dress and bridesmaid were undeniably pretty). Her knickers had been abandoned in the other room; above the tops of the white stockings her thighs and the lovely bottom were mercifully unblemished except that the insides of her legs shone with the clear honey dripping down from the swollen leaves of her cunt.

The Captain pulled out of Jives, leaving the field to Kim, who seemed only too keen to take his place and whose enthusiasm was clearly what Jives needed to raise her to the heights. Astrid was equally delighted to feel her vagina stretched once more by her employer's practised tool. He relished the lascivious situation as the three couples shagged away in unison. Or at any rate in fairly close harmony, as the operations of Sergeant Raddle were now growing jerky and irregular.

A well-known composer and pianist, unhappily no longer with us, was noted for the panache with which he ended his concert performances. He would play the triumphant final chord twice over: instead of *TUM* he substituted *ti-TUM*, as if tapping a nail lightly to get the hammer squarely aligned before slamming it home. This was the burly sergeant's way of finishing off. The Captain followed suit to the same rhythm a split second later, his knees quivering with the nervous discharge as a thick, creamy release of a more material kind raced through his cock and spurted into Astrid in a succession of hot gushes. 'She do make a lovely bride, don't she?' Jives commented, referring to Helen's spasms on the other side of the glass even as the Captain was shaking with his own orgasm.

'Bugger the bride,' he replied. 'Can't you see I'm just having intimate relations with the bridesmaid?'

189

TWELVE

THE ENTERPRISE CULTURE

Tue, Aug 18

Cottage has been so busy and crowded since late Saturday afternoon. Began when phone rang – it was Captain down at Upchester station with that Helen Lascelles. Mac got dressed and took car to fetch them while I tidied up a bit and made myself pretty in black bikini bottom and my halter top with black and yellow stripes that makes Mac call me her little honey-bee. Tied my hair with a black ribbon.

Helen and Captain weary and travel-stained so Mac made them get in bath together. Captain had back to taps so I draped towel over plumbing to make it a bit more comfortable for him. Doubt if he noticed – leaning forward most of time. Helen sat between his legs, facing him, with her thighs on either side of his hips. I perched on loo while Mac stripped down to bra and panties and knelt by tub to administer thorough soaping. How cute Helen looks with her bare twat! Water slopped all over floor. (That was only the beginning. By Sunday morning there was going to be huge damp patch on kitchen ceiling and it was dripping from light bulb but Derrick knew what to do and made holes in plaster to drain it.)

Anyway, while they were being washed and played about with by Mac and by each other (no room for me to do anything but watch), between the two of them they did their best to explain what had happened. Seems they were all down on beach at lunch-time having the regular Saturday barbecue.

Captain had laid on lots of extra wine in those boxes with little taps, so party was quite rowdy and everyone had turned up. Usual jokes about sausages and drumsticks and 'got any hot stuff for us?' About half the women kept their beachwear on, though that was mostly pretty skimpy. Half of the others stripped right off and the rest went either topless or bottomless. Motel G-strings most popular uniforms for the guys but they tended to get discarded as soon as cocks were too big for them to contain. Helen and Captain came down dressed in denims (he told Helen this was important) but took them off at bottom of steps.

CAPTAIN: Remember Mr Black?

MAC: You mean that big Nigerian guy?

CAPTAIN: No, that was Mr Brown. Mr Black's a redhead. You know him, Mel.

ME: He was my partner when we won that game on the beach. Not my type. A wanker.

CAPTAIN: Well, he had his plonker in Helen's mouth . . .

ME: What was she wearing when she got her denims off?

HELEN: What I had on when you stripped me off just now – that tight black strapless top of mine that makes me look as if I haven't got any boobs.

ME: But you . . .

CAPTAIN: Great effect. It emphasises this part. (*He lifted her up on his legs so her bare twat came up out of water and ran finger up along slit. Big splash when he let her down again.*) Anyway, he was getting her to suck him like that when she broke away from him . . .

HELEN: I was gagging.

CAPTAIN: . . . she broke away from him and stood up. His spunk splashed the top she was wearing and sprayed all over her tummy and this lovely smooth fanny (*hitching her up again and letting her settle down on his big plunger which was sticking up out of bath water*). So I grabbed hold of her hand and ran down to sea with her, ripping off my G-string on the way.

HELEN (*to Captain*): Wow, you do feel big!

CAPTAIN: I certainly feel pretty great. You make me feel – how shall I put it? – *masterful*, Helen.

HELEN (*to us*): Anyway, we went romping out into the waves, hand in hand. When I was up to my waist in the water and it wasn't quite reaching to his balls he started rubbing me with the palm of his hand to clean me up. It made me all shivery. I threw my head back and gazed up at the sky.

CAPTAIN: She was howling like a wild animal – it must have been the salt water that triggered her off.

HELEN (*to Mac*): Oh yes, Mac, go on massaging my nipples with the soap like that. They've been chafing against that silly black top all day. It's much too tight.

MAC: They're getting really hard now. But I don't know if it's the effect of the soap or of having a man up you.

HELEN (*to us*): Well, my eyes were rolling round out of control and suddenly I noticed this smudge of black smoke coming up from behind the cliffs. The Captain here said it was just some farmers burning stubble so I didn't think much more about it and let him fuck me standing up in the water.

CAPTAIN: I was standing, of course, but Helen wasn't. She was lying back, floating, and I waded in between her open thighs.

HELEN: Oh, that's right – that's how my black top got wet through. It dried on me afterwards and I think it must have shrunk a bit. No wonder my tits are all sensitive!

CAPTAIN: Once I'd got stuck into her I pulled her up by her armpits and she put her arms round my neck. Felt rather like it does now, except that we were bobbing up and down in the waves. She started going on about the smoke again so not needing the distraction I waded up to the beach with her. She felt heavier and heavier as we came up out of the water with me holding her under her bottom. We got a cheer from the barbecue crowd.

HELEN: That's right. A couple of blokes got hold of my legs and another one held me under arms with my head resting on his stomach – well, on his prick really, which seemed to be stiff enough to support the weight of it.

CAPTAIN: So Helen was stretched out flat, held up as if she was floating in the water again, and I was standing there moving in and out of her with everyone looking on till I shot my load up into her belly.

ME: Bet that felt good!

CAPTAIN: Yes, but I'm not going to let myself think about it now in case I come too quickly. It's been a hectic day and I just want to relax. This is luxury – sitting here in a hot bath with my prick swelling up into this lovely little wanton's cunt while a beautiful, lustful woman soaps and massages us and one of the prettiest girls I know sits there watching.

Well, I have to admit I felt flattered. I opened my knees and made sure he could see me put my hand down inside my bikini briefs to frig my slippery slit. Helen told us how after that public fuck she went round flirting with the guys on the beach and getting some of their wives jealous, though some of them were turned on and wanted to do threesomes with her.

And then came the big disturbance. A little group of revellers had gone splashing out for a swim and a bit of what Captain called 'wet partying'. (That would have done as description of what was happening in bath.) Suddenly they were all shouting and screaming and waving their arms. After a while Helen realised what they were yelling: 'FIRE!'

Everyone dropped what they were eating or drinking and disconnected themselves from whoever (whomever? whomsoever?) they were screwing and scrambled up steps to clifftop in a blind panic. Captain told Helen to get dressed and they both slipped into their denims before following others up to meadow.

It was like some pagan ritual, Helen said. There was the Honeymoon Palace Motel blazing from end to end and all these naked and half-naked bods hopping about as if they'd flipped. By now the sky was black with smoke that blotted out the sun, so all that bare flesh shone lurid red from the flames. The fire had taken hold completely – no way to get to phone and no chance of anyone saving their belongings. Helen said she was devastated.

But Captain didn't seem too surprised and knew just what to do. Logic of whole operation was quite elegant. Only way to raise alarm was for him and Helen, the only ones dressed, to borrow car and drive to town. They took Range Rover belonging to old Des, who was furious but could hardly refuse.

HELEN: I must have been a bit hysterical. And I felt sort of jealous (*to Captain*) when you stopped to kiss Mrs Nugent goodbye. Could see your hand on her bare bottom and playing in between her legs as if she was something special to you.

CAPTAIN: I was just telling her I'd try to keep in touch. We put a lot of effort into trying to sort out her problems.

HELEN: Yes, but I suppose it's just that she was so pretty and so – so grateful. (*To all of us*) Funny thing, though: what I missed most was my teddy bear. But as soon as we were out of sight of the fire the good old Captain here pulled off the lane and dived into some bushes. Guess what? He came out with half a dozen suitcases, his and mine, ready packed and hidden away there. Pennies began to drop. I thought he was planning to make getaway and let others stew in their own juice . . .

MAC (*feeling in between them in water*): He must be stewing in your juice by now, poor man.

CAPTAIN: Reckon I can hold on a bit longer. We'll wait till I'm thoroughly marinated before we see if I've worked up enough pressure to blow her right off me.

HELEN: Anyway, that wasn't quite his plan. He had to act responsible and get fire brigade in case the insurance people got suspicious. So he put his foot down and we rocketed over all those pot-holes, heading for fire station. It was so bumpy I fucking nearly came in my jeans, didn't I?

MAC: Calm down, dear, or you'll make lover boy here shoot off before he wants to.

HELEN: Remember how narrow those lanes are? Well, imagine what I felt like when I heard this fire engine coming towards us! Someone must have seen all that smoke and raised the alarm. There were hedges on both sides. Captain Marvel here didn't even slow down. Some close shave! (*To Captain*) How much did they miss us by?

CAPTAIN: Crikey, we've got to be talking fag papers.

HELEN: So we just drove straight to the station . . .

ME: The fire station?

HELEN: No, stupid, the train station. I hope poor old Des and his Doris get their Range Rover back. Still, they won't be needing it till they find some clothes to wear, will they?

We just caught a train stopping at Upchester and here we are.

MAC: Here they are, as large as life and twice as lecherous. What's your next move, Captain?

CAPTAIN: I'm not going to move, Muriel. I'm just going to sit here having a good feel of her and let her cunt muscles get tighter and tighter till she jiggles and squirms and we both go over the top.

MAC: No, I mean what are your plans now the motel's gone?

CAPTAIN: First we hang around here, if you don't mind, till the insurance money comes through – I must get on to them first thing Monday. Then we do a runner. We'll be off on a cruise to let all the fuss die down, if there is any. And after that it'll be London. I'm planning to use my capital to set up a little business publishing dirty books.

MAC: Where there's muck there's money, eh? Get your knickers off, Melanie.

ME: And this top?

MAC: No. It gives you a bit of style. I like feeling your tits through it. And the contrast with your bare back. Come here, my little honey-bee, and unclip my bra.

With Mac nude and me bottomless we both got into bath. Strictly standing room only! We stood between Captain and Helen. He put his hands on my hips and started kissing bum – Helen did the same to Mac and soon they were both doing wicked things with their tongues. Maybe it was a kind of reflex but as soon as we felt that contact we both arched our bodies back and jutted our hips forward and tried to make the mouths of our cunts kiss. No good – there just wasn't room for that kind of acrobatics. So we went into tight clinch and did it with our other mouths and tongues while the two love-birds down in the water used *their* mouths and tongues between our open legs.

All this hanky panky was getting Captain worked up to boiling point. He's always said how exciting it is for him to look up a girl's crotch from underneath. And Helen was so mad to suck out Mac's liquids that she was wriggling up and down on him.

Suddenly it hit us all at the same time, wiping us out like an earthquake.

An earthquake and tidal wave. I said there was no room for me and Mac in bath but when everyone quaked and collapsed like that there just had to be room, even if arms and legs were hanging over edge and most of water had sloshed out over floor. Yet there still seemed to be enough water to make us splutter like we were going to drown. And not just water. Even though Captain's prick had been up Helen's twat as far as it would go when the earth moved for all of us, most of the fuckjuice had been squeezed out of her by her writhings when she got dragged off him. The bath water seemed to be full of these sticky, ropy skeins of spunk which kept getting into my mouth and my hair.

Well, we'd just begun to calm down and feel uncomfortable crammed into bath-tub like that. I was already thinking it was a bit awkward having to share one bloke between us three girls when door opens and in breezes Derrick, starkers and fresh as a daisy. 'Got a little surprise for you,' he says.

Next thing I knew, bathroom and not just bath-tub was full of bare flesh. In barged Darcy and Susie followed by Tim and Gail. We all roared with laughter and in no time at all four stiff pricks were ready to service five juicy cunts. How we managed it I can't say – hardly enough room for the nine of us to stand, even with four in bath. But we thought it would be more fun to have sex stuffed in there like sardines rather than spilling out into bedroom or going down to garden.

Spilling's the word. Not much bath water left to spill, of course, but plenty of sperm splashing from those cocks. Don't really understand the mechanics – or do I mean hydraulics? It was gushing all over the place and yet we all agreed that our mouths and cunts seemed to have been stretched full of spunking cocks over and over again. As if the gods had been showering their ceaseless blessings on us and into us from great, fleshy cornucopias (spelling? Maybe it should be *cornucopiae* – Mac would know).

This was beginning of orgy which is still going on. Into its fourth day now. Pace has slowed down a bit and some of the pressure's off because we finally gave up trying to get comfy in bathroom. Most of daytime action has been outside in garden. We don't seem to be too popular with the cats! Talking of cats, I must have a word with Susie O'Flammery. She's a sweet kid and I love the yeasty taste of her but I don't think it's quite decent the way she keeps letting Derrick take her into dark corners for a kiss and a quick fuck. It's supposed to be share and share alike, isn't it?

And now I can hear Captain, Derrick and Darcy on stairs. They're calling for me. Must break off now. They want me badly and I can't wait for it . . .

The dream began pleasantly enough. Mary Muttock was wandering over the sunny playing fields of Cunlip College, elegant in the academic gown that afforded some slight protection from the rays of a sun that might otherwise have scorched her pale limbs and breasts. In one hand she held her silver hip flask and in the other a swishy cane. It was good to see so many Cunlip girls again, and to see them just as they had been two years ago when she still queened it as Principal. Yes, Miss Muttock; no, Miss Muttock. Certainly, Miss Muttock, and how would you like it? Swish! Swish! Ouch!

Everywhere she looked she encountered happy, smiling, naughty girls. Many of them were demure and pretty in the pale blue, knee-length, short-sleeved summer dresses. These dresses fastened as high as the neck and buttoned down the front; the girls wore them with white socks. Others sported crisp, white shirts, usually without the striped Cunlip tie, their sleeves rolled up to the elbows, and short grey skirts. A number of the girls had removed their skirts to reveal standard issue navy knickers, while in one or two cases Miss Muttock noticed they had retained the skirts but dispensed with the knickers. Swish! Ouch! Swish!

She came across a little trio having fun on the Upper Field. Anne Amory looked quite cute in a straw boater. Apart from that, all she had on was her white shirt just reaching to the level of her pussy, her college tie and long white socks. When Anne turned round for a moment, Miss Muttock could see the curve defining the bottom of the girl's buttocks. If you lifted the shirt she would be both kissable and floggable. But the girl turned back to stand facing the Principal with her legs crossed, her thumb in her mouth and her other hand pretending to hide her cunt.

The outfit of Anne's friend Carla Merryweather was calculated to produce something like the opposite effect – as well as socks she wore the grey college skirt, but above the waist she was quite bare. Well, not quite: like Anne, she too was wearing a tie.

To entertain the two chums, little Nikki Culpepper, with her short, straight brown hair and a pale green T-shirt which reached down to just above her belly button, was up to her usual tricks. She stood with feet apart and hands on hips, flaunting her sex. Mary Muttock took a swig from her flask and crawled right up to her. The impudent girl was fucking herself with a banana, like something out of the jungle.

The jungle. Yes, the wooded parts of the grounds had grown, multiplied and crowded into a shade around her, a lurid green shade raining with sweat. The hairy coconuts that hung in clusters and split to spill their sweet white milk on Mary's breasts reminded her how hotly she yearned for fulfilment. She broke off a dangling bunch of bananas, selected the biggest one for herself and handed two others to Carla and Anne. They all followed Nikki's example until the tropical heat steamed the lenses of Miss Muttock's schoolmarmish glasses into white blindness.

She waded on through the swamp. At each laborious step her projecting banana butted into the trunks of ancient trees or the stems of creepers as thick and hard as giant cocks. It got rammed so far up her that she had to introduce a second one and then a third and even then she was gasping for more.

Suddenly there was a commotion of bats and parrots and a lithe figure came swinging down through the trees, a proud and striking specimen of *homo semierectus*. It was the Captain, his balls curtained with a skirt of dense pubic shag hanging from belly to thighs. Out through this curtain stretched his great white creeper, which started off at an upward angle but curved down until the hooded tip drooled over his knees. This was a creature to be baited and relished. Miss Muttock was sure he must have come from her own family tree, or one close enough to allow cross-breeding. But however lewdly she presented her open sexmouth to him, swaying her hips in time with the pounding of those jungle drums and coaxing that monstrous trunk of flesh until it stood straight up his belly and forced his chin back – no matter what she did to bring out the *animal* in this musclebound hunk, he always ended up fucking Anne and Carla and Nikki. Unless her steamed-up spectacles were playing tricks on her, he even had all three of them at once. His prick was so long he could thread them all like beads on a bare bodkin. And there was still a clear nine inches left for Mary Muttock. Yet whenever she got near enough to spike herself, his swollen fruit exploded and the lenses of her glasses were coated with thick honeydew that took an eternity to drain down and restore a modicum of vision, albeit clouded with lust and frustration.

Out of the primordial slime a hot, toothless mouth opened and clamped itself softly, insidiously, around her ankle. She was sinking into the pullulating bog and as she sank deeper the mouth opened wider and slowly slipped up her leg until it battened on her thigh.

Even when she had dragged herself from the swamp, torn her way out of the jungle and hurled herself, sobbing, on the silky white sand of that interminable, horizonless desert, the creature's mouth was still sucking at her thigh, sapping her will. She forced herself forwards over the smooth sand. If only she could gain that rounded dune and crawl up to its towering pinnacle . . .

The pinnacle hardened between Miss Muttock's teeth as she opened her eyes. Sunlight filtered in through the tent formed by Gloria's chestnut hair. The young American's breast was soft, so soft, and she knew that the trembling of her own thigh against the open cunt was bringing her lover to the edge of ecstasy.

'Oh yes!' panted Gloria. 'Do it like that, and I guess we ain't gonna need that husband of mine! This is just wild!'

Miss Muttock, however, was rather glad that the wildness was somewhat tamer and more domestic than the savagery through which she had struggled to reach this blissful oasis.

* * *

'Next time we'll try actually scoring,' says Rod. He and Sally are back in Mrs Buxton's semi in East Acton, drinking tea in the kitchen. They have been playing tennis down at the recreation ground. Rod used to play a bit at school and he is trying to teach Sally, who has a natural flair and the fluency that comes from watching hours of Wimbledon on TV. All she needs is a bit of technique to help her body to do what her mind wants. And maybe, she thinks, that's what Rod needs in his love-making if he's going to have any hope of actually scoring.

He looks really handsome standing there beside the kitchen sink, all tanned in his brief white shorts and tennis shirt. Why did she ever see him as rat-like? As she gets to know him better she is beginning to discern something almost noble in those narrow features. He has the mien and bearing of a thoroughbred stallion. If only he had the staying power!

Sally feels relaxed. It's good to have the place to themselves for once. This is probably the first time she and Rod have been alone together in the house since the dramatic end of their honeymoon. Her mum has gone to have tea down the road with her nan, and from there they will be going straight on to bingo.

Sally sips her tea, confident in the knowledge that she too looks good perched on the stool in her tennis clothes. Her simple but expensive white dress has a row of purple buttons down the front and narrow purple piping round the edges. Her rippling blonde hair is gathered back in a band of matching purple. The dress hasn't got a belt but is beautifully tailored so that it gives her slightly more of a figure than she's actually got, clinging to her flat but somewhat broad waist and then flaring out over her soft but rather narrow hips. It's a very short skirt, of course, just like the ones the prettiest girls wear at Wimbledon. Maybe the lacy knickers would be a bit too revealing for the centre court, though. Down on the courts Rod gets a lovely view of her crotch when she stretches up to serve, as well as a glimpse under her right arm of the yellow hair he is so fond of. And she reckons that when she stoops to pick up the ball she has an appreciative fan club in the teenagers on mountain bikes and old men on benches behind the wire netting. She knows that Rod adores her long, smooth legs. He can't take his eyes off them now as she puts down her cup and nurses one knee, the other leg dangling down from the stool.

'You know what?' he says, finishing his own tea. 'I just adore your legs. They're not like what I think of as a married woman's legs.'

'Well, I don't know if it's got anything to do with it but I'm not eighteen yet, am I?' And in some ways, she thinks, though this certainly has nothing to do with it, I'm not one hundred percent married, worse luck!

Sally draws up her other knee and hugs them both, knowing that this will show off the plump sexlips bulging through her knickers, the crispness of the open lace contrasting with the creamy softness of her thighs and offsetting the springy yellow tufts that will have worked their way out through the interstices.

Rod comes across and stands in front of the high stool. He puts his hands behind her neck and hugs her to him; she responds by opening her knees and letting him press the hardness inside his shorts against that tempting bulge. He mops his brow and says he feels like a shower, so she follows him upstairs. Sally has been missing her regular daily fixes with the Captain and is simply dying to have her cunt filled up again.

In the bathroom Rod turns his back on her. While he undresses, Sally slips off her panties and has a pee. He pulls the plastic curtain across but before he can step into the bath she moves up behind him, reaches round to the front and fondles his balls. 'I like you sweaty,' she reminds him. 'I like the idea of an athlete trying to fuck me, an athlete in the peak of condition. The peak of *physical* condition, if you know what I mean.' She tugs playfully but meaningfully at his flaccid cock. It begins to fill out at her touch.

Of course Rod knows perfectly what she means. They go into her pretty bedroom, which is tiny and cluttered with the dolls of her innocent childhood. They stand in a close embrace. Rod's hands wander down her back and come to rest on the tops of her bare thighs. As his tongue slides in between her teeth the tips of his fingers discover the absence of knickers; her bottom feels cold, cold from the evaporation of the sweat that has filmed it since their game.

He backs off and starts to undo the purple buttons, working

downwards from the top. Is that why women have their clothes buttoning the opposite way to men, Sally wonders, so that it's easier for blokes to undo them? A warm smell of new-mown hay is released as the dress falls open. The pink nipples are immodestly visible and indeed emphasised by the openness of her skimpy lace bra; she guesses Rod will decide to leave this on while he enjoys her. He drops to his knees to continue the downward progress. When he exposes the triangle of blonde curls that cover her well-formed mound and don't quite hide the line of juicy pink running down to disappear between her thighs, he slides his hands up the backs of her thighs until they curve outwards under her loose skirt. He pulls her towards him by the buttocks and buries his face in her damp heat.

By now Sally is mad with lust. She knows, though, that if she gives way at once her excitable husband is bound to spill his seed, as he always does, before getting into her vagina. Not that this can't be fun – it was a lot of fun to have him doing that on honeymoon, when she was getting plenty of cock from the Captain, Talbot and the other men who had her. But now she's back home – if she can still think of the house she grew up in as home – trying to settle down as a decent married woman, she feels she would like to give nature a chance. Not much point in having a womb, she thinks, if you don't take chances with it. She always gets embarrassed when her mum asks her if she's on the Pill . . .

So Rod needs to be kept talking. Not that this has ever worked, it's just that he does seem to be able to contain himself a bit longer that way. He can't even begin to talk while he's licking her like that, so she shrugs off her dress and falls back on the bed. Rod stands up and runs a greedy eye over his wife, sportily half-clad in her tennis shoes and socks and lace bra. The pink gash between her legs pouts open.

He throws himself down on her and thrusts his fingers into the pulp of her sex, but Sally makes him lie beside her, his erection pressing against her thigh. 'You never really told me about your first time,' she giggles. 'You told me that silly story about your brother wanking over the TV but you've kept pretty tight-lipped about yourself.'

Rod's fingers are toying with the folds of Sally's vulva. 'No one could call *you* tight-lipped, Sal,' he grins. 'Tight up there inside but no one's going to do themselves an injury trying to get into you. OK, then, here goes. I must have been about sixteen when it happened. There was this little tart from the girls' school who used to chat me up at the bus stop. She was quite pretty but what really excited me was that when you got close up to her she had this kind of sexy smell.'

'And did you get close up to her?'

'Sometimes when there was nobody waiting for the bus she'd shove herself against me and try to make me kiss her. We'd play a sort of game, with her swooping her mouth up at mine and trying to force her tongue in, while I kept twisting my head round to get away from her. All the time we kept holding each other round the waist. For me this kissing game was just an excuse for rubbing against her body. I could feel her titties getting hard through her thin summer dress and I got really stiff myself inside my trousers. Like when I used to play husbands and wives with Craddock, except that instead of his hard dick pressing back at me there was just this softness down there where her legs joined. I was dying to have a look at her under her dress but didn't dare.

'Whenever we could, we used to sit together on the bus, upstairs in the back seat. The one of us on the outside could look back down the stairs and see that mirror the conductors use to find out what's doing on top without coming up. We took to flirting and messing about with each other, first through our clothes and then putting our hands inside them.'

'Didn't you get caught when people got up to go downstairs?'

'Now and then. But we just about got away with it by pretending it was a sort of friendly fight we were having – you know, what they call horseplay. The big day for me was when I stuck my hand right up under her dress and found she hadn't got any knickers on, like you just now, Sal. "I don't wear them in the summer," she said, all matter of fact. "Only when I'm having my monthlies." I didn't know what she was talking about.

'One day it was really quiet – only three or four others upstairs and they'd all paid their fares. Well, this girl undid my trousers . . .'

'You haven't told me her name.'

For a moment Rod is embarrassed; he has not done so because the girl's name was Sally. What is more, it is for this reason that he was first attracted to Sally Number Two when she came to work in the office. 'It was Jane,' he lies. 'Anyway, she pulled my thing out of my pants and rolled it between her hands till it was huge. Then she stood up facing me, made me shift across into the middle of the seat and got up on it with her knees on either side of me. When she lifted the front of her dress I got my first ever view of her whatsit. Of any girl's whatsit. Because her thighs were so wide apart all the sexy bits were sort of hanging open. I could see they were wet.

'On both sides of her slimy groove and just above it there was all this light brown hair. Looked incredibly shaggy to me then, though it was only her first growth. Much more than what I had sprouting round my willie. Anyway, she let her dress down so I couldn't see any more and squatted back on her heels. I thought she was going to sit right on my dick and make it go up inside her. But no – she had it standing up straight against my belly with her groove pressed along its length. Like this.'

Rod rolls on top of Sally and presses the underside of his long prick into the channel between her lovelips. She feels it rubbing against her clitoris. 'Go on,' she whispers.

'She put her arms round my neck and we kissed. It was a lovely feeling being so close, especially when the bus went over bumps and this – this Jane – slid up and down against my stiffness. We came to some road-works, all ramps and rough bits. Well, you can guess what happened. Suddenly there was all this pressure down between my legs. I felt the thick creamy stuff racing up my shaft, so much of it I think Sa – Jane – must have felt it too as it rushed up past her sensitive parts. And then it came squirting out, scalding hot. Seemed like buckets of it. All over, er, Jane's belly and fur, all over my shirt and the inside of my trousers. What a mess! Some of it must have slopped down on the seat. Well, she made me give her my hanky and did her best to mop it all up. She promised to wash the hanky and let me have it back but she never did. The other day she told me she'd kept it just like that and took it to bed with her to remind her of that time on the bus.'

'The other day? So you're still seeing her?'

Rod is not going to tell her that right up to the time of their marriage he was still meeting this first Sally every few weeks and that they would go to the common and lie under bushes where she would pull his thing out and suck him off till he came . . .

'Oh, I just happened to bump into her in the street.'

'I hope you weren't both waiting for a bus.'

Rod has worked his way down his wife's belly until his mouth is level with one of her breasts. He presses his lips against the stiffness of the lace. The tip of her nipple stretches up, trying to burst through the little holes, and just manages to make contact with the tip of his tongue. He slips the white strap down over her shoulder and uses his teeth to drag down the cup. Out springs the soft white mound and he dilates his lips to fasten them on it with enthusiasm.

During this operation the heavy knob of his penis has dropped to a lower position. Sally can feel it nudging against the entrance to her cunt. She lifts her thighs and wraps her legs round him. Rod's response is to press forward so that the whole length of her canal is forced open as the slender prick stabs into her. She sighs. At last!

Rod, however, seems hardly aware of his triumph. Other thoughts preoccupy him. Lifting his head and allowing the stretched teat to drop down out of his mouth, he grins and addresses her. 'I've got a surprise for you, Sal.'

'Can't wait for it.'

'Want a place of our own?'

'Can't wait for that, either.'

'Well, fancy moving down to the coast, then? We're going back into the property market, you and me. Nugent and Nugent – how does that sound?'

'Come on, Rod. You know the market's not even bottomed out yet.'

'Got to operate in the margins, see,' Rod explains as his flesh swells inside her. 'The Honeymoon Palace Motel . . .'

'Completely burnt out, wasn't it?'

'Yeah, we don't even have to pull it down. I done a deal the other day with old Haggler's solicitors – been meaning to tell you I phoned them but wanted to wait for the right moment. We get the land dirt cheap because it's falling into the sea. Put up about a hundred low-cost, short-life residential units and rent them or flog them off as sheltered housing for old folks. No problem about the erosion. They're not going to last that long, are they, the old dears. We'll have our own little bungalow and office down there and the beach all to ourselves – those steps are lethal for wheelchairs. And that's just the start. As soon as this blasted government gets the economy kick-started out of recession we'll start diversifying. Brilliant, eh?'

Sally is indeed impressed by Rod's commercial initiative but even more by the way he has penetrated her and is now slowly gliding up and down the tight length of her sheath. She reaches round behind her left thigh and cups his testicles in her warm hand. His mouth drops once more to her eager nipple and draws it in. A coating of saliva leaks from his lips and flows down the white curves of the breast.

And now his buttocks are jouncing and jolting as if driven by steam as the rod of iron pistons back and forth in the well-lubricated cylinder that sleeves it. He is doing it to her, giving it to her with all the vigour she so longed for on her bridal night.

Sally does her best to think dirty. 'Fuck me!' she cries. 'Rod me with that great shaft of yours. Come on, spunk in me till your stuff comes out of my ears. Oh, oh – O-O-OHH! NO-OHHH! Y-Y-YES!!'

The muscles of her abdomen go rigid and her sucked nipple takes on an active role, doubling its length and thrusting up to fuck Rod's mouth as Sally hits her peak. Her cunt grips her husband's newly empowered cock, which reacts to the contraction by swelling up until, in her ecstasy, it seems to her that he must be on the point of splitting her open. A second violent orgasm judders through her body, followed by wave after wave of aftershocks.

Rod draws back about six inches, letting the huge, angry head of his prick churn around in the sensitive opening of her vagina. Once again he relinquishes the purple nipple. He raises himself on straightened arms. His elongated, almost aristocratic features grin down at her as his loins quiver, his cock rams all the way in and he proudly sluices his high-pressure streams of sperm into the innermost depths of her hot cunt.

'Oh, Rod,' she yells. 'At last! Oh, how you can fuck! Do it again, quick! Fuck, Rod, fuck!'

Letter from Esme

Dear Readers

In case all you readers are starting to feel the cool October air blowing a chill of the impending winter your way, hopefully our October Nexus titles will warm you up a little. I know I like to get really cosy and curl up with a good naughty read when it's cold outside. The Nexus publisher says I need something hot inside me in the morning to keep me glowing in the winter months, and I'm sure he doesn't mean porridge!

Here's the rundown of the Nexus books available in this month of October and upcoming November. They all differ vastly in terms of setting and period as the publisher believes in giving people a variety of themes.

In *Time of Her Life*, the heroine, Abigail, has unlocked the secret of time-travel. She journeys across the centuries and fulfils her submissive desires in a time when wanton hussies were disciplined by stern noblemen. Will she even want to return to the twentieth century?

The Palace of Honeymoons has no mention of time-travel, however. For the Palace in question is a hotel where young couples can find their erotic dreams come true. It's positively bristling with modern equipment: two-way mirrors, video cameras and all manner of kinky accessories ensure every sexual whim and fancy is catered for and our hero – that lascivious Captain – can indulge his voyeuristic tendencies.

The phenomenal demand for Black Lace books has far outweighed the most optimistic expectations of the publisher. This proves that there are thousands of women out there only too keen to get their hands on licentious material. Just as I suspected! October's book is *Pleasure Hunt*. It is by the same author as *Web of Desire*, which was published in July, and tells the story of Olympia Deschamps – a young woman on a mission to gain entry into the most exclusive society of French Libertines. Living in Paris in the present day, Olympia is carrying on the tradition of her ancestors; to seek out pleasure as a committed sensualist who will thirst still, even when her lust has been quenched.

Next month sees the release of *Return to the Pleasurezone*, the sequel to the very successful *Adventures in the Pleasurezone* by Delaney Silver. *Forum* magazine really liked this book and it's also one of my particular favourites. If this is how sex will be in the future, then book me a ticket on the next time machine.

Talking of travels in time, again, our other book is set in a very different era; Victorian times to be precise. Annie is taken into service as a very special kind of maid. If you have a fondness for pretty young posteriors, *Annie* is the book for you.

The Black Lace book for November is a real bodice-ripping yarn called *Outlandia*. Shipwrecked on a desert island in the nineteenth century, Iona Stanley has to learn to fend for herself. When she is crowned living goddess of the island and worshipped by a host of virile young men, things don't seem so bad after all. I'm not surprised.

As the living goddess of Ladbroke Grove I have to bid farewell for the time being.

Cheerio for now.

Esme

THE BEST IN EROTIC READING – BY POST

The Nexus Library of Erotica – almost one hundred and fifty volumes – is available from many booksellers and newsagents. If you have any difficulty obtaining the books you require, you can order them by post. Photocopy the list below, or tear the list out of the book; then tick the titles you want and fill in the form at the end of the list. Titles marked 1993 are not yet available: please do not try to order them – just look out for them in the shops!

CONTEMPORARY EROTICA

AMAZONS	Erin Caine	£3.99	
COCKTAILS	Stanley Carten	£3.99	
CITY OF ONE-NIGHT STANDS	Stanley Carten	£4.50	
CONTOURS OF DARKNESS	Marco Vassi	£4.99	
THE GENTLE DEGENERATES	Marco Vassi	£4.99	
MIND BLOWER	Marco Vassi	£4.99	
THE SALINE SOLUTION	Marco Vassi	£4.99	
DARK FANTASIES	Nigel Anthony	£4.99	
THE DAYS AND NIGHTS OF MIGUMI	P.M.	£4.50	
THE LATIN LOVER	P.M.	£3.99	
THE DEVIL'S ADVOCATE	Anonymous	£4.50	
DIPLOMATIC SECRETS	Antoine Lelouche	£3.50	
DIPLOMATIC PLEASURES	Antoine Lelouche	£3.50	
DIPLOMATIC DIVERSIONS	Antoine Lelouche	£4.50	
ENGINE OF DESIRE	Alexis Arven	£3.99	
DIRTY WORK	Alexis Arven	£3.99	
DREAMS OF FAIR WOMEN	Celeste Arden	£2.99	
THE FANTASY HUNTERS	Celeste Arden	£3.99	
A GALLERY OF NUDES	Anthony Grey	£3.99	
THE GIRL FROM PAGE 3	Mike Angelo	£3.99	
HELEN – A MODERN ODALISQUE	James Stern	£4.99	1993
HOT HOLLYWOOD NIGHTS	Nigel Anthony	£4.50	
THE INSTITUTE	Maria del Ray	£4.99	

Title	Author	Price	Year
LAURE-ANNE	Laure-Anne	£4.50	
LAURE-ANNE ENCORE	Laure-Anne	£4.99	
LAURE-ANNE TOUJOURS	Laure-Anne	£4.99	
Ms DEEDES ON A MISSION	Carole Andrews	£4.99	1993
Ms DEEDES AT HOME	Carole Andrews	£4.50	
Ms DEEDES ON PARADISE ISLAND	Carole Andrews	£4.99	1993
MY SEX AND SOUL	Amelia Greene	£2.99	
OBSESSION	Maria del Rey	£4.99	1993
ONE WEEK IN THE PRIVATE HOUSE	Esme Ombreux	£4.50	
PALACE OF FANTASIES	Delver Maddingley	£4.99	
PALACE OF SWEETHEARTS	Delver Maddingley	£4.99	
PALACE OF HONEYMOONS	Delver Maddingley	£4.99	1993
PARADISE BAY	Maria del Rey	£4.50	
QUEENIE AND CO	Francesca Jones	£4.99	1993
QUEENIE AND CO IN JAPAN	Francesca Jones	£4.99	1993
QUEENIE AND CO IN ARGENTINA	Francesca Jones	£4.99	1993
THE SECRET WEB	Jane-Anne Roberts	£3.99	
SECRETS LIE ON PILLOWS	James Arbroath	£4.50	
SECRETS TIED IN SILK	James Arbroath	£4.99	1993
STEPHANIE	Susanna Hughes	£4.50	
STEPHANIE'S CASTLE	Susanna Hughes	£4.50	
STEPHANIE'S DOMAIN	Susanna Hughes	£4.99	1993
STEPHANIE'S REVENGE	Susanna Hughes	£4.99	1993
THE DOMINO TATTOO	Cyrian Amberlake	£4.50	
THE DOMINO ENIGMA	Cyrian Amberlake	£3.99	
THE DOMINO QUEEN	Cyrian Amberlake	£4.99	

EROTIC SCIENCE FICTION

ADVENTURES IN THE PLEASURE ZONE	Delaney Silver	£4.99
EROGINA	Christopher Denham	£4.50
HARD DRIVE	Stanley Carten	£4.99
PLEASUREHOUSE 13	Agnetha Anders	£3.99
LAST DAYS OF THE PLEASUREHOUSE	Agnetha Anders	£4.50
TO PARADISE AND BACK	D.H.Master	£4.50
WICKED	Andrea Arven	£3.99
WILD	Andrea Arven	£4.50

ANCIENT & FANTASY SETTINGS

CHAMPIONS OF LOVE	Anonymous	£3.99
CHAMPIONS OF DESIRE	Anonymous	£3.99

CHAMPIONS OF PLEASURE	Anonymous	£3.50	
THE SLAVE OF LIDIR	Aran Ashe	£4.50	
DUNGEONS OF LIDIR	Aran Ashe	£4.99	
THE FOREST OF BONDAGE	Aran Ashe	£4.50	
KNIGHTS OF PLEASURE	Erin Caine	£4.50	
PLEASURE ISLAND	Aran Ashe	£4.99	
ROMAN ORGY	Marcus van Heller	£4.50	

EDWARDIAN, VICTORIAN & OLDER EROTICA

ADVENTURES OF A SCHOOLBOY	Anonymous	£3.99	
THE AUTOBIOGRAPHY OF A FLEA	Anonymous	£2.99	
BEATRICE	Anonymous	£3.99	
THE BOUDOIR	Anonymous	£3.99	
CASTLE AMOR	Erin Caine	£4.99	1993
CHOOSING LOVERS FOR JUSTINE	Aran Ashe	£4.99	1993
THE DIARY OF A CHAMBERMAID	Mirabeau	£2.99	
THE LIFTED CURTAIN	Mirabeau	£4.99	
EVELINE	Anonymous	£2.99	
MORE EVELINE	Anonymous	£3.99	
FESTIVAL OF VENUS	Anonymous	£4.50	
'FRANK' & I	Anonymous	£2.99	
GARDENS OF DESIRE	Roger Rougiere	£4.50	
OH, WICKED COUNTRY	Anonymous	£2.99	
LASCIVIOUS SCENES	Anonymous	£4.50	
THE LASCIVIOUS MONK	Anonymous	£4.50	
LAURA MIDDLETON	Anonymous	£3.99	
A MAN WITH A MAID 1	Anonymous	£4.99	
A MAN WITH A MAID 2	Anonymous	£4.99	
A MAN WITH A MAID 3	Anonymous	£4.99	
MAUDIE	Anonymous	£2.99	
THE MEMOIRS OF DOLLY MORTON	Anonymous	£4.50	
A NIGHT IN A MOORISH HAREM	Anonymous	£3.99	
PARISIAN FROLICS	Anonymous	£2.99	
PLEASURE BOUND	Anonymous	£3.99	
THE PLEASURES OF LOLOTTE	Andrea de Nerciat	£3.99	
THE PRIMA DONNA	Anonymous	£3.99	
RANDIANA	Anonymous	£4.50	
REGINE	E.K.	£2.99	

THE ROMANCE OF LUST 1	Anonymous	£3.99	
THE ROMANCE OF LUST 2	Anonymous	£2.99	
ROSA FIELDING	Anonymous	£2.99	
SUBURBAN SOULS 1	Anonymous	£2.99	
SUBURBAN SOULS 2	Anonymous	£3.99	
THREE TIMES A WOMAN	Anonymous	£2.99	
THE TWO SISTERS	Anonymous	£3.99	
VIOLETTE	Anonymous	£4.99	

"THE JAZZ AGE"

ALTAR OF VENUS	Anonymous	£3.99	
THE SECRET GARDEN ROOM	Georgette de la Tour	£3.50	
BEHIND THE BEADED CURTAIN	Georgette de la Tour	£3.50	
BLANCHE	Anonymous	£3.99	
BLUE ANGEL NIGHTS	Margaret von Falkensee	£4.99	
BLUE ANGEL DAYS	Margaret von Falkensee	£4.99	
BLUE ANGEL SECRETS	Margaret von Falkensee	£4.99	
CAROUSEL	Anonymous	£4.50	
CONFESSIONS OF AN ENGLISH MAID	Anonymous	£3.99	
FLOSSIE	Anonymous	£2.50	
SABINE	Anonymous	£3.99	
PLAISIR D'AMOUR	Anne-Marie Villefranche	£4.50	
FOLIES D'AMOUR	Anne-Marie Villefranche	£2.99	
JOIE D'AMOUR	Anne-Marie Villefranche	£3.99	
MYSTERE D'AMOUR	Anne-Marie Villefranche	£3.99	
SECRETS D'AMOUR	Anne-Marie Villefranche	£3.50	
SOUVENIR D'AMOUR	Anne-Marie Villefranche	£3.99	

WORLD WAR 2

SPIES IN SILK	Piers Falconer	£4.50	
WAR IN HIGH HEELS	Piers Falconer	£4.99	1993

CONTEMPORARY FRENCH EROTICA (translated into English)

EXPLOITS OF A YOUNG DON JUAN	Anonymous	£2.99	
INDISCREET MEMOIRS	Alain Dorval	£2.99	
INSTRUMENT OF PLEASURE	Celeste Piano	£4.50	
JOY	Joy Laurey	£2.99	
JOY AND JOAN	Joy Laurey	£2.99	

JOY IN LOVE	Joy Laurey	£2.75	
LILIANE	Paul Verguin	£3.50	
MANDOLINE	Anonymous	£3.99	
LUST IN PARIS	Antoine S.	£4.99	
NYMPH IN PARIS	Galia S.	£2.99	
SCARLET NIGHTS	Juan Muntaner	£3.99	
SENSUAL LIAISONS	Anonymous	£3.50	
SENSUAL SECRETS	Anonymous	£3.99	
THE NEW STORY OF O	Anonymous	£4.50	
THE IMAGE	Jean de Berg	£3.99	
VIRGINIE	Nathalie Perreau	£4.50	
THE PAPER WOMAN	Francois Rey	£4.50	

SAMPLERS & COLLECTIONS

EROTICON 1	ed. J-P Spencer	£4.50	
EROTICON 2	ed. J-P Spencer	£4.50	
EROTICON 3	ed. J-P Spencer	£4.50	
EROTICON 4	ed. J-P Spencer	£4.99	
NEW EROTICA 1	ed. Esme Ombreux	£4.99	
THE FIESTA LETTERS	ed. Chris Lloyd	£4.50	
THE PLEASURES OF LOVING	ed. Maren Sell	£3.99	

NON-FICTION

HOW TO DRIVE YOUR MAN WILD IN BED	Graham Masterton	£4.50	
HOW TO DRIVE YOUR WOMAN WILD IN BED	Graham Masterton	£3.99	
HOW TO BE THE PERFECT LOVER	Graham Masterton	£2.99	
FEMALE SEXUAL AWARENESS	Barry & Emily McCarthy	£5.99	
LINZI DREW'S PLEASURE GUIDE	Linzi Drew	£4.99	
LETTERS TO LINZI	Linzi Drew	£4.99	1993
WHAT MEN WANT	Susan Crain Bakos	£3.99	
YOUR SEXUAL SECRETS	Marty Klein	£3.99	

Please send me the books I have ticked above.

Name   ....

Address   ....

           ....

           .... Post code   ....

Send to: **Cash Sales, Nexus Books, 332 Ladbroke Grove, London W10 5AH**

Please enclose a cheque or postal order, made payable to **Nexus Books**, to the value of the books you have ordered plus postage and packing costs as follows:

UK and BFPO – £1.00 for the first book, 50p for the second book, and 30p for each subsequent book to a maximum of £3.00;

Overseas (including Republic of Ireland) – £2.00 for the first book, £1.00 for the second book, and 50p for each subsequent book.

If you would prefer to pay by VISA or ACCESS/MASTERCARD, please write your card number here:

— — — —   — — — —   — — — —   — — — —

Signature: _____